THE
GIRL
MADE
OF
CLAY

ALSO BY NICOLE MEIER

The House of Bradbury

THE GIRL MADE OF CLAY

NICOLE MEIER

LAKE UNION
PUBLISHING

Text copyright © 2018 by Nicole Meier
All rights reserved.

Published by Lake Union Publishing, Seattle

www.apub.com

Amazon, the Amazon logo, and Lake Union Publishing are trademarks of Amazon.com, Inc., or its affiliates.

ISBN-13: 9781503904637
ISBN-10: 1503904636

Cover design by Faceout Studio, Tim Green

Printed in the United States of America

In memory of ARJR, the first sculptor in my life.

PROLOGUE

The fire came without warning. Just as the predawn mist began to clear, the first flames licked the sky. It started with a dull crackle, followed by a hiss, and then an ominous coil of inky smoke snaked upward. It wasn't long before flashes of bright orange lunged in hungry strokes across the pale horizon. A merciless heat spread as the flames gathered strength and tumbled outward, taking down everything in their way. A searing, ripping fervor enveloped and consumed all that it could. Later on, after the ashes settled, someone would say they'd heard the fury of it, likening it to a rabid animal rushing through dense underbrush. Much later, another would claim they saw a figure flee the scene and disappear at the water's edge without a trace, like a ghost into the fog. But no one was really sure. The only surety was the fire itself: a living, breathing thing that rose up and gutted and destroyed.

CHAPTER ONE

SARA

If Sara had known what was waiting to greet her that morning, she would've stayed in bed. At 6:45 a.m. she startled awake. The stillness of her room had been disturbed, though she noticed the alarm had yet to sound. *Probably the dog,* she told herself as she sat upright and peeled away the covers. Her toes were the first to slip reluctantly from under the warmth as she let them drift just above the braided rug. Reaching for her robe, she glanced across a tangle of sheets. No Charlie. Again.

She still couldn't understand why her husband had agreed, after all these years, to increase his schedule. Why now? Perhaps if she really allowed herself to give it serious thought, she'd admit she knew the reason.

A dog's yip traveled through the house, commanding her attention. Like it or not, it was officially time to greet the day. Sara hadn't any time for brooding. She was needed elsewhere. Another yip was followed by a dramatic shushing. *Sam.*

"I'm coming, I'm coming," she grumbled under her breath. Her view of the vacant bed caused her to yank a forceful knot into the sash of her robe. She sighed. Strong coffee was in order. Arriving in the kitchen, she squinted, her eyes adjusting to the light of day. Two expectant faces peered back at her, and Sara's mood lifted.

"Well, hello there." She smiled wide, doing her best to erase any signs of agitation. "How long have you two been up?" She glanced from the dog to the boy who hovered with his pet in the middle of the tiled floor. Sam's deep-brown eyes blinked back from under a fringe of long lashes, and Sara's insides melted a little. How she loved those eyes.

"Acer woke up first, then me," Sam announced matter-of-factly.

Her son was clutching a cereal spoon in one hand, and just beyond him, on the farm table she adored, sat a half-full breakfast bowl surrounded by splashes of milk. Apparently Sam had taken matters into his own hands in the absence of his parents.

She scanned the bright kitchen, the hub of the house. While the other rooms in their midsize Craftsman were perhaps "overly decorated," according to Charlie, this space—with its warm oak beams, distressed white cabinets, and slate-gray countertops—was where the family spent most of their time. Sara loved to stand at the deep farm sink and gaze out the window to watch Charlie chase a soccer ball around with Sam in the yard. A year ago, on a whim of inspiration, she had a contractor take down all the upper cabinets and replace them with open shelving she'd seen on a home renovation show. It turned out pretty well, if she did say so herself. She loved how inviting this part of the house felt. Her little desk was tucked into a corner, allowing her to sip coffee and take in the natural light while organizing bits of her life.

"Did you use your inhaler this morning?" She glanced out the window. Tree pollen had been considerable this fall; streaks of yellow dust were in evidence all over the neighborhood yards.

"Yep, did my inhaler."

"What about your nose spray?"

"Yes, Mom." She detected a note of irritation.

"Okay, good then." Sara knew this part of their morning had become robotic and repetitive, but she couldn't help it. As Charlie would say, micromanaging was in her DNA. Sam scooted out his chair and went back to his Cheerios. Sara relaxed. He was good about taking care of himself. She really needn't worry so much.

With his back to her now, he hunched over his spoon and made slurping noises. Her son's caramel-colored hair shot up in a collection of wild tufts at the crown, evidence of a hard night's sleep. The hem of his pajama shirt crept up, revealing a peek of his curving spine. At ten years old, Sam was getting too big to cuddle, but at that moment she had a strong desire to pull him in for a tight hug. She stepped forward to place a hand on his shoulder, but just then Acer appeared by her side, shifting his weight and whining. *Right,* she thought. The dog had to go out.

Why couldn't all this happen after her coffee had been poured?

She ushered the dog through the sliding glass doors and out onto a patch of grass that needed mowing. Charlie used to be good about taking care of things like that.

"Your cell phone's been buzzing, by the way," Sam said over his shoulder.

"It has?" A pebble of anxiety materialized in Sara's gut. If someone was trying to reach her before dawn, it likely wasn't good news.

Where was her phone? She'd been overcommitting herself lately, and the toll of her volunteer schedule had been catching up to her—last night she'd neglected her usual routine of charging all her devices before collapsing into bed. Her eyes now skimmed over an open laptop and an adjacent cup of disregarded tea. Her heart beat in double time as she sped up her search.

Never in a thousand years did she ever think marrying a commercial airline pilot would entail any real sense of danger. But that was eighteen years ago, before 9/11 and before a recent run of terror alerts flooded the airwaves. Just last week, several major airports had been shut down and occupied by Homeland Security in response to so-called credible threats. Thankfully, nothing had come of it, but the ordeal had caused Sara's anxiety levels to spike for days.

"I think I heard it from over there." Sam gestured in the direction of her pine desk.

"Thanks, buddy." She patted him on the head and scurried to retrieve the device.

Three missed calls from an unknown number. An unsettling prickle crept along Sara's scalp, and as she hesitated, the phone suddenly illuminated. With a jumpy finger she punched in her access code and played the waiting voice mails.

"Yes, I'm trying to reach someone named Sara. This is Carrie from Pacific Memorial Hospital. Could you please contact me when you get this? Ask for the nurses' station." A number was rattled off too quickly. Sara swore, unable to locate a pen in time.

Her heart quickened. Why was a hospital calling her? *Oh, please, no.* Was it Charlie? Where was he flying this week?

Abandoning the remainder of the messages, she hastily searched for a callback number. Her teeth latched on to a cuticle and gnawed as she scanned the screen. Pacific Memorial was somewhere on the coast, wasn't it? It wasn't the name of any of the local hospitals, as far as Sara could recall. At least not any of the big ones in Portland. Panic bloomed as she pressed "Redial" and waited for the line to pick up.

To her dismay, the only voice that answered was that of an automated recording. Sara listened to the directory of extensions but realized she had no idea who she was calling. All the previous message told her to do was to ask for the nurses' station. Which one? She was keenly aware of the jackhammering of her heart as she dialed zero and willed a live body to greet her on the other end. No such luck. Her request was immediately transferred back into the maddening black hole of hospital extensions.

"Dammit!" She went back to the voice mails.

"Hi, I'm calling for Sara, I believe. It's important that you call back. Pacific Memorial. Ask to be put through to the third-floor nurses' station. Thank you." No number. These people were going to get an earful if she ever got through.

The next message was a male voice, deep and stern. "Hello, this is Dr. Burke trying to locate a"—the voice broke off, as if the caller were reading from something—"a Ms. Sara Harlow for a Mr. Thomas Robert Harlow. It's imperative you call Pacific Memorial as soon as possible. If this is the wrong number, I apologize. Thank you."

Harlow. The name hung in the air like an omen.

Sara listened to the last message twice. Her ears somehow didn't feel as if they were cooperating with her brain.

She'd been wrong. She should be relieved. These calls weren't regarding her husband at all. But the revelation didn't quell Sara's dread whatsoever.

They'd been about her father. Something had happened. Something big enough to send people calling for her.

But the question was, did she want to call back?

CHAPTER TWO

SARA

Sara had to get out of the house, to create distance between herself and that damned phone. It was ridiculous, really, that a handful of voice mails could set her spinning. But they had done exactly that.

After scooting Sam off to school and leashing the dog, she zipped up her fleece jacket and set out on a brisk walk. She'd hoped the crisp fall air would jar the dread from her brain.

This was typically her favorite time of year, when the autumn season blew across Oregon and magically transformed the foliage of her Portland suburb into a rainbow of warm, spice-colored hues. A cold snap had caused the big maples lining her street to shimmer with leaves aglow in color. Ash and aspen trees also showed off, displaying a rich spectrum of impressive ochers and scarlets. Hundreds of pine needles had been released and showered down to create a woodland carpet on the nearby walking trails. The entire display held the power to make Sara feel fuzzy inside.

Normally.

But today her feet moved in an unsteady clip. Her limbs wouldn't quite perform and instead acted like unstable rubber bands. Her insides were just as jittery. Regardless, she willed her body to move. She usually did her best thinking on walks like these. And now, more than ever, she needed to think.

Acer yanked her forward, weaving along the narrow sidewalk with his nose pushing downward. This was his big moment outdoors, and Sara knew he wasn't going to let anything stop him. He tugged again, clearly oblivious to his owner's inner turmoil. *So much for loyalty,* she thought.

Loyalty. *Now there's a laugh,* she said to herself. *Does TR truly expect me to be loyal, after all this time? After everything?* Knowing him, he was probably just holed up in a room, plugged into an IV and recovering from a bad bender. She snorted, offended at the thought. He should know better than to reach out to her.

But her father had summoned her anyway. "TR." The great Thomas Robert Harlow. And she was expected to respond.

Yet there was also something grimmer to consider: Did TR ask someone to contact her? Was he on his deathbed and wanted to have one final conversation with his estranged daughter? Was his time limited?

Or was he lying helpless in a gurney in critical condition, completely unaware? Perhaps he had no idea that his daughter had been informed. Maybe the nurses took it upon themselves to hunt her down without his consent. This idea was equally upsetting.

Her sneakers created a muted crunching over the damp leaves as she moved along her street a little faster. She wasn't certain she wanted to revisit any deep-seated feelings toward her father that might arise from seeing him. But if this crisis with TR really was a life-or-death matter, the grieving little girl in her wasn't sure she was willing to let him slip away either.

A young jogger passed by, casting Sara a funny look as he sped across the road. She realized she had been shaking her head forcefully, going over the options as she walked.

It would have been nice to discuss things with Charlie right now, to have another adult with whom to share her precarious situation. But he was maddeningly MIA.

Even if she were to get ahold of her husband, Sara knew what he would say. He'd shrug and claim it was up to her. Charlie liked to consider himself an even-keeled type of guy. Always neutral. Sometimes she just wanted to shake loose some sort of uncontrolled passion from the man she'd been married to for nearly two decades. There were instances when it was all she could do not to shout, "Throw a plate against a wall! Scoop me into your arms and tell me you've missed me! Anything!"

But then again, that's what she'd been so desperately seeking when she met Charlie. A calm soul. Something so opposite from her past, so opposite from her father.

Now Sara was just plain seeking him. Before leaving the house, she'd shot up a series of red flares in the form of harried texts. Charlie, I'm having a crisis. Please call me.

The only response was dead air.

What was she doing?

She stopped, sudden urgency sweeping over her. "Come on, Acer," she called. "Let's cut this walk short and head home. There's something important I need to take care of."

~

Sara had been placed on hold twice now. The minutes on the wall clock ticked by, and suddenly she worried she'd foolishly wasted too much of the morning debating. Her foot twitched as she suffered through recorded promotional messages regarding the hospital's "excellent staff" and "winning reputation." *Not so much,* she thought, since a confused receptionist had already rerouted her and transferred her to the wrong floor more than once.

"Answer!" she hollered into the receiver. She shook her fist in midair just as a voice echoed back in response.

"Hello, third-floor nurses' station. How can I help you?"

"Yes, I'm returning a call I received earlier this morning. This is Sara Young. Well, you probably have me down as Sara Harlow." Her tongue grew unpleasantly thick at pronouncing the name she hadn't uttered in so long. The name she'd shed so many years ago. "I think I'm calling about a patient of yours?"

"Sara Harlow Young, you say?" The girl's voice answered back in staccato. Sara suddenly felt as if she'd said something absurd.

"Yes, that's right. Dr. Burke called me."

"Okay, hold please." Click.

"No!" Too late. She'd been placed into the void of the annoying promotional loop once more. What was it with this place?

Instead of allowing herself to fall down the rabbit hole of imagining TR dying, she racked her brain, trying to remember where she'd last heard he was living. As the years went by, she'd stopped monitoring. There was Madrid, then Greece, then stateside in New York City, a stint in Santa Fe, and back to New York. At some point the news articles fizzled and then dried up completely. They had been Sara's only source for tracing her father's existence. He seemed to have vaporized into obscurity a decade ago. Even the salacious tabloids tired of covering the washed-up, wild-heart personality after a while, regardless that his artwork was still considered prestigious in certain circles.

"Hello, Ms. Harlow?" A different woman's voice came across the line this time, her tone laced with weariness.

Sara's back stiffened against the frame of the kitchen chair. "Yes. Hello. That's right." *I used to be that person. That girl with the name I've worked so hard to forget.*

A rustle of papers came through the line. "Ms. Harlow, I'm an RN at Pacific Memorial Hospital. We've been trying to track you down. One of our patients in the burn unit has been asking that we locate you."

Burn unit.

"So he's . . . alive?" She could barely get the words out.

"Yes," the woman answered. "He's badly injured, but he's going to be all right."

A buzzing settled over Sara, as if someone had suddenly filled the room with mind-numbing static. Her father was alive, and he was apparently hurt.

And he'd asked for her.

"What does that mean, exactly?" Visions of bandaged limbs and seeping, raw wounds came to mind.

The woman cleared her throat. Spurts of intercom announcements crackled in the background. "I apologize if this is all a bit of a shock to you. But there has been an accident. A Mr. Thomas Robert Harlow has been injured and is currently in our care. The only name we could get out of him was yours. I'm calling to inform you of his condition. We can only release information to a family member. Are you related to Thomas Harlow?"

Her throat constricted, and the words wouldn't come. On reflex, she opened her mouth wide and attempted to gulp for air. Only a guttural sound escaped.

"Ma'am?" The weariness changed to concern.

Sara's mouth hung open as she tried to process. "I . . ." A wave of grief rolled through her. She squeezed her eyes shut while faraway memories flashed behind her lids. A little girl on the beach holding her father's hand, a roomful of people with champagne and flashbulbs, loud arguing, the earthy smell of wet clay, a man enveloping her in a clumsy, drunken embrace, and her mother slumped and wailing on her knees.

He'd left her alone as a child, with an adult's mess to clean up. He'd claimed Sara was the best thing in his world, his "little muse." But it hadn't been enough. He went away, leaving Sara alone with her unstable mother. For that, she swore she'd never forgive him.

"No," Sara stammered as the tears threatened to pool. "You've reached the wrong person. I'm not related." With a shaky motion, she pressed "End" and let the phone slip to the tile floor.

CHAPTER THREE

SARA

Watery ice settled inside the glass tumbler as a stream of honey liquid filled the lower half. Sara watched behind a set of drooping eyelids as her friend prepared her second drink of the evening. Sara was drinking more than usual, but at the moment she didn't care.

She glanced over at Birdie, her heart thawing a little. Warm, inviting Birdie. Lucky for Sara, her next-door neighbor's living room was always open for late-night company. And tonight she needed a friend. She'd left a note for Sam, in case he woke up and wondered where she went. She nodded and raised her glass in salute, thankful for a port in the storm.

Over the course of the day she'd tried to distract herself with running Sam between school and soccer practice, drafting emails, and trying to reach Charlie. But all this couldn't ease her gnawing guilt. She'd thought more than once about picking up the phone and calling the hospital back.

"Tell me again what happened with Charlie." Birdie's hazel eyes were glassy and slightly bloodshot, probably from long hours working behind a bank of steaming restaurant equipment. Plus the hour was late, but her friend swore this was her time to relax, take a load off, and decompress after a long day's grind at her restaurant. Sara could appreciate that.

The ice slid past Sara's teeth as she tipped back her drink. She was more thoughtful now, the nightcap putting a soft focus on her present surroundings. Her neighbor's house was comfortable, with a Northwest cabin feel. Leather sofas and downy cushioned chairs faced a stacked stone gas fireplace that now burned on a low flame. Wide-planked wood floors spread out along the single-story bungalow style house, a contemporary touch Birdie and her partner had recently added to the century-old home. Sara envied the relaxed vibe of the place, something she'd tried desperately to achieve in certain parts of her own home but couldn't quite accomplish.

She curled her socked feet underneath her and considered Birdie's question. "I don't know. But when someone takes forever to call their fucking wife after she texts that she needs him, that's a problem. Is it not?" The alcohol was causing her to curse, something she'd been trying to stop since Sam was old enough to repeat her language. It wasn't totally her fault; she blamed some of this on Joanne. Her mother had always treated her like an adult, even when Sara had been a small child—no filters, no boundaries.

Joanne Harlow hadn't exactly been a figure of maternal perfection. She'd been an emotional wreck for years after TR's departure. There was a lengthy, dark period, during Sara's youth, when the shades were always drawn and the house was never cleaned. Sara had been too young to be counted on to warm the microwaveable dinners and make sure the dirty underwear made it through the wash, and Lord knew her mother couldn't have been bothered. Looking back on this as an adult, Sara understood Joanne's inaction to be a result of depression, but back then it had just seemed purely neglectful.

Birdie raised an eyebrow. Sara didn't normally lose her cool in front of other people.

She took another sip of her drink. The Charlie thing was worrisome, true. But it was taking a back seat to the alarming news of her father. What Sara desperately wanted to confess to Birdie was her underlying predicament with TR. Being aware of him lying in a hospital bed, perhaps vulnerable and alone, was creating a well of mixed feelings she couldn't ignore.

But unraveling her childhood story required more detail than she was prepared to share. Even now. Even with Birdie, the friend whom she trusted the most. Birdie would likely wonder why Sara had hidden elements of her past; she'd want to know about TR's history. Sharing any of this now meant the opening of an old, fragile wound that Sara had worked so hard to protect. It was far easier to steer the conversation back to Charlie. There'd be fewer questions that way—and less shame than in exploring why she, her father's only child, wasn't running to his bedside.

"It's just that he's been doing this a lot lately," she continued about Charlie. "Leaving for long periods of time, being unavailable."

Birdie's solid frame sank back into the folds of an overstuffed armchair. She gazed thoughtfully into her whiskey. "Maybe," she said without looking up, "you should ask him where he's been."

Sara startled. "What do you mean? Like ask if he's been fooling around or something? He just says he's been busy with work."

She'd considered this possibility before. It was hard to imagine her husband with another woman, but it happened in marriages all the time, right? People grew apart; they made mistakes. But she knew Charlie well; his excuse was always the airline.

"Perhaps," Birdie said, abruptly leaning forward and narrowing her eyes. "But hold him accountable, Sara. You need to face this. I mean, I like having you as my post-work drinking buddy, but hiding out here isn't going to solve your problems."

Sara blinked. She'd forgotten Birdie could be brutally blunt sometimes. She took another long sip, allowing the heat to travel down her throat as she pondered her friend's advice.

She *had* asked Charlie where he'd been when they'd spoken earlier. It had taken hours to track him down. When she finally reached him, Sara was nearly inconsolable.

"I'm sorry, hon," Charlie had said over the phone. "I thought I mentioned my flight changes to you."

"You did, but didn't you read your phone and see that I needed to talk to you?" Every fiber of her being shook as she responded. She hadn't even informed him of the calls from the hospital yet, and she was already becoming more upset. What was worse than her escalating worry over the TR situation was being met with Charlie's apathetic I-can't-believe-you're-making-such-a-big-deal-out-of-this tone. She detested that the most—as if her fears were unfounded.

"What if something had happened to Sam and I needed to get ahold of you?" She'd been incredulous. "What if I had been hit by a car and he was left all alone?"

A puff of exasperation blew through the earpiece. "Well, it didn't. Nothing fatal happened. You and Sam are fine, Sara." She could almost hear Charlie's jaw clench as he said her name. She'd been noticing this kind of interaction between them lately, her harried and him evasive, placating.

It wasn't always this way; in the beginning there'd been a lot of good years, trips together using Charlie's airline miles, where they'd cozied up under beach umbrellas and hardly kept their hands to themselves, tender times when he consoled her over the madness surrounding her unpredictable mother, and later around Sam's deliciously lovable infancy and toddler stages. When everything smelled like warm milk and baby's breath. But somewhere along the line things shifted. It was like the invisible force that once pushed them together was now drawing them apart. Lately, Sara felt as if her very presence somehow bothered Charlie. Like he'd rather be elsewhere.

"I think you're missing the point," she said to him, measuring her words.

"And what point is that?" Again with the placating. "That I'm working and wasn't reachable for a few hours? It wasn't on purpose, Sara. I was flying."

Sara bit down hard on her lower lip before responding. She'd practically paced a hole into their bedroom rug, dividing her worry between one man who appeared to be slipping from her life and another man who was being thrust back into it.

Before allowing her to answer, Charlie had mumbled something about how they'd talk things over when he returned at the end of the week, and then the line had gone dead. She'd been cut off.

That was how she found herself slinking across the darkened front yard and into her neighbor's living room, just after she'd put Sam to bed.

Sara wondered how to share with Birdie the real reason she'd come knocking on her door. She yearned for an objective opinion. All day long her mind had played tricks on her. Perhaps the old man had summoned her because he'd finally grown up and changed his ways. Could it be possible? But Sara just couldn't bring herself to find out. She feared falling back into his orbit might mean she'd be once again be discarded.

Plus, what would she tell the people at the hospital if she did call back? That she'd had a bout of amnesia and only now just remembered their patient was indeed her father?

How could she reunite with the one person from her past she'd tried so hard to forget? It hadn't been easy. The media and, for years, even her own mother had a difficult time giving up the subject. For one thing, there was the inescapable fact that Sara was TR's spitting image, as Joanne used to say. The thick head of strawberry hair, the green eyes, the nose with a prominent bump at the ridge. These were all his traits, passed down to her.

And then there was the sculpture.

A painfully recognizable piece of art that was created in Sara's very likeness. A little girl laughing and hiking up her overalls at the water's edge, forever encased in bronze and paraded around from one traveling exhibit to the next. It was the piece that rocketed TR and his artistry into instant limelight and out of his family's lives. The precious piece of Sara's life, her history, that TR extracted for his own gain and used as a golden ticket to a famous career.

A ticket away from her and into a whole other world.

Sara had come across articles over the years. Ones portraying her father as an arrogant and reckless artist known for his string of eclectic celebrity girlfriends and his ability to close down a nightclub or fill an exclusive art gallery. From a distance, TR's life had played out like one never-ending party.

Now their worlds were colliding: her father apparently needed her after so many years of her needing him.

From where she sat, Sara had a decision to make. She couldn't turn to her mother; Joanne had passed away several years ago. Birdie was clearly fading after her hard day at work. And Charlie wasn't planning to return home for several more days. This choice was solely up to her.

Maybe TR had realized the error of his ways and called Sara wanting to make things right. Maybe now that he was injured and facing his mortality, his view on the world had been altered.

It was that little *maybe*, finally, that had her saying good night to Birdie and stumbling back to her house to ponder how she was finally going to reconnect with her long-lost father.

CHAPTER FOUR

TR

No one ever warned TR how lonely a thing like pain could be. Epic, mind-numbing pain. The kind that pulverized you with a singular blow and threw you down into a dark, cavernous ditch from which you couldn't climb. That's what it was. God-awful. Until the drugs came. And then it was a rushing blur of pleasurable sauce dispensed through the veins, sending all that damned pain into hibernation for the time being. That was the state into which TR's once-colorful life had now dwindled. A sad song set on a never-ending loop of the unbearable, followed by the gentle softening of Lady Morphine.

All the while images faded in and out, distorted as if obscured by a funhouse mirror. He'd tried to blink them away, pushing back the guilt right along with them. But Marie's angry face floated to the forefront anyway. And Bo's, too, his face twisted with the expression TR had come to associate with him almost immediately after they met—a mixture of scorn, anger, and disappointment. TR had left the people in his life behind. Or maybe it was the other way around. Either way, it haunted him.

He was able to gather bits of outside information as the days progressed. The local authorities appeared, wearing shiny badges and false sympathy. They unceremoniously laid out a list of events surrounding the fire, not so subtly prodding TR to fill in the missing blanks. They sought details regarding any other people on the property, and TR was nervous as to whether details of the fight had been divulged.

But he kept these thoughts to himself. Most of his time in the hospital was spent either knocked out by pain meds or drowsily attempting to spoon-feed himself chocolate pudding with his left hand. Enduring an interrogation was the last thing TR wanted.

As far as he could tell, he was burned up pretty badly, and it hurt like a son of a bitch. White-coated doctors loitered in hallways, putting their heads together and rattling off terms like "surgical skin graft."

The whole affair made TR nauseous. Partly because anything medical made him uneasy, and partly because it was imperative both hands remain intact.

But the idea of getting back to work seemed implausible at the moment. In his current state, a good percentage of him was bandaged and oozing.

He'd been told it was coming up on two weeks in that bed, being fed rivers of fluids through a blasted tube that plunged into his skin at the center of an ugly, purple welt. And things were starting to itch. But primarily TR worried about getting some kind of pain-free rest.

Even that had proved difficult so far. Most of the time he nodded off, he'd jolt right back awake after dreaming he was running from the blaze. Flames so hot they felt like the gnashing teeth of an attacker, snapping viciously at his right side. He'd come to in a swath of perspiration, immobilized by fear and heavy narcotics, desperately pinging the nurses' station for help.

Just as he'd told the cops, TR recalled smelling smoke and then running from the fire. Despite uncertainties surrounding Marie and the nasty fight that had erupted between them like a bed of provoked snakes, he chose to offer little detail on how the fire had started or how he had ended up soaked with seawater and slumped on the sand. He wasn't ready to think about that yet.

After jotting down notes on a pad, one of the detectives explained how TR had been found in his pajamas, facedown in the secluded cove just below the property. The edges of his right side were charred up and down, and his house up on the hill was engulfed in flames. One detective made an inquiry about alcohol and flammable art supplies. A bolt of fear had shot through him. But it seemed they had no real clues.

TR asked critical questions of his own. Was anyone hurt? How much of the house and its outer structures were left unscathed? What had happened to his collection of art? He couldn't lose his entire life's worth of work. Was anything spared? His tongue was so thick with emotion that he'd choked on the words as he waited to be told the fate of his beloved sculptures and drawings.

The investigators just looked on with pitying expressions, as if to say, *A tragic case if there ever was one.*

What did they know? These small-town hacks. TR would be goddamned if he'd let them see him crumble. His thumb slammed down on a red button until, at last, a familiar dulling of medication slipped over him like a soft veil.

~

In his alert moments, TR was aware he was beginning to lose track of time. Close to two weeks had only been broken into dismal increments of searing pain and drug-induced sleep. How much longer could this go on? Wanting to seek the comfort of his own bed, he'd asked the staff to contact Marie.

"She says you aren't welcome back home," a nurse offered apologetically. They both knew he'd be discharged soon, and he appeared to have nowhere to go.

TR had sagged back into his pillows at the realization he had few options left. He could only think of one other person who might be willing to take him in, but he dismissed the notion. It was ludicrous.

Helplessness was creeping in.

And then something surprising happened.

TR didn't realize it right away. How could he? He wasn't in his right mind, and the hospital was a constant sea of strange faces. All types of nurses and specialists had been coming and going at odd hours; the only thing differentiating these women was the color of their hair and the occasional tight ass. He knew everyone in that sterilized ward considered him too doped up to notice. A pathetic old man with sour-smelling skin, unwashed hair, and clad in a papery gown.

But they were mistaken. TR may have been immobile and pushing seventy, but he was still a red-blooded male with an eye for beauty. Even if only half-awake, an artist always observes.

He was rousing from another night of fitful sleep, and the optics were hazy at best. Suddenly he sensed a certain energy present in his bland little room.

Here came an inexplicably familiar woman, appearing to be in her early forties, wearing mop of fiery hair and lips pursed so tight it looked as if they'd been glued shut. Accompanying her was a bird-boned boy, the type who looked as if he might be a touch too fragile for this world, traipsing behind and staring down at some kind of device.

They must be in the wrong room, TR thought. *Probably someone else's family.* All the family he had was either dead or wanted nothing to do with him. Mostly.

"Don't know who you're looking for, sweetheart, but it ain't me." It came out like a jar full of gravel. TR cleared his throat and cursed under his breath. Somewhere along the line he'd been intubated, and the damn equipment had made his insides raw. The doctor told him it had been necessary due to smoke inhalation and things would heal over time, but TR wasn't so sure. Nothing on his body felt like his own anymore.

The woman and the boy looked back at him with matching stunned expressions.

"Did you hear what I said?" TR tried again. He squinted. Now that he was more awake, his vision was sharpening, as was his pain. A stirring of recognition emerged.

The redhead stepped forward with hesitation. She adjusted a leather tote bag over one shoulder and extended a palm to block the boy from advancing.

"No, TR," she said. "We're in the correct room."

His ears pricked. He grew uneasy. Only his friends called him by this nickname. To the rest of the world he was either Thomas, or Thomas Robert, depending on how snooty the social circle. Gallery owners used to love to employ all three names when he was exhibiting. *You simply must see our collection of Thomas Robert Harlows!* They'd draw it out like he was a damned member of high society or something.

TR suited him much better. Less stuffy. Only those close to him knew this.

TR examined her. There was something he couldn't quite put his finger on. He didn't recognize the voice, that was for sure, but still there was a ring of familiarity. It was how the eyes met up with the bridge of her nose. That lightly freckled peach-toned skin. Much like his own, actually.

And suddenly he knew.

He shook his head. The drugs must have been playing tricks on him. Either that, or he was about to bite the dust and this was some kind of angel. Or ghost.

But no, the woman lingered, her torso rising with a visible inhale. "It's me, Sara. We came because you asked us to."

The words permeated his skin, settling deep into his chest.

His dry lips felt cracked, his tongue gone numb. Time stood still. TR's heart felt as if it might seize. He widened his gaze and glanced from the woman to the boy and then back again.

Was that really her?

"Sara?" he whispered. "You came?"

"Yes." Her soft chin betrayed her otherwise stoic demeanor, quivering just the slightest. A hand shot back behind her, checking on the security of the boy.

Sara. Maybe it was the drugs, but it was as if something suddenly warm seeped from his heart and filled his whole spirit. Here she was. His little muse who once danced with square feet in the bubbling sea foam. The impish creature who used to slip her tiny hand into his and ask to watch him work. The ten-year-old who got swooped up under the protective crook of her mother's arm, whose life he didn't mean to miss but somehow did. His girl.

It was real, but what was he to say to this grown woman?

The silence in the room was stifling.

Everything was so maddeningly muddled. He had the faint memory of an exasperated nurse asking if there was a family member to notify, a next of kin. Apparently, Marie had hung up on them one too many times. He did offer Sara's name in a foggy state. But he hadn't expected her to materialize at his bedside after all these years.

He felt the heat from her accusatory glare. If he were at home, TR would pour himself a stiff drink.

Glancing beyond her, he gestured. "Who is *we?*"

The young boy in a navy hooded sweatshirt peered up at him. A scrawny thing, really. But he had a tender face, made up of long lashes and an aura of innocence. It was the kind of face that made one want to pick up a brush and paint something.

TR wasn't usually much for kids. But for some inexplicable reason he had the sudden urge to reach out and run a finger across one of those unblemished cheeks. His left hand rose an inch, but the tubes reminded him he was hooked to an IV.

The boy eked out a barely audible, "Hello," before his eyes went back to his mother for help.

Sara shifted. An oatmeal-colored knit tunic hung down around her frame, practically swallowing her whole. What was she hiding from under there?

"This is, um . . ."

TR realized she was nervous, the way she kept gripping the purse strap that was looped over her arm. Her lips pressed together again, as she appeared to be deliberating. Then she rolled her shoulders back and straightened.

"This is Sam. My son." She placed her arm around the boy now with a softening behind her eyes. Her voice was edged with a distinct weariness.

"We only came because the hospital insisted. They said you were in an accident. I don't know what's going on, but for your sake I suggest you wake up and tell me."

For the first time in weeks, TR actually felt like laughing. A chuckle started at the base of his belly and rolled out deep and low. The amusement hurt his ribs, but it delighted him nonetheless.

He wagged a finger. "You're much more assertive than you used to be, kid."

A shocked expression crossed Sara's tight features just before she jutted her chin defiantly. Her arms whipped into a tight fold.

"I believe I'm entitled to an explanation."

For which part? TR wondered.

He regarded her again. Somewhere in there was the little girl he once knew. Sara was attempting to keep a poker face, but he wasn't buying it. This girl obviously came with an agenda.

"First of all, why don't you get that boy a seat?" TR needed to get control of this situation. With his free hand, he propped himself against a lump of unsatisfying hospital pillows and motioned to a faded blue armchair in the corner. He ran a dry tongue over a set of filmy teeth. "And second, be a doll and get me a glass of water, would you?"

If it were possible to see steam come out of someone's ears, he would have sworn that's what was happening with Sara. He watched as her eyes narrowed into angry slits. After a beat she strode over to the chair and wordlessly yanked it out for her son. A paper cup was snatched from a nearby dispenser and filled from the bathroom sink. It was delivered to his bedside table with such succinct violence that half of its contents sloshed out over Sara's shaky hand.

"Satisfied, old man?" Her complexion was now a deep crimson.

My girl grew up to be a spitfire, TR mused. He stifled a smile. *Good for her.*

Taking his time, he sipped at the tepid water and tried to ignore the faint taste of corroded metal. If only his cup were filled with a splash of booze instead.

TR needed to get out of there. But instead he was laid up, alone and helpless. The cops had informed him, in no uncertain terms, that the main structure of his home was not to be occupied. And apparently, so had Marie. It was deemed unsafe due to the fire.

That part really riled him. What right did anyone have to keep him out of his own place? *That was the real crime,* TR thought. But there he was anyway. Stuck in that prison-style bed and wondering how to appeal to his estranged daughter's sense of humanity. He'd quite literally and figuratively burned all his bridges at home and now hoped to seek shelter with his only daughter.

Think, you idiot, he told himself. But the fog was slow to clear.

TR had zero idea how to ask for help.

CHAPTER FIVE
SARA

It was all Sara could do to keep her composure. Truthfully, she'd come to find out whether TR had anything important to say to her. That, and out of a worry her father could possibly die before she had the chance to confront him. The last time she'd seen him was when she'd been sixteen years old, over a disastrous reunion in Los Angeles when she and her mother had discovered TR at an art opening.

Now there they were in the same room together. *And the first thing he does is ask for a cup of water?* No hello. No claims that he missed her. Nothing.

Her brain was having trouble processing the difference between the enchanting father of her youth who used to usher her into his cozy art studio, providing a sanctuary of creativity and peace from the outside world, and the crotchety blowhard before her now. But TR was clearly in some kind of delusional fantasy if he thought his long-lost daughter had driven all this way to be treated like a moronic groupie.

Life had had its way with TR. Hard living had left a physical imprint. Deep lines ran up his forehead, connecting like the rungs of a ladder and disappearing into his whitened hairline. Prominent parentheses clung around his eyes and mouth. Sun damage had given him an almost leathery hide, indicating little consideration for self-care.

The tissue of his face seemed to be slightly bloated as well. Sara wasn't sure if this was perhaps due to alcohol abuse or just the effects of his accident. The nurse out front said he'd been through a lot. So perhaps there was no real way to know. Sara made a mental note to talk to the attending physician as soon as she got the chance.

She had so many things she wanted to say. So many angry questions that had burned a hole in her for her entire adult life. And now TR was a captive audience, tethered to an IV and bound in first-aid dressing.

"Tell me, my boy," TR croaked in Sam's direction. "How old are you?"

"He's ten," Sara heard herself snap a little too quickly. "And I'll be the one asking questions for now, if you don't mind."

TR flinched.

Part of Sara wished to bring her fists down onto the bedside table and demand TR explain where he'd been. Didn't her father care to know about how she'd survived in his absence? Was he oblivious to it all? She wanted to shake him by the shoulders and make him understand the pain he'd caused her, the pain he'd caused Joanne.

Standing there in that foul-smelling room, she steadied herself. She'd tried to locate him once upon a time but hadn't been successful. That was before the ease of tracking someone via the internet and social media. Before she was an adult and the hole in her grieving heart had yet to close up and seal itself off from him entirely. But she realized he needed to know of the damage he had caused. How his leaving had robbed her not only of a parent, but also of the art she so loved. She had been forced to give up on her creative dreams to take care of her ill mother.

Anguish began to bubble to the surface, ready to spill from the giant fissure in her heart—but Sara had to consider Sam.

Her son was sitting so quietly behind her. Patient and wide eyed. Clearly waiting for some kind of explanation or a proper introduction that would allow him to know this stranger who was his maternal grandfather. All she'd told him on the drive over was that her father hadn't "participated" much in her life, but he was now sick and asking to see them. Sam had looked confused and asked questions, but Sara's answers had been clipped as she glossed over any real explanation.

How could she protect Sam and deal with her own eruption of feelings? On top of this, Sara sensed that the two males in the room had further questions about one another. Until that day, neither knew the other existed. Sara had omitted so much whenever Sam had asked.

But TR knew I existed, Sara thought. *And what good did that ever do?*

She glanced at the clock on the colorless wall opposite the bed. She was suddenly tired. It had already been a long morning.

Bringing Sam along wasn't her first choice. God knew what they might be greeted with when they got there. But without Charlie around to take over, and Birdie and Eileen having to work, Sara saw no other option. She told herself that if the nurses warned them TR was in scary shape, she'd leave Sam in the waiting area with a book.

But a part of her reasoning for bringing Sam along was because she wanted to show TR she was all right. Despite his leaving her behind, with a heartbroken mother and no tangible explanation, Sara turned out okay. And she had her beautiful son with her to prove it.

She also came to see if her father was clinging to a lifetime of remorse from his deathbed.

The old man, however, wasn't dying. True, he was injured badly, as was evidenced by the way he winced at even the smallest of movements. But it was clear the old goat was going to carry on. And by the way TR was acting, he was likely going to carry on without showing his own flesh and blood even the smallest scrap of repentance.

"How long have you been in here?"

"Too damn long!" His bushy brows leaped together into a deep scowl.

"Well, the nurses tell me you've been badly burned. In a house fire. Is that right? Your house?"

"Yes." He shrank a little deeper into the mattress, and Sara got a strange sense he was hiding something.

She realized how much he'd aged since she'd been a little girl. His skin was sallow and his shoulders hunched. Broken capillaries flecked his nose, like mini bursts of purple explosions. Sara couldn't decipher whether they were a result of old age or indicators of someone who had hit the bottle one too many times in his day. His once-rugged jawline was now covered by the beginnings of a beard. White, salty flecks of stubble traveled unevenly down his neck and melded into his reddened skin.

And then there were his eyes. Gone was the bright light Sara had held in her memory. TR always had the expression of one constantly marveling at beauty. But all Sara detected in him now, as this sixty-nine-year-old man lay slack in this hospital bed, was a dim shadow of defeat.

TR had never been considered a classically handsome man. But as publications used to describe him, he carried a kind of outdoorsy and rugged charm. His reddish hair was regularly sun-kissed blond, making him look like he belonged at the beach. He was often photographed wearing a sly, playful grin that evidently kept TR in the epicenter of women.

But where were his admirers now? Sara wondered.

For the first time since she'd arrived at the hospital, she noticed the absence of any flowers or cards. Where were all the well-wishers of the man who once traveled with an entourage, who entertained the rich and famous on rented yachts and in private European villas? What had become of TR's so-called friends he'd reportedly collected in well-known circles? Had they abandoned the washed-up man now that he'd progressed toward obsolescence?

A careful knocking came from the other side of TR's door.

As if on cue a young-faced doctor slipped into the room. Sara was a little surprised. She estimated this guy must be a decade her junior, with his healthy head of styled brown hair and the physique of someone who hit the gym on a regular basis. She only hoped that what he lacked in years he made up for in competent knowledge.

"Good morning," he announced, and offered a broad smile.

Sara did her best to quickly wipe the concern from her face. She smiled back. The doctor made eye contact with each of them and swiftly pulled out a clipboard before scanning it.

"I'm Dr. Burke. And you must be?"

Sara hesitated, wondering what was written on that clipboard. "I'm Sara."

"My daughter," TR interjected, a little too loudly.

"Wonderful," Dr. Burke said. He faced Sara. "Are you the family member who'll be in charge of home care once our patient is released?"

Home care?

The air in her lungs emptied. Sara felt as if her stomach had dipped down into her knees.

"I'm sorry. What exactly do you mean?"

Dr. Burke cleared his throat. He must have had plenty of experience dealing with shocked family members, because he calmed his tone. "I'm hoping you're here, Sara, to look after your father. While his injuries were quite serious, consisting of second- and third-degree burns, he's progressed very nicely. Especially for someone his age. The skin graft surgery went well, and his wounds are beginning to heal. We'd like to see him return to the comfort of his home, but this can only occur if someone is around to care for him."

"But I'm not—"

Dr. Burke's brow knit into a frown. "Is there a problem?"

Was the room suddenly ten degrees hotter? Sara could feel a slick sheen of perspiration developing at the base of her back. She twisted her face into an uncertain question and shot an angry look at TR.

"What my daughter means to say, Doc, is that my house has been pretty charred up from the fire. I'm not allowed to go back there yet. The cops say it's a no-no."

The doctor's face relaxed a little. "Well, then, if that's the case, then perhaps he can return home with you, Sara. You live in the area?"

"Well, sort of. I, um . . ." What could she say? *I live in a nice house about an hour and a half away, but I have no interest in taking in my father because my resentment is more significant than his health?*

Everyone in the room stared.

"No," she blurted. This wasn't going to happen. She had no intention of taking care of TR. "My dad seems to be getting such great care here. I think it's best if the hospital looks after him until he's able to get back on his feet. You know, in case of any, uh, complications?"

Dr. Burke's frown returned. "We planned on keeping him for a day or two more, that's true. But considering your father is lacking any kind of health care insurance, we thought it might be best—"

"You don't have any medical insurance?" She was incredulous. Here TR was, a world-renowned artist who'd once been photographed with the president, and he couldn't even bother to muster up a bit of lousy insurance?

TR refused to meet Sara's glare. He shrugged. "Don't believe in it."

She pinched the bridge of her nose. "Good God, TR."

Dr. Burke continued. "So you see—"

"No, no. There must be another way. I'm not the right person for this." The very idea of TR coming home with her was absurd. "Wait!" She snapped her head up. "He may not have insurance, but he's got money. I mean, do you know who this is? This is *Thomas Robert Harlow.* The artist? His work has been exhibited in the Met, for Christ's sake!" It was uncouth. She recognized this. But the situation seemed to call for it. Her father was rich.

Wasn't he?

TR mumbled something under his breath.

"What is it?" Sara demanded. "Speak up."

Her father scowled from under the covers. His tone turned surly. "My situation has changed."

She cocked her head. "What does that mean? Your financial situation?"

"That's right. It's complicated. The best option is that I go with you for the time being."

Oh, what a fool she'd been! TR had no intention of a heartfelt reunion, to try to make things right. Her father appeared to have no more money, no more friends, nothing but a burned-down house. He'd called because she was the only one who would come.

She was his last resort.

As Sara refused to acknowledge the fresh stinging behind her eyes, someone tugged on the hem of her sweater. She wheeled around to discover Sam pulling at her.

Sweet Sam.

In all the commotion she'd nearly forgotten her son was there, taking it all in. Sara scolded herself for being so preoccupied. What must her ten-year-old be thinking?

Kneeling down to eye level, she met his gaze. "What is it, honey?"

"Mom," Sam whispered. "You're just going to leave him here, all alone?"

Yes, because that's pretty much what your grandfather did to me when I was your age.

Even so, Sara melted as she stared into the quizzical expression of her only child. What kind of a mother was she if she couldn't demonstrate compassion in front of her son? What message would that give?

She shook her head. No, she wouldn't be the one to repeat history. TR might have sucked at being a parent, but she did not.

"Oh for God's sake," Sara's voice echoed off the sterile walls and into the hushed space. "Fine. TR can come home with me. But only for a brief stay. I mean it. A few days, and that's it."

TR pumped his head as if he understood, but Sara had a terrible feeling he didn't.

CHAPTER SIX

SARA

Sara slipped from the bedroom just after sunrise on Saturday morning, leaving Charlie to sleep soundly. It had been two days since she'd agreed to take in TR, and her nerves were a tangle of knots. Clutching a pair of sneakers in one hand, she made for the front door. A happy jingle trailed behind her. She looked back to catch Acer's sinewy shadow down the hall.

So much for being alone.

Not to be forgotten, her eager Labradoodle trotted to the front door and planted himself next to a hook with his hanging leash. His caramel tail thumped the floor expectantly. Sara tried shushing him, but he whined in response.

"Yes, okay, we're going on a walk," she whispered low. Running a palm along his velvety ears, she treated him to a much-appreciated scratch. "You don't miss a beat, do you, pal?" Acer cocked his head.

She peered outside. Hazy morning light filtered through the front window. A twinkle of frost winked at her from the lawn. Reflexively, she pulled a barn jacket off the coat rack and shrugged it over her thin sweatshirt. Hints of winter were moving in quickly.

Securing Acer with one hand, she stepped out into the still of the morning. She loved this part of the day, when everything appeared fresh and new. A chance to start over.

A solitary male jogger dashed by. Pulsing bass thumped from his earbuds, breaking the stillness. Sara nodded in greeting and strode in the opposite direction. The dewy sidewalk rose up to meet her as she quickened her pace and willed her weary body to awaken.

It was unusually early, but Sara had to get out of the house. It was important to escape before falling into a chance encounter with her husband.

Otherwise, confessions would need to be made. She wasn't quite ready for that.

Charlie had returned home late the previous evening, announcing that he had the weekend off from work. Sara had hoped maybe they could talk, even though he appeared to be too worn out to hold a conversation. She'd pushed anyway but was only able to get out the bare facts regarding her father. After she'd revealed that TR had been hospitalized, Charlie had raised his eyebrows, asked after his condition, and then expressed a hint of concern for how this might affect Sara before falling asleep partially dressed on top of the bed.

Sara had stared down at him, thwarted. The cloying odor of stale airplane ventilation filled the space between them. In all the years they'd been together, she still couldn't get used to that smell. Sensitive to this, Charlie used make a beeline for the shower whenever he came back from long trips.

Now Sara was lucky if they were even in the same room for very long, let alone doing thoughtful things for one another.

So much had been neglected lately. They wouldn't necessarily quarrel about anything, which she supposed was a positive. But they wouldn't really discuss anything either. All of Charlie's travel was installing an emotional distance between them. He seemed to be putting in more and more time at work over the past few months, and Sara couldn't understand why. When she'd asked Charlie, he'd claimed it was the "peak" of his piloting career and he was in demand. He seemed to thrive off it, actually. But at the end of his trips he'd return home depleted. As a result, Sara grew resentful, and he mirrored her mood.

Lately, communication between them had dwindled down to routine schedule updates and status reports regarding Sam via text. Every so often there'd be small bursts of face-to-face time in between Charlie's trips. But even those were rare. It was no kind of way to have a healthy marriage, and Sara was pretty sure they both knew this. Yet nothing changed.

Sooner or later a conversation needed to happen.

Sara disliked the idea of having to face her unassuming husband and lamely admit she'd given the okay to host her wild and negligent father for an undetermined amount of time. Without consulting anyone. Even herself.

The guilt of this constricted her. Sara had said yes to the doctor's unyielding request well before she could fully process what it meant. There hadn't been any time to fret over the implications. But now that it was happening soon, Sara worried TR's presence might have a negative effect on her household. Namely, her rocky marriage.

How was she going to tell Charlie?

The last thing she needed right now was another problem between the two of them, straining the already fragile seams that held them together. If they didn't have space or time to connect now, what would that look like once a practical stranger moved into the house?

What have I done? Sara worried.

A squirrel darted out from the base of an oak tree. Acer stood at full attention, his frame a taut ball of excitement. The squirrel sprang forward, and Acer followed suit. Sara skidded behind, her arm feeling as if it were being ripped from its socket. Acer may have been lean, but he was all muscle.

"Stop it!" She yanked her elbow backward. "I'm not in the mood."

Acer yipped. Two chocolate eyes met hers, cast in a shade of dejection. His fuzzy head lowered, and he obediently slunk along the path.

"Sorry, pal." Great, now she was taking it out on the dog. She offered a pat. "Just not today."

Perking at the affection, Acer assumed a speedy gait.

Get your thoughts together, Sara. She needed to be calm when she returned home to discuss things with Charlie. That was the whole point of the walk, to quiet her jittery nerves and make a plan. Walking faster, she rehearsed variations of her speech in her head.

Somehow she'd convince her husband that TR's visit wasn't going to affect them too much. It would be a blip on the radar. A brief act of mercy. That was all. The old man would heal and then move out. Simple as that.

But in her heart, she wasn't so sure. When had anything regarding TR ever been simple?

~

When she'd properly worn out herself and the dog, Sara returned home. The front entry was partially blocked as she stepped inside. She discovered a prone Sam rooting around in a shoe bin. The lower half of his camouflage-patterned pajama bottoms stuck out from under a bench. Farther inside the house, pots and pans clanged on the stove. Acer danced around and sniffed at a tantalizing bacon aroma.

"What's going on?" Sara unleashed the dog and kicked off her shoes. It was surprising to find everyone awake. Lately, Saturdays were for sleeping in.

"Mom, I have a soccer game, and I can't find my cleats!" Sam surfaced from under the bench, sporting a bad case of bedhead and a frantic expression. "Have you seen them?"

"This early?"

"Yeah, I have to be at warm-ups at eight."

Puffing out her cheeks, she checked her phone. Had she really been walking for over an hour?

"Shoot, honey. Sorry. I must've forgotten. But don't worry. I'll help you. Did you try the garage?"

Sam smacked his forehead and ran off.

Sara went to investigate the activity in the kitchen. Charlie was up, dressed in a wrinkled concert T-shirt and fleece sweatpants. A pair of silver tongs dangled from his hand. In front of him was a sizzling fry pan. Sara noticed he was humming something, but she couldn't quite catch the tune. Sunlight flooded in from the bay window behind him. It highlighted little flecks of gray in Charlie's gradually thinning hair. It struck her that her husband was aging more rapidly lately. At forty-five, his looks were shifting. But she decided the change suited him. A silver fox. Seeing him unguarded like this gave her an unexpected pang of nostalgia. She used to love leaning on the counter beside him, sipping coffee and looking on as he cooked breakfast on lazy Saturday mornings.

"Good morning." Charlie glanced up and smiled.

Sara's heart caught. It had been so long since she'd witnessed this sight. Nowadays Charlie always seemed too busy to make breakfast. He usually opted for snatching a granola bar before heading out the door. Even when he was home for longer stints, he made a habit of taking off for a morning run, leaving Sara to sip coffee alone until Sam wandered in. Seeing him now, like this, gave her hope.

"Good morning to you." She glided in and helped herself to a stool. *This is good,* she thought.

"Out early with the dog, I see."

"Yeah. I tried to let you sleep in." She smiled, easing her way into the conversation. After all, it wasn't such a big deal, was it?

"Thanks," he replied.

She studied him a second longer before choosing her words. "Now that you're up, I was thinking—"

"Mom!" Sam shouted from the open garage door. "I think I left my cleats at Adam's house. Can you call his mom?"

Not wanting to give up her place in front of Charlie, she barked back. "Sam, really? Are you sure you left them there? Because it's seven fifteen in the morning, and I don't want to bother Mrs. Hogan so early on a weekend."

Charlie sniggered.

"You're not helping."

He shrugged and offered her a slice of greasy bacon. "You always tell me organization is your department. I'd help out, but I'm on bacon duty."

"Oh, brother." She rolled her eyes. "You're incorrigible."

"Mommm!" Sam was beginning to melt down.

Sara threw up her hands. "Fine. Fine. Fine." Tromping into the other room, she retrieved her phone and began dialing. So much for a quiet discussion over breakfast.

The other line picked up after five long rings. Sara bit her lip. She knew it was too early. "Hello, Maggie? It's Sara. Sorry to call at this hour but—"

"Oh, hi, Sara. That's okay, we're up over here." Of course they were. With her organic green teas and glowing skin, Maggie was one of those perfectly relaxed moms who seemed to have things under control 100 percent of the time. Sara couldn't remember when she'd ever witnessed her friend late or frazzled for anything.

"Never mind!" Sam hollered from his bedroom, drowning out Maggie's response. "Found 'em!"

Sara shook a fist in the air. "Oh shoot. Sorry, Maggie. False alarm in the Young household. I'll fill you in later. Have a nice Saturday!" She punched the "End" button before her friend had a chance to respond.

"Samuel Alexander Young!" she scolded. "No more monkey business. Get your gear packed up. We're leaving in ten."

The response was a loud scuffling followed by a banging of drawers. She sighed. It wasn't even 8:00 a.m., and she was worn out.

Returning to the kitchen, she checked on Charlie's progress. A heap of bacon was displayed in the center of the table, along with frozen waffles and strawberries. But Charlie was already on the move. Gulping down a glass of juice, he ran past her.

"I'll take him," he called over his shoulder. His bare feet sped down the hall.

"You will?" Sara felt as if she were playing catch-up, but if Charlie wanted to take Sam to his umpteenth game of the season, then fine. She was relieved not to have to rush back out again. And today, of all days, she wasn't in the mood to make small talk with the other parents who usually clustered around one another on the sidelines. But at this rate she and Charlie would never have a moment to talk.

"I missed the last game, so now that I'm here, I want to see him play. Just have to change my clothes!"

Perhaps Charlie was glad for the excuse to run out with Sam so he wouldn't be stuck alone at home with her. Trying to convince herself she was merely being paranoid, she trailed her husband into the bedroom.

Sara flopped down on the unmade bed while Charlie rushed around, getting dressed. Acer wandered in, and Sara shooed him back out.

"Besides," Charlie's muffled voice now echoed from inside the walk-in closet. "I wanted to catch up with Sam. You know, see what he's been up to lately. I only have this weekend to do that, because remember, I leave again on Monday."

Sara nodded and then froze. Charlie still knew nothing about her little excursion to the coast. After their not-so-pleasant phone conversation earlier that week, she'd decided to keep all updates at a minimum until he finally returned home.

She sprang up. She hadn't considered Sam would blow her news to Charlie before she had the chance to explain.

"I think I'll come too!" she announced, arriving at the mouth of the closet.

Sam yanked on a tube sock and glanced up with surprise. "Really? I just assumed you'd want the morning off."

Yes, she wanted to say. *I'd very much like the morning off, but not at the expense of Sam spilling the beans before I do.*

Scooting past him, she pulled a baseball hat from a high shelf and covered her windblown hair.

"Sure," she said. "I'd love to come."

~

The race to the soccer fields was the typical Saturday mad dash of parents and kids all squeezing into a tiny parking lot and then hustling in the direction of the waiting coaches. A sea of color-coded kids in matching jerseys and knee-high socks poured over the grass and ran around like ants at a picnic. Then a whistle blew. It was fun and team building and, for the most part, good for Sam. But soccer also put Sara's nerves on edge because this type of aerobic activity inevitably trigged her son's never-ending asthma. It served as a seesaw of continual excitement and dread.

This was the part of Sam's life that Sara tried and usually failed at— not being what other parents referred to as a helicopter parent. But she couldn't help it. They didn't know what it was like to watch their child fall into a fit of wheezing coughs while he searched for air. The other parents had no clue how vigilant Sara had to really be.

Oh, that's just his exercise-induced asthma, no worries, she'd reply glibly to onlookers as she'd scurry onto the field, waving at the referee to call time-out while producing an extra inhaler from her pocket so Sam could catch some relief. This had been the story of her son's entire life.

Sara blamed the labor and delivery team who insisted on taking Sam prematurely. If only her beautiful baby hadn't been yanked from her womb at thirty-seven weeks. If only the procedure that was meant to help him hadn't caused Sam to swallow large amounts of amniotic fluid in the process. But the doctor had convinced Sara a C-section was the responsible route, claiming Sam had stopped thriving and would have a better chance outside the womb.

To this day Sara regretted that decision, even though she and Charlie had both agreed to it at the time. The sound of Sam's desperate pulls for his first breath still haunted her. Just after surgery, she was groggy and confused. Despite this, her instincts told her something was wrong. Before she could understand what was happening, she saw Sam being whisked away with a great sense of urgency to be plugged into machines and monitors in the neonatal nursery. Sara never forgot the feeling of emptiness in her arms when he left. It was a void she never wanted to know again.

If she thought about it long enough, she could still touch the raw grief that lay just behind her heart. The agony of not being able to swaddle her new baby, to nurse him and to doze by his side for five excruciatingly long days was virtually unbearable for both her and Charlie, who'd taken on the stress by mostly pacing around in the background. The day they handed her pink-cheeked cherub back to her, Sara swore she'd never let go.

"Mom?" Sam stood next to her now, a soccer ball rolling around under his neon-colored cleat. "I have to go."

Sara snapped out of it long enough to give him a hug and slide an inhaler into his free hand. She breathed in the scent of his hair. He squirmed but let her hold on for a second longer. "Go get 'em."

"See ya!"

Charlie, who had been chatting with the coach, wandered back over to the sidelines. "Should be a good game. They're apparently playing a team that came over from the coast."

Sara swallowed. The coast.

"Charlie?"

"Yeah?" He dragged his focus from the field. This was her window.

"Speaking of the coast, I uh, I have something to tell you."

"What's that?" He turned his head, only partially listening.

"I took Sam to the coast the other day. While you were out of town."

"That's nice." His eyes tracked the cluster of boys on the field.

"That's not all."

"What'd you guys do, go to the aquarium or something?"

"Not exactly."

Charlie threw her a puzzled look.

She glanced around, making sure none of the other soccer families were hovering too closely. She didn't feel like having to share her news with twenty other parents.

"Well, you're not going to believe this, but we went to see my dad."

Charlie turned, his face scrunched into a question. "Really? You and Sam went out there? That seems unlike you. You never want to talk about your dad. You called him a 'selfish boozer' who you'd never give the time of day."

"Yep. That's the one." Charlie knew most of her childhood story and had backed her decision not to locate her father when they were announcing their wedding, and again when Sam was born. Sara had explained that reaching out to her father would likely be a big disappointment, so Charlie never pushed. She'd appreciated that about her husband. He couldn't really relate, seeing how his parents were overly involved in his own life, but he'd supported her anyway. "Well, I wasn't sure how critical his condition was. I felt like I needed to go. You know, in case it was dire?"

"Okay . . . but last night you said he was going to be fine. You said he was hurt in a house fire, but he was recovering. Didn't you?"

"Yes. He is. I mean he's pretty badly burned. He needs someone to look after him when he gets out in a couple of days. And, well, I don't know how this happened, but I kind of agreed to take him in for a while until he can get back on his feet."

Charlie flinched ever so slightly.

"Ha! I know, crazy right? So anyway, for better or for worse, he's coming. Soon. Actually, he'll be here Monday. Just thought you should know."

The whistle blew and the game started, leaving Charlie's mouth hanging open and Sara holding her breath.

CHAPTER SEVEN

SARA

After being considerably stunned, Charlie lobbed some pointed questions her way regarding the decision to bring TR into their home. Namely how it would affect Sam and whether or not they needed to lock up their liquor cabinet. Sara couldn't blame him. She'd painted a pretty wild picture of her father over the years, so Charlie was right to worry.

"Well, he's injured and he's older now," she'd told Charlie. "I get the feeling he's moving a lot slower these days."

He'd only scratched his head.

"I can't explain it really, but it was just something I felt I had to do. Don't get me wrong; I'm still angry with him. I don't know. Maybe there's a small chance he's changed." She'd felt stupid saying this out loud. It made her sound gullible. And Charlie knew Sara suffered no fools. "Besides, it's just for a few days. How much could possibly happen?"

They'd talked more over the course of the next twenty-four hours, until work called and Charlie was back to packing his travel bag. Sara got the feeling he wasn't totally sold on her big idea to care for TR, but he agreed nonetheless.

"Thankfully, Sam will be in school most of the time your dad's here," he'd pointed out.

Sara had agreed but quietly wondered what she'd do with Sam during the hours he wasn't in school. She'd have to figure the logistics out as she went, she supposed.

After Sara watched Charlie drive away, she couldn't shake the nagging feeling of desertion that moved in with his departure. While the two of them had carved out time to talk over the weekend, none of the discussion had been about them; ironically, it had all been about her father. Sara shook her head. Even when he wasn't around, TR's larger-than-life presence overshadowed her own.

And now here she was, winding her way up the coastal highway to pick him up, wondering if she'd made a big mistake.

Collecting TR and transporting him to the car proved to be a production. For someone who fled a house fire with nothing but the clothes on his back, the man sure had accumulated a lot of stuff. Aside from the plastic bag bursting with medical supplies—bandages, anti-bacterial ointment, anti-inflammatory cream, painkillers, gauze, and other various sanitary odds and ends—he'd also obtained a ridiculously large cluster of Mylar balloons along with an obscene floral arrangement.

"Where did all of *this* come from?" Sara asked, attempting to lug a lead-heavy vase in one arm and balance a slippery bag in the other.

TR offered a sideways grin. Something like a secret hung just at the edges of his upturned mouth. She didn't know why, but seeing him possess such a display of gifts instantly drove a shard of anger through her. She had no idea who'd sent her father the well wishes, but it had to have been from someone close to him. Perhaps a friend or a lover. Someone who'd had access to her father's life where she had not.

She observed her sixty-nine-year-old father clutch his balloons like a triumphant toddler, while an amused staffer wheeled him toward the exit.

"All you're missing is a sucker," she grumbled under her breath.

"I have friends, you know," TR said, prickling.

"Really?"

TR pointed his chin staunchly forward as Sara hustled to keep up with the pace.

"Well, if you must know, they're from my manager, Edward. He found out I was in the hospital and wanted to express his condolences."

"You're not dying, TR."

"Felt like it."

"Uh-huh."

Sara was stumped. Did TR even still have a manager? Hadn't the work all but dried up lately? She studied her father distrustfully. If not, that meant he might have money, or at least options.

Rounding a corner, she was jolted from contemplation as she nearly collided with a harried nurse. *"Uff!"* Sara came to an abrupt halt as the vase slipped precariously low. Her load jostled. Sara's feet tangled as she struggled to save the display from crashing to the floor.

Gratefully, at the last minute, she righted the vase. She blew a huff of hot air up, removing hair from her dampened forehead. "Can we slow down a minute here?"

"Sorry." The orderly eased up on the wheelchair.

"Thanks." She wondered if the hospital staff was all too eager to boot TR and his cranky ways to the curb. This was only her second time visiting with her father, but it was enough to tell her he was going to be a handful.

Once he was delivered into the passenger seat, Sara shut the door and thanked the orderly. She clumsily pushed a folded five-dollar bill into his hand.

"Oh, you don't have to tip me, ma'am." The kid blushed. "It's part of the job."

"Take it. I'm sure you guys earned more than your paycheck taking care of this one." She angled her head in TR's direction and offered an awkward smile. Something in her suddenly had the urge to cling to this employee and beg him to admit her father back upstairs. Back to where trained professionals who knew what they were doing could take over. Because Sara was the exact opposite. An ill-equipped, estranged daughter with no idea what she was getting into. Thankfully, it was only going to be a few days.

TR coughed on the other side of the glass.

"I'm coming." Sara signaled. Scrambling to open the driver side, she asked if he required water. The smoke damage had dissipated, but TR's voice still sounded like sandpaper against a washboard. She wasn't going to lie. It unnerved her.

TR waved her off, assuring her everything was fine. Sara hesitated. There wasn't anything left to do except start the engine and embark on the long drive home.

~

By an hour into the drive, neither one of them had uttered more than two sentences. Silence settled over the car like an oppressive blanket, the weight of nothingness stifling them both.

With every bump in the road, every balk of discomfort from a wounded TR, Sara pursed her lips and tried to determine whether it was yet the time to ask questions. Being completely alone with this man, after twenty years of distance, was surreal. From time to time she'd steal a glimpse at his mottled, sun-spotted hands, his heavy brow, and his time-altered stoop. The years had clearly morphed his features, and she wondered just how much it had changed the person on the inside.

Part of her wondered whether she was dreaming. Here he was, her absentee father. Finally. But the close proximity of this now practical stranger was also decidedly uncomfortable. Which one of them was going to speak first? she wondered. Undoubtedly, there were subjects lingering on both of their tongues, but Sara and her father were either too stubborn or too nervous to begin.

Building up her courage, she glanced over once more. To her dismay, TR had nodded off. His head slumped to the side of the car, one cheek pressed against the glass. Sara couldn't tell if he was truly asleep or just resting his eyes. She cleared her throat once. Nothing. Deflating, she opted to let him nap.

TR jolted with a start when they finally arrived home and the engine cut. Sara raised an eyebrow. He was either a light sleeper or had been playing opossum the whole time to avoid conversation. She suspected the latter.

"Here we are," she announced to him cautiously. His expression was slightly dazed.

"This is it, huh?" A cough sputtered out, followed by a phlegmy clearing of the throat. He let out an exaggerated groan as the door swung wide. Sara hesitated. She had a grim feeling this was a snapshot of her life for the immediate future.

After shuffling and complaining his way to the entry, TR managed to get himself inside. Sara followed behind, carting his belongings and doing her best to bite down on her judgment. He was the one who'd asked to come, wasn't he? She wanted to point out that this was what a person got when he lacked any kind of insurance and was forced from the hospital. But she thought better of it. Best not to start off on the wrong foot.

Using a free limb to shut the door, Sara set down his things. "Here we are."

"So you said."

"It should be quiet today. No one else is home except for us. And everything is on one level. There aren't any stairs for you to navigate." It was a strain to keep her tone upbeat. "You'll also have your own room. So you can enjoy a bit of privacy."

Sara watched his eyes skip over the space. He glimpsed the walls. "There isn't any art hanging anywhere." It came out in a disdainful grunt.

Sara's cheeks grew hot.

Without waiting for a response, her father continued to survey the area. He took in the overstuffed twill sectional that had seen its share of use, the muted gray chenille pillows tucked into the corners, glass table lamps, and an array of framed family photos. The wood floors had been mopped, save for a half-chewed pinecone snuck in by Acer. A pair of Sam's shoes lay haphazardly near the rug. The morning mess in the adjoining kitchen wasn't tidied; she'd run out of time, and breakfast dishes still needed to be done. Sara gazed on all of it with new eyes.

What must her life look like from the outside?

TR's expression remained flat. Did he approve? It didn't matter. She didn't care.

Acer noticed them and barked from the other side of the glass slider.

"You've got animals?" TR asked nervously. His feet inched backward.

"Just one. A dog." She nodded and gestured toward the backyard.

"Humph."

Had her father been afraid of dogs when she was little? She couldn't recall. They'd never been a family with pets. It wasn't an option. Her mother claimed she was allergic to fur. Sara hadn't considered the lack of any pet odd until she married Charlie and he claimed otherwise.

Ignoring Acer's barking, Sara moved past her motionless father. "Well, let's get you settled into your room."

He grunted in reply.

As she gathered up his things, Sara's mouth went dry. Now what? She was officially in foreign territory. She was faced with a man she barely knew, a person who was more a stranger than a father, and things felt acutely awkward. Aside from the stubborn pride that lingered between them, the pair really didn't have all that much in common. Mutely, she led him down the hall.

She tried reminding herself she was the one with the advantage. After all, it was she who had the luxury of returning to her own house. If anyone should be uncomfortable, it should be her homeless father.

She peeked over her shoulder to make sure he was following.

TR's face was arranged into an uncertain expression. Sara wondered if he'd hoped for some kind of celebrity fanfare or rolling out of the red carpet upon his arrival. But a welcome home party was definitely not going to happen. Her family was busy elsewhere, and she'd purposely kept the news of her houseguest a secret from the neighbors. She hadn't even confided in Birdie yet. TR's existence was best kept quiet for now. At least until she could gauge his behavior.

Arriving at the threshold of the pint-size guest room, Sara forced a polite smile. She refused to let him know this whole event had the ability to unnerve her.

"Well, this is it." She ushered him inside. "It isn't much, but you'll have your own bathroom. That's one thing I loved when we bought the place, an abundance of bathrooms!" Okay, now she was just filling dead air with random statements.

TR shot her a funny look and hobbled inside. "I'm just glad to get away from that damned hospital bed."

Was that his idea of a compliment?

Brushing past his crankiness, Sara ran a hand over the quilted bedspread. "Well, my in-laws tell me this mattress is quite comfortable."

TR held tight to his sour-lemon expression.

She pointed toward the small closet. "I picked up a couple of things for you and hung them in there. It's not much, but hopefully it's enough to get you by for now."

The day before, she'd stopped by a big-box store and chosen a package of boxer shorts, several pairs of warm socks, sweatpants, and a few flannel shirts on sale. She knew her father would require loose clothing because of his burns, and she assumed he didn't have anything beyond his pajamas with him at the hospital. It had been strange to shop for a man she hardly knew. She'd scrutinized the clothing racks, wanting to please him but also confused about why she cared. Purchasing the undergarments felt necessary but bizarre, not to mention an awfully intimate thing to do. But she'd been hopeful as she handed over her credit card to the cashier. Maybe TR would appreciate the gesture.

Watching him now, she wasn't so sure.

"Well, perhaps you want to put your feet up for a while." She hustled out of the room, hoping he'd take the cue and stay put. He was already starting to irritate her. "I'll be out there, cleaning up my kitchen. Holler if you need anything."

Clicking the door, she exhaled. This was going to be a lot harder than she anticipated.

~

Hours later, after Sara had just returned from dropping Sam at his evening soccer practice, TR emerged from his room at dusk resembling a deranged vampire stepping from his den. In the half-light, with his wild hair and bloodshot eyes, he startled Sara with his sudden presence. Who was this untamed creature wandering her living room?

The dryness in Sara's throat returned. The pullover gray sweatshirt she'd purchased for him was rumpled, a heavy line of slumber creased his left cheek, and his eyes drooped at half-mast. He coughed a few times and then straightened.

It struck Sara that even in her father's absolute worst state, he had an uncanny way of filling a room. When she was a child, he'd often made her feel special by casting his glow directly onto her. But inevitably that glow waned, and she was forgotten when the attention from an adoring crowd increased with his newfound notoriety.

At times, this made for a confusing childhood. TR could make an entrance, and people, mainly women, would stop and stare. Likely this was in part because he was a known artist. Everyone loved a celebrity. But with TR there was something more. His presence always had a kind of magnetic pull. It wasn't because he was particularly tall or arresting. And Lord knew he had the propensity to be brash. Despite this, something effortlessly alluring radiated from his person. TR carried his own brand of confidence mixed with mischievous charm.

This charisma used to serve as a type of relief for Sara. Depending upon which way the wind blew, Joanne's mood could turn on a dime, enveloping their small household in a cloud of gloom. Recognizing this, TR would swoop Sara into his comforting arms and shelter her away behind the walls of his art studio—back then, a humble outer building in the form of a glorified shack served as his workspace. There he housed precious blocks of clay, firing equipment, and a special stool with a workbench saved for Sara. TR would plant Sara on that stool and spin fantastical stories about how her miniature clay creatures could come to life if she constructed them with the right dose of magic. Sara loved those moments with her father.

But every once in a while, his charm would also be accompanied by a hint of danger. Something would set him off, a failed effort with a sculpture or an argument with Joanne, and this made him erratic. Sara knew something unpredictable, like an outburst, might come at any given moment. It wasn't that he was verbally abusive per se; he just ran his mouth with brash opinions, often at the expense of others. It kept the people who knew TR on their toes, wondering what he might do or say next.

Today, it turned out, was no different.

At first glance, she could tell he was disoriented. His arms and his mouth hung slack. TR went from one corner of the rug to another, looking dazed and dragging a palm over the backs of furniture.

He must have taken some of those pain pills, Sara thought. Worry coiled itself around her middle. How unstable was he?

Spying her at the kitchen sink, TR perked somewhat. "I find myself in need of a little refreshment." His chapped lips smacked together.

Sara lurched forward, hoping to head him off at the pass. "You must be thirsty after your long nap." She was aware of how desperately false her graciousness sounded. It wasn't how she wanted to come across; she wanted to remain in charge.

TR slid languidly into an armchair. "Indeed."

"How about some water or juice?"

"Fine. Fine." Her father's head bobbed as if on a spring. "Although . . ."

Here it comes.

"If you were to tip a skosh of bourbon into that water and add a cube or two of ice, that would be even better."

Sara bristled. The old man clearly hadn't changed. She hadn't forgotten how he treasured his highball brimming with ice and liquor. While he rarely lost control, there was a period at the end of his time with Joanne, when they were fighting, that it was typical of him to be well lubricated by dinnertime. Sara figured it was a miracle he'd survived the past two weeks in the hospital being alcohol free. But then she remembered the morphine.

"Sorry." She folded her arms. "We don't keep bourbon in the house. I'll bring you some apple juice, though."

"Ah, a bit of a teetotaler, are you?" The condescension hung low.

Sara turned and snatched a glass. The cupboard banged louder than she intended. "No. Not at all," she called into the other room. "It's just not wise for someone in your condition to consume alcohol."

"Humph."

Wonderful. It was only day one, and he was already at it. Sara gritted her teeth. She wasn't sure she was going to have the fortitude for this. Thankfully, Sam would be away at soccer practice for another hour. TR needed to pull himself together if he wanted to spend any time around his grandson.

Delivering his drink, she produced a coaster and willed her nerves to settle as she lowered herself onto the nearby couch. TR blinked and said nothing.

"Are you in much pain?" she asked.

"Some." TR regarded her but looked away quickly, as if he were embarrassed to admit weakness.

"Do you recall much about the fire? Was it an accident? Like something electrical?"

"Hmm. Don't remember everything, but yes, it must have been an accident."

"Must have been?" Sara peered suspiciously at her father. It seemed like a rather odd way to phrase the event that had landed him in the burn unit of a hospital.

"That's right."

"And you realized just in time to get out?"

He looked at her. "I'm here, aren't I?"

This wasn't proving fruitful. He was either hiding something or too doped up on pills to have a clear conversation. Sara wasn't sure. Either scenario made her uncomfortable.

Sara wondered what he was thinking as he sat staring into space. Part of her yearned to study every inch of him. She had a profound urge to know this man who'd been missing for so long, to take in his features, his mannerisms, and even the way he cradled his drink. It was silly, but she'd missed out on so much that she wanted to catch up on. But another side of her was enormously uncomfortable. There wasn't any closeness here.

She fiddled with the corner of a pillow self-consciously. The dishwasher hummed mechanically in the background.

At last TR brought the juice glass to his lips. He pulled a face and muttered something inaudible under his breath. Sara assumed she didn't want to hear what it was.

Now what? TR continued to lounge with a stoned expression. Sara hadn't the faintest idea of what she was supposed to do next. She realized how difficult this was really going to be. And it scared her.

～

Lying in bed that night, listening to the weighted silence of the house, Sara ran through a list of questions that Joanne had never answered. A whole lifetime of mysteries.

But all her inquiries would have to be put on hold. Because the man parked in her guest room wasn't a friend and he wasn't family.

He was a stranger.

CHAPTER EIGHT

TR

Suburbia, as it turned out, was completely void of pleasure. Without it TR wasn't sure what in the hell he was supposed to do with himself.

On Wednesday morning, two days after he'd arrived at Sara's, he rolled over in bed and winced at the stream of light leaking through the blinds. The lids of his eyes squeezed shut. The sound of cars rushed by on the busy street outside. A sprinkler hissed to life. He pushed his face into the pillow and groaned. Beyond his own stench, he smelled something floral. Lightly pleasant. But it wasn't enough. He ached to fill his lungs with the vigor of briny air.

TR missed the sea. The roar of the crashing waves. The thick canvas of the bucketing fog.

He missed simple things too. Like the single hand-rolled cigarette he permitted himself after a long day's work. He missed the ability to create on a whim. He missed waking up next to the soft curves of Marie.

Despite missing home, he wasn't ready to go back even if he could. That would mean facing the damage from the fire, on top of everything else, and at the moment that was too much to bear.

After seeing his daughter, a guarded stranger, at the hospital, TR realized he'd been given an opportunity. Marie kicking him out had caused Sara to take him in. Never in a million years would he have believed it. But here he was anyway. Of course, he wasn't sure how this experiment would go. After all, Sara was awfully angry. And he, too, was fairly uncomfortable being on foreign ground. But he couldn't ignore the tiny seed of hope that sprouted the day she arrived. He hadn't felt that kind of hope in years. For that reason, TR needed to see if closeness was at all possible with his long-lost daughter.

But so far things hadn't been easy.

Surely, given his terrible state, he should be allowed some creature comforts while he was laid up, miles away from anything familiar. But no. His daughter was not of the same belief.

TR's healing process was to be a quiet affair.

This was mainly due to the rules. Ridiculous, uptight, bourgeois rules. There was to be no cursing, no cigarettes, and cruelly, no booze of any kind. To TR's great disappointment, not even the smallest nip of a warm nightcap was offered on his first evening spent in a strange place. One might argue that given his condition, such a gesture would have been the hospitable thing to do.

But not in that house. "I don't think we need to overdo things right now" was his daughter's dismal directive. Looking around, TR doubted his daughter even knew the meaning of the term. This bland existence was not the life he'd expected any daughter of his to be living. No, sir.

And perhaps even worse, there'd been no visitors either. Not that he had many friends left anyway. Seemed they'd all evaporated with the money.

But still. Seeing as the husband was off traveling for work and the kid was otherwise occupied during the daytime, a visitor or two would have been a welcome distraction from the pain.

His presence, however, was not to be made known.

What did that even mean? TR had wondered.

So for two days he'd kept mostly to his room. After leaving him in the hospital over the previous weekend, Sara had returned Monday, tight-lipped and orderly, briskly signing her name to forms and jotting instructions for home care.

When he'd asked after the whereabouts of the kid, she coolly informed TR that the boy was at school. *That's what children do*, she'd said pointedly, as if TR were an idiot. He assumed she was implying he would know such things if he were a real parent. And the one time he'd actually gotten a glimpse of the boy in the house, Sara had rushed the kid away to his bedroom before TR even had the chance to get close.

They were off to a rocky start.

On that first day, during the drive home, unnecessary conversation had been avoided at all costs. This was partially due to the winding roads that lulled TR into a sleepy state, and also because he worried over what he might say. He didn't know yet how or when he'd tell her about Marie . . . or Bo. But to do so on their first day reunited seemed too soon. Instead, he'd watched from the corner of his eye as Sara gripped the wheel with whitened knuckles and scowled through the windshield. Why had his daughter agreed to take him in? Obviously, she was mad about it. So why do it?

And was she always this angry? He couldn't recall.

The last time he'd seen Sara she'd been about sixteen or seventeen years old. A beautiful, fair-skinned teenage girl. The event had been an art opening, if memory served. He believed it was the one celebrating his light and ceramic installations at a fussy gallery in Los Angeles.

TR hadn't spoken to his ex-wife, Joanne, for a long time. This didn't mean he hadn't tried to communicate; in fact, he was in the habit of sending handwritten cards with the odd check whenever he could. He hoped to somehow make sure Sara was cared for. But he almost never received a reply. The regret and worry he'd carried around over Sara's well-being never left him. It was an anvil that had the potential force to bring him to his knees, if he allowed himself to dwell on the mistakes of the past. But Joanne had all but hidden from society and taken their daughter along with her. Booze and women helped to numb TR's pain and guilt over his failed marriage and nonexistent role as a parent. That, and the slow march of time.

Despite this, Joanne must have read about the event in the press because there she was that evening, uninvited and inebriated. Regardless of their strained relationship, she showed up, pushing her way through a host of flashbulbs and partygoers. She was dressed in a too-short cocktail dress and dragging an embarrassed-looking Sara behind her.

"Say hello to your *daughter*, TR," Joanne had slurred slightly, the waxy red of her lipstick bleeding into the fine lines around her mouth. A horrified Sara was practically thrust into the middle of the crowd.

TR had been a bit boozy that evening as well, with so many people toasting the exhibit and plying him with free drinks. This clouded his judgment, but he specifically remembered trying to hug Sara and pull her to the side for a conversation. He'd been distracted by Joanne's wild appearance but genuinely glad to see his daughter after so long. The rush of conflicting emotions had been virtually overwhelming.

Joanne ruined it all before it could even begin. He remembered accusations flying, cameras flashing, and then both women rushing toward the door.

What happened that night still wasn't entirely clear. But that was Joanne for you. Unstable and emotional. TR was sorry Sara got tucked so tightly under his ex's wing, but what could he do? His reasons for having to be gone were incontrovertible.

And now here he was, decades later, under his grown daughter's roof. Grateful yet confused.

At the onset, TR had been appreciative of a real mattress and decent night's rest. He'd already suffered through weeks of nurses waking him on the hour to check his vitals and peer suspiciously at his wounds. Now at his daughter's, he was free from that relentless schedule. Gone was the stink of antiseptic and urine that drifted in every time the door leading to the corridor opened. Gone were those nosy cops too.

But his misery wasn't over quite yet.

Each morning, just outside the guest room door, the footsteps of his warden could be heard. It was bad enough she had to dress his wounds. But Sara would start by poking her head around the corner and instructing TR to get up and wash. Like he was a damned moron.

It was emasculating as all get-out.

"You're going to have to hold still," she'd say, approaching him, her face forming a tight pucker. Sara didn't admit it, but TR got the sense the medical aspect of his care might've set her teeth a bit on edge.

She'd start by laying out a complicated collection of first-aid materials. In his opinion she was overthinking it. What was wrong with a simple piece of gauze and a Band-Aid? Hell, even a paper towel and some tape would suffice. But no, Sara went by the book, never skipping a step of the instructions doled out by the hospital nurses. She'd make a big production out of going into the bathroom and washing her hands and then coming back out to unwind bandages and uncap ointments. For his part, TR was instructed to sit still on the edge of the mattress as she drew the table lamp nearer to gingerly peel back the old dressing and scrutinize the burns on his right side.

Her breath was soft as she delicately pressed a warm washcloth to the tender area. TR would try to cooperate, remaining quiet and focused on Sara. While the act itself was fairly painful, he welcomed the experience. How lovely to have his daughter's face hovering inches from his own, allowing him the freedom to study the girl he'd missed for so many years. It was peculiar to see her all grown up, her strawberry hair pulled loosely down around the nape of her neck, her peach complexion now marked with spots of sun damage and a scattering of fine lines. He longed to know her again.

The problem was Sara wanted to know things about him too.

"So tell me more about how you escaped the fire," she'd probe. "You were inside the house when you smelled smoke? Did any alarms go off? Were you able to save anything?"

"Yes, I was inside asleep and managed to run out when the smoke came. I only got out with myself and nothing more." He winced then, acting as though speaking were too much amid the pain. And sometimes it was. But mostly he was afraid if they started discussing the fire, he'd inevitably slip and disclose information about the complications in his life. He hadn't figured out how to handle everything himself, let alone how to broach any of it with her. He hoped to establish some kind of civil relationship with Sara before admitting things about his life that might hurt his daughter.

And so their routine went each morning. A few questions and a lot of avoidance.

He'd then make his way into the kitchen for medication and breakfast only to find a lukewarm cup of weak coffee and a plate containing a single runny egg. While he attempted to sit and eat in peace, she'd run the blasted vacuum cleaner over the rug as if her life depended on it. The constant whirring drowned out any chance of connecting with his own thoughts.

His daughter made it known she intended for him to suffer.

But today was playing out differently.

As he stood adjacent to the small bathroom vanity and ran a steaming washcloth over his face, TR detected voices coming from the kitchen. Until now, everyone practically walked around on tiptoe in that place. Like they were afraid to bother one another. But a sudden crashing of silverware against dishes in the sink, accompanied by an outburst, told him something was off.

The dog barked.

A male voice rose and then clashed with Sara's.

Must be the husband home from his trip, TR thought. *Charles or Chuck something.* He replaced the towel and strained to listen. If he was to walk out into trouble, TR wanted to know what he would be getting into. He glanced at his naked and still-bandaged reflection in the oblong mirror. He frowned. Not exactly in fighting shape.

The kitchen was just a ways down the hall, and the conversation was mostly muffled. TR still recognized the tense tone. He'd experienced many a row with girlfriends over the years, most recently with Marie, and could identify that type of bitter exchange anywhere.

Unevenly, he shuffled over to the closet and jerked a borrowed robe off the hook. He grunted at the sight of the worn terry cloth. *Also probably the husband's.*

The voices escalated.

TR felt a little sweaty. He wasn't sure what to do next. His eyes flicked around the room for some sort of weapon. Perhaps he needed to defend Sara. If this guy turned out to be bigger than him, he didn't have much in the way of protection.

TR cursed. There wasn't anything but a cashmere throw and some old magazines stacked on a vintage wicker chair. This was exactly why he kept a baseball bat tucked into the shadows under his bed back home. Being a celebrity, you never knew when some crazy would wander onto your property. One had to be prepared.

"Screw it," TR muttered.

He flung the door open. Pain flared down his side like electric currents, but he moved out anyway. He wanted to size up this mystery husband of his daughter's who, up until that point, had yet to materialize. The voices continued. His bare feet slapped faster along the hardwood floor.

They must have heard him coming, because all sounds ceased. Arriving out of breath in the kitchen, TR came face-to-face with a weepy-eyed Sara and a man wearing a pilot's uniform and a grimace.

Both of them met TR with shocked expressions.

The curly-haired dog wagged its tail and formed nervous figure eights around his ankles.

TR ran his left hand through his matted hair and tried to regain composure. The pain of moving quickly had left him nauseated and panting. Needles of agony crept down his skin. Nevertheless, he gritted his teeth and plastered a phony grin across his face.

"You must be Chuck!" he bellowed. "I was wondering when you'd get home from your trip so we could be properly introduced."

The pilot's jaw unhinged.

TR wondered if his burned flesh still smelled of overcooked meat. He took a step back but didn't break eye contact.

"*TR,*" Sara hissed. Her eyes bulged like emerald stones.

The husband immediately averted his eyes. "Whoa."

"What's wrong?" TR couldn't make out what was happening. Both Sara and her husband were recoiling, not from one another but him.

Just then a slight breeze trickled in from an open window. The temperature caused TR to feel a little funny. He dumbly followed Sara's gaze downward.

"Oh, Christ!" His good hand swatted the gaping terry cloth robe shut. They were staring at *him*. "Left the barn door open! Ha! A little too much to see so early in the morning, eh?" He forced a laugh. In his haste, he'd forgotten the sash to the robe.

"Good grief, don't you wear pajamas?" Sara made a face.

TR's memory lighted on the extra pile of clothing Sara had provided. He shook his head. "Nah, never had any use for them."

"Evidently."

Hoping to change the subject, he scanned the room for coffee.

"I didn't make any yet," Sara snipped. She obviously knew what he was seeking and made her way to the space-age machine resting on the counter.

"This is my husband, Charlie, by the way. Not Chuck." She jerked her head over her shoulder. Ignoring both of the males in the room, his daughter popped some kind of pod into a container and pressed a button. Within seconds, dark-brown liquid flowed into a cup.

"Nice to meet you." Charlie stepped forward and attempted to shake TR's good hand. "Although, I gotta say, we haven't heard much about you. Like ever." He laughed uneasily and then looked over at Sara at this last bit.

His daughter's eyes shifted to the floor. Her cheeks flushed pink.

TR was beginning to understand that maybe Sara hadn't even told her family about him. To this group of people, he was just a stranger. Well, he supposed this was only fair. Hurtful, but fair. He *had* led the life of a stranger.

"Right," TR announced in a delayed response. "Well, here I am!"

Sara nodded and handed him his coffee. Her sigh landed at his feet like an anvil.

"Here you are."

TR pretended he wasn't sure if she was referring to him or the drink. Then his heart skipped a beat when he saw she'd handed him some kind of dark roast. A deep, nutty aroma wafted up and tickled his nose. Sara had been holding out on him after all. Maybe in all the chaos of the morning she'd forgotten to punish him with whatever weak doughnut store crap she'd provided on earlier days. Or maybe he was getting on her good side.

As he took his first inhale of real caffeine, he studied Charlie as he edged toward the door. A lean fellow, really. Kind of willowy like their son—who must have been at school, for he was nowhere around. Same brown eyes too. Seemed polite enough once the yelling had stopped, TR guessed. But slippery. Like a fish that didn't want to be caught. The indecent exposure thing probably didn't help, but this guy clearly wanted to be elsewhere.

TR cast a sidelong glance to check whether his daughter noticed the same thing. The violent way she was scrubbing the counter with a soapy sponge told him she most definitely did.

"Well, I'm actually just off to work. Maybe we can catch up next time," Charlie said, snatching up a travel case and backing out of the room.

Sara's entire demeanor deflated. TR wondered if their quarrel had anything to do with the fact that this character was never home.

Easing out a nearby bar stool, TR positioned it just so in order to climb up without inducing too much discomfort. He perched his elbows on the breakfast counter and clasped the coffee cup. Feeling more alert for the first time in days, he observed the details of his surroundings.

The place was cozy. He had to admit. Bright daylight entered through a sizable bay window, casting a cheery glow on shelves that were stacked with blue and white dishes and glass mason jars filled with snacks and cookies. A comical little handmade bowl balanced near the porcelain sink. Heavy red glazing was glopped around its lopsided exterior.

He smirked. Something the kid must have made in school.

TR mused at this grown-up daughter of his. She certainly was the hostile type. But seeing her at home, he discovered she was also the kind of person who went to the trouble of displaying her son's handmade knickknack, no matter how terrible it was. She was clearly proud of the boy. And, from the little he'd witnessed, she appeared to be a devoted mother.

He liked that. But his smile was quickly replaced by a low feeling. He hadn't stuck around long enough to collect Sara's childhood knickknacks, and this realization troubled him. He'd left and not returned. And now his kid was an adult. TR was suddenly and acutely aware of the need to make up for lost time. To perhaps see if he could reverse some of the damage that might have been done. How on earth he was going to accomplish such a thing was beyond him, but he was willing to try.

"Well, girl." He set down his cup and strummed his fingers on the polished surface in front of him. "I guess it's just you and me now."

"Right." Sara turned to face him and offered a sad smile. "Just you and me."

CHAPTER NINE

SARA

Always be careful what you wish for. Sara considered this statement as she stood in the kitchen, opposite TR.

Today her wish came true. Not only had TR risen with things to say, but also he'd come barreling into the kitchen on red alert.

The day had not started well.

For one thing, there was the awful fight with Charlie. Sara had knots in her stomach just thinking about it. But he'd left her little choice. After learning her husband had come home for a night's sleep in his own bed only to rush back out for a double shift, she'd exploded. Charlie of course had snapped into full defense, claiming she didn't support his work and making a point to hurl a mountain of guilt in her direction whenever he did return. Having her father there didn't help. Charlie had accused her of being overly emotional from the stress of having to take care of TR. What did he know about the stress she was under? Her husband wasn't ever home long enough to appreciate how hard she was trying to keep it all together. How many times was Sara left with the view of Charlie's back as he put distance between them? And there he went again; practically sprinting for the exit once TR emerged.

TR. She snorted. Her father's timing couldn't have been worse.

She hadn't even had the chance to finish making her point to Charlie before hurricane TR struck. The old man had shown up with his bloodshot eyes full of innocence as his bathrobe hung wide open for the entire world to see. *Un-freaking-believable.*

No wonder Charlie ran.

Sara rubbed her temples and looked on as her oblivious father relaxed in her kitchen. He made little smacking sounds as he slurped greedily at her good coffee. Was he actually moaning?

Where had she put the aspirin?

It was bad enough she had to set everything aside to tend to her impetuous father. But Sara had the needs of Sam to consider too. Luckily, he'd taken the bus to school earlier that morning. But he would be home soon, and Sara was going to have to run interference.

She was exhausted just thinking about it.

Sara ran cool water from the faucet over her hands. "You know," she announced to TR over the running water, "Charlie's got a lot of demands at work. Being a pilot, it's a busy life. It's just how things are right now. He'll be back soon."

"I suspect so."

Sara looked away. It was no business of her father's that her marriage was splintering.

"It was all planned, you know. Him leaving today? Just part of the job." She wondered if TR was buying her bullshit. He only nodded once, so it was difficult to tell.

Swatting off the faucet, she twisted a dishtowel through her wet hands. The shakiness was faint but still there.

True, she was aware of the latest cause of her husband's annoyance. Sara hadn't shared much with her husband about TR in the past. She had given him the brief version: that after becoming famous for his sculpture work, he had summarily ditched Joanne and Sara for greener pastures. Charlie had asked a few times to know more; in the beginning he lightly suggested Sara try to find him and let her father know how she felt. But Sara always brushed him off. It was mostly too painful to revisit the sins of her father. Eventually, TR's name vanished from their discussions altogether, sending the subject of her father into deep hibernation.

The parent Charlie knew most about was Joanne. And for much of the time, that had felt like more than enough. Yet there was Sara's father, suddenly taking up residence in their guest room and making an appearance in Charlie's favorite robe without warning. That was unfortunate.

Couldn't Charlie see Sara was upset too? Where had he been? When she'd asked, he'd been dodgy with the details.

She wasn't buying "the airline needs me" bit anymore. He was a grown man with seniority and a good reputation within the company. Because of this, Charlie had always been able to dictate his schedule. So what had suddenly changed? Didn't he want to be around her anymore? Certainly, he couldn't believe the company was more important than his family. Sam needed a father, and she needed a partner.

Sara refused to acknowledge the pinprick of fear over the idea he might have found someone else, someone better, with whom to take up company. She refused to be abandoned.

She'd been driving home this very point when TR had intruded. *We're supposed to be a team, Charlie. You can't just return home for one night and then take off again so soon.* Sara had wagged a finger and reminded him she had never signed up to be a single parent.

Her husband's blood had been boiling, that much was clear. But she'd never know what he was thinking because, once TR had inserted himself into the picture, Charlie had taken off like a shot.

Sara surveyed the room and sighed.

Dishes were piled up on the counter, the refrigerator was near empty, and the dog required a walk. There were only a few hours until Sam would be returning on the school bus, and by the way TR was throwing back Vicodin, she would need to make a run to the pharmacy.

And she could forget her duties to the PTA this week. There just weren't enough hours in the day.

After watching TR drain two cups of coffee, Sara decided he was caffeinated enough for a little light probing. There was a lot to discuss with her father, an unending list of topics, but she knew she wasn't emotionally ready to touch any of them yet. These were heavy subjects that might cause her to unravel. She needed to prepare for that. What she was willing to dive into, however, was the fire.

Edging around to his side of the counter, Sara kicked her legs lazily over a stool. She did her best impression of a relaxed vibe. It was essential to act casual if she were to catch him off guard. Maybe that way he'd share a bit more information.

"So"—she twisted a lock of hair—"I noticed the lilies in your room are beginning to lose their petals. They were so nice. Who did you say sent those to you?" She recalled TR's defensive retort when she'd first raised an eyebrow back at the coast.

"Flowers?" The upbeat demeanor her father had a minute ago now appeared to wilt slightly. He looked away and feigned ignorance, pretending to inspect something at the bottom of his cup.

Doing her best to mask new irritation, she tried again. "You know, the arrangement you got in the hospital? The giant vase we brought home with us? The one that spilled water all over my back seat?"

TR pressed his index finger to his cheek. Peachy sunspots mottled the skin. A puffy, crescent-shaped scar ran over his knuckle. Sara wondered what had caused it. A flash of grief moved through her. Her father's hands, which were once so familiar, were now a curious roadmap of the many years she'd been denied.

TR moved his jaw around in contemplation and finally answered. "Ah yes. Those flowers. Lovely display."

"Uh-huh."

Really, was her father prone to dementia or just faking it?

A hand shooed the air between them. "We can toss them if they're dying. Nothing lasts forever."

Sara frowned. "That's not what I was asking."

"Oh?"

Oh, for goodness' sake. "TR, who sent you the flowers?"

"I thought I told you they were from my manager, Edward. Wonderful fellow."

She narrowed her gaze. "Edward who?"

"Why does it matter?"

Because I get the strange feeling you're not telling me a whole lot. She sucked air through her teeth and faked a smile. "Because I thought you might want to use my phone and tell him where you are, that's all. If he went to the trouble of sending you that bouquet and big batch of balloons"—which had met their demise in the hot car—"then he's probably worried about you. Maybe you should touch base."

Her father squirmed in his seat, readjusting the sash of his robe. Sara twisted up her mouth. *You aren't fooling anyone,* she thought. Not thirty minutes ago he'd carelessly flashed the whole house. Suddenly he was concerned with modesty?

"Ah yes. I think I will call him. But later. I believe he's traveling at the present. Busy guy."

"What about other people in your life who might be concerned? A girlfriend perhaps?" Sara knew enough about her father from past headlines to know he liked to keep the constant company of women.

"Mmm," he responded. "I don't think any girlfriends are worried about me at the moment." His eyes drifted to the ceiling, studying something invisible.

"Well, maybe we should check on the status of your house. The police paid you a visit in the hospital; from what I understand, they reported a lot of damage. We should call them—and maybe call a restoration company to go check things out."

To her surprise, TR landed a fist on the counter with a sudden thump. "No!"

An uneasy flutter materialized in Sara's chest, yet something deeper in her core forced her to speak anyway. "No? Don't you want to know when your house will be habitable again? Aren't you worried about your things?"

Gathering himself up, he tightened his robe. Sara watched the wave of emotion recede behind his eyes. "Yes, I'd like to know about my things. There are a lot of works in progress waiting for me to return. But with my pain level, I'm just not ready to travel to the coast. I need more time. You know, to heal. At the moment I'm not feeling too well. I need to rest."

Sara frowned. For someone so prideful, it seemed odd he was admitting he was too fragile to be productive.

"Okay. You just let me know if I can help."

Before the words had left her tongue, TR gave up his post and drifted in the direction of his room. He jutted a thumb into the air. "Righty-o!"

He shut the door on Sara and any chance for discussion.

Well, that went nowhere.

Sara slouched and stared blankly at the wall. The two of them had been circling one another for days, avoiding genuine conversation. At first she believed this was because her father's system was chock-full of heavy narcotics. But now she wasn't so sure. Was TR purposely acting dopey just to avoid her questions? Did he have something to hide beyond the transgressions of his past?

Sara went over to the laptop resting on her desk. Up until now, she'd stayed away from all things TR on the internet. But perhaps it was time to do a little digging.

Where to start? She tapped the desk and debated. The mystery of her father's life went so far back.

There had been a time for Sara when TR had been accessible. Her memories of this period were securely locked away, and it often hurt to retrieve them. But they existed. When she was around seven or eight years old, Sara was one of the few people allowed into TR's inner sanctum. Even at a young age, she realized this was a unique privilege.

Many of her childhood days were whiled away on a rustic wooden bench in the corner of TR's messy studio. This was Sara's favorite place to quietly examine her father's work. She'd forever remember the cool, earthy smell of the clay slabs and the surety of them against the flesh of her tiny palms. She could still picture her fingerprints creating faint impressions around the edges of the mud, recording her very existence. She used to love the pleasing way her father sank a sharp cutting wire into the doughy mass, choosing a section with care. Sara would always be gifted a small slice, which usually resulted in a painstakingly molded dog or horse.

Her creations were scrutinized with her father's detailed eye, their attributes commented on and then praised. It was in that studio that she first blossomed. The clay work itself was an instant love for Sara. Her father seemed to acknowledge this passion, and he encouraged it, celebrating her pieces as if she were a peer and not some silly child squandering away the hours in her father's office.

This recognition from her father, in and of itself, had filled her up enough to replace everything else that was missing in her life. It didn't matter that there weren't any other siblings or that her mother was preoccupied with her own self-inflicted melancholy. Back then, the art had been everything.

Hours would fly by as Sara also studied her father's craftsmanship. She admired the way his rough hands formed obscure shapes in his work, the way the tendons in his forearms flexed and bowed. Her hand would quietly skim the tray of intricate carving tools that seemed to call to her like rare and precious objects yearning to be touched. When left alone, she'd let her fingertips graze the rolls of wire mesh used to support malleable clay forms. Everything had a purpose, and she wanted to understand what.

Watching her father sculpt was like witnessing a magician produce something out of thin air. TR was the enchanted wizard, and Sara was his little fairy muse. At least, that was the story she used to tell herself.

But those days had long ago vanished.

Dismissing these memories to the far corners of her mind, Sara pushed open her laptop. The screen illuminated, and instantly unopened emails and calendar updates filled the screen, each digital notification a red flare that had been shot up, signaling for help.

Casting her guilt aside, she cleared them to the bottom of her screen. She'd come back to her duties soon. At the moment, there were more pressing matters to address.

"Okay, TR," she whispered toward the computer. "Let's see if we can uncover a few things."

Her fingers moved in nimble strokes across the keyboard. Pausing after a few clicks, she checked over her shoulder. All was still. She relaxed a little. TR must have been napping. That was good. It was best to be cautious when googling someone in the next room. But then again, Sara thought, this was TR's doing. If he'd just been upfront with her in the first place, she wouldn't have to resort to online snooping.

The first few items she came across were ones she'd seen many times before. A smattering of old images and articles, mainly from arts and entertainment publications, featured TR in his glory days. Looking young and virile, he posed in eclectic galleries and discussed his works at museums. There was even a Wikipedia page dedicated to him.

Sara clicked the link and scanned the biography.

Thomas Harlow Young (born June 7, 1949, in Los Angeles, California) is an internationally acclaimed sculptor, painter, and installation artist renowned for large-scale sculptures that emphasize the human figure. Harlow's most recognizable work, *Girl Rising*, is a clay-to-bronze statue, created in the image of his daughter, Sara, depicting a child playing at the rising surf . . .

Sara snapped the computer shut. Pinching the bridge of her nose, she tried to rid the statue's gleaming, metallic image from her brain. A bitter taste coated her mouth.

She hated that thing. She always had. For everything it represented and everything it took away. And yet the public loved it. Sara always considered it ironic how people believed the statue was a testament to TR's connection with his daughter. It's true, she'd posed for the piece and spent countless hours with him in the studio while he molded, shaped, and reworked the sculpture. Sara had been nothing but eager to hold steady and play her father's all-important muse.

But in the end, it was the thing that pulled them apart. After the statue was so well received, TR was suddenly lured away to make appearances at the request of important people in the art world. He'd frequently head off on exhibit tours and then return at all hours of the night from parties and work events. He claimed he needed to be away, to network and follow the art. Tension in their house mounted on the daily, as Joanne accused TR of all sorts of infidelities, and her father slowly began to check out from their lives. The fights escalated until one day he simply went away. Sara asked her mother if TR had left word, sent her any messages. Surely her father wouldn't forget his muse. But Joanne remained tight-lipped, giving her daughter little hope. Sara was left behind to feel like nothing but a figment of her father's spectacular imagination.

Steeling herself against further self-pity, Sara straightened and opened the laptop once more. She'd been able to disregard discomfort brought on by the sculpture before, so she could do it again.

Hitting the "Search" button, Sara entered what she knew about TR's coastal property. Which wasn't much.

The truth was she hadn't the slightest indication how her father had been living. All she knew was that he existed alone in some rambling house out on the Oregon coastline. His artwork hadn't shown in years, so she wasn't sure what he did out there day after day. The only shred of information TR shared was that his house was secluded from the road and it overlooked the Pacific Ocean.

Sara tried getting more out of him when he'd first arrived. She'd lobbed a few questions while changing his bandages. *What about the accident?* she'd asked. Didn't he want to get to the bottom of that? But TR was guarded and turned indignant. He'd waved her off and claimed he didn't want to talk about it.

It left her suspicious.

For example, how did the fire start? Was it a mishap or something more ominous? After scouring the local paper back at the hospital, the only thing she'd been able to uncover was a small mention in the police log reporting a fire at a private residence located above a cove. The house had been badly burned and its owner seriously injured. No probable cause identified.

TR must have been living up there like a hermit, because as she searched online now, she found the event had attracted little to no attention from anything other than local media.

Sara was dumbfounded.

What had really happened?

There was something about the way TR eluded her that made her suspect there was more to the story. She was determined to find out just what that was. But it would have to wait because, at that moment, TR ambled back into the room and announced he was out of pills.

Once more, her investigation was put on hold.

CHAPTER TEN
SARA

Sara and TR fell into a steady rhythm. The cadence of time was kept even by routine first-aid checks and the running of errands, with sleep and meals bookending it all.

Sara did her best to keep Sam occupied with the normalcy of school and planned afternoon activities. And Charlie, though he maddeningly announced he'd extended his already lengthy work shift, made an effort to call each night for video chats with Sam. Not wanting to intervene, Sara would tiptoe by, doing her best to remain unseen on the periphery. She'd wait until they were done and then say hello. She'd ask if his flights were going smoothly and make an attempt to connect, despite Charlie's brief answers. It wasn't easy. Despite the fact she and Charlie weren't exactly communicating, at least Sam was getting the benefit of catching up with his father in some capacity. For that, she supposed she should be grateful.

It was how to limit her ten-year-old's exposure to his grandfather that stumped Sara. She still felt unsure of how TR's influence, or lack thereof, might affect Sam. The three of them were under one roof. And in the evenings, she had no choice but to cautiously let the two of them interact.

"Tell me about your day, boy," TR would inquire around suppertime.

"It was good. You know, the usual school stuff. I'm in charge of the class turtle this week."

"Turtle!" TR practically leaped back at the announcement.

Sam giggled, enjoying a fresh audience. "Yeah, he's twenty-six years old and eats dandelion leaves from your hand. And he only poops like once a month."

"You don't say!" TR scratched his stubble, dumbfounded. "That's just about the damnedest thing I've ever heard. And I've heard some things!"

Sam's answers were unguarded and honest. Sara hadn't given him reason to be leery. But he must have sensed Sara's hesitation around her father, because he'd speak only when spoken to, not yet brave enough to start a conversation on his own accord.

Up until this point, their communication had mainly consisted of passing food items at the breakfast counter or trading remarks over the dog. TR usually went back into his room when Sara would sit down in the evenings to help Sam with his homework. Sara wasn't sure what Sam thought of his grandfather yet. She supposed he really didn't have much to go on.

She guessed this would eventually change.

TR, for his part, had succumbed to playing the role of a willing patient, after a few stumbling blocks. At least, as much as an egotistical old goat could without conceding his principles too much. God forbid he attempt to step out into the sunlight and stretch his legs from time to time. And the introduction of anything remotely nutritious, like a kale salad or cold-pressed juice, resulted in a fit of ridiculous proportion. Sara could forget any of that nonsense. As far as TR was concerned, she was *barking up the wrong tree.*

"I'm going to walk the dog," she'd announced earlier. "Why don't you put on that jacket hanging in your closet and come with me? It would be good for you to get your muscles moving for a bit."

TR pulled a face. "Why would I do that? It's raining out there."

"Only a little drizzle; it won't hurt you. Don't you think you need to build back some stamina after the hospital?" She'd hoped getting him out on a walk might put them in neutral territory, where she could have a captive audience and probe more about his life. And, as an added bonus, get him back to health so he could leave.

"Maybe later," he said, and wandered back to the security of his bedroom.

It was not lost on Sara that, for the second time in her life, she'd become the child caregiver of an adult parent (who maddeningly acted like a child)—just as in her rocky relationship with Joanne.

It was a function she'd learned growing up with an irresponsible mother. Despite her disapproval of Joanne's wacky choices (purchasing a pair of neon thrift-store beanbags as their living room furniture) and her mother's oftentimes lack of understanding of a situation's gravity (the time she laughed off overfilling the bathtub until water pooled onto the floor and dripped one level below), Sara knew if she did not step in with a dose of common sense, things would inevitably turn out far worse. After Sara moved out and got an apartment of her own, Joanne would often do crazy things. She'd sign up for luxury European river cruises with money she didn't have, only to call Sara crying and ask her to help figure out how to cancel nonrefundable tickets. Or she'd meet a man in the meat department of the grocery store and invite him over, diving headfirst into dating someone whom she knew nothing about, only to complain to Sara her new beau was married and she didn't know how to unravel herself from the situation. These rash decision-making routines of her mother exasperated Sara. Joanne never learned; she never changed. Everything was always filled with unnecessary drama. And yet, without Sara's help to fix her mother's mistakes, Joanne would surely fail.

Sara didn't have it in her to turn a blind eye and walk away. Just as when she was younger and took it upon herself to scrape together dollar bills from the bottom of her mother's purse for groceries and make sure her depressed mother got out of the house from time to time, she assumed a similar role as an adult. It must be something in the makeup of her DNA that caused her to stick around and clean up the mess. A combination of guilt and sense of duty forced Sara to the front lines when a parent was flailing. Feelings aside, things needed to be handled.

And who else was she going to count on if not herself?

~

The following day Sara learned she wasn't alone in her search.

It was coming on three o'clock, and she was just collecting her purse before heading out the door. Sam's school would be letting out soon, and she wanted to be there when it did. Recently she'd taken to picking Sam up rather than relying on the bus. Right now, with Charlie gone so much and TR taking up her energy, it was important to spend time alone with her son. The fifteen-minute car ride allowed for a kind of welcome decompression on both their parts, before returning home and walking into whatever awkwardness TR had up his sleeve.

Her thoughts had been cluttered as she rushed along her front walkway. Overnight, the wet weather had made for a treacherous path. Carefully, she picked her way along the slickened moss that peeked through a herringbone pattern of brick pavers.

The slam of a car door averted her concentration. Sara snapped her head up. In doing so, her feet came dangerously close to slipping out from underneath her.

"Whoops!" Throwing her arms out for balance, she stuttered to a stop.

Two men dressed in formidable dark blue came her way. Sara gripped her jacket as the policemen approached in lockstep. Glancing beyond them to the street, she noticed a nondescript four-door sedan parked at the curb. She couldn't tell where the plates were from, but her first thoughts went to Charlie. And then to Sam.

Her limbs went numb. Sara steadied herself and braced for the worst.

"Ma'am?" One of the officers produced a laminated badge in his meaty hand. Sara was too frantic to read his identification.

"What's happened?" She searched his solemn face.

"I'm Detective Hernandez. This is my partner, Detective Muth. We're detectives from the Sandpoint Police Department."

"Sandpoint?" She let out a whoosh of breath. Her eyes darted to the matching emblems of their uniforms. Blue patches were sewn onto the shoulders with a seaside scene depicted on the logo.

Of course. She should have known. This was some business about TR. Why shouldn't it be? Everything else had been lately.

But it still didn't explain why these were men all the way out here, poking around in a Portland suburb. They were well out of their jurisdiction. In slow motion, her brain began to connect the dots.

"We're following up on an investigation of a matter at Thomas Robert Harlow's home. We understand he's your—"

"Father. Yes." Sara finished his sentence, eager for him to get to the point. "You must be here about the fire."

Had there been a development in the case? Were they possibly there because TR was considered a suspect? It seemed absurd to consider, but what if her father had done something rash in order to gain insurance money? After all, back at the hospital he'd indicated he was out of savings. If TR wasn't going to cooperate, maybe this detective could enlighten her.

"If he's at home, we'd like to speak with him." He hooked a thumb through his belt loop, a holstered gun protruding from his hip. Sara reflexively rubbed at the hairs standing on end along her skin. Was it possible TR was more dangerous than she knew?

Sara glanced down at the gun once more and smiled uneasily. *Stop freaking out.* It was silly to be nervous, but she couldn't shake the feeling.

"Yes, he's home. But I have to be somewhere. Could you come back? That way I can—"

"Sorry, ma'am." The taller of the detectives shook his head. Sara noticed his hair was cropped too closely, revealing the imperfections of his scalp. She tried to concentrate on what he was saying. "We need to get back to Sandpoint as soon as we're done. You go on ahead. If Mr. Harlow is inside, we'll take it from here."

Sara hesitated. How was she supposed to get to the bottom of this mystery if she was cut from the picture? Checking her watch, she realized she hadn't any choice. The school bell had already rung.

"Okay, I guess," she stammered. She had no choice but to step aside.

"Thank you, ma'am."

"TR's inside. Just knock loudly. He's a heavy sleeper." And he doesn't like to be disturbed unnecessarily, she wanted to add, but thought better of it.

Jogging to her car, the investigators and their questions hovering at her door, she secretly prayed the men wouldn't be able to rouse TR and would be forced to come back.

It might be her only hope of finding out the truth.

~

It had killed her to drive away without knowing anything. When she returned later with Sam, TR had been no help.

"What did the police want?" She'd cornered him in the living room with her hands on her hips.

"Oh, nothing, really. Just a routine follow-up to let me know they're ruling it some kind of accident and that the place is still unlivable."

"Really? What else did they say?" This was the first she'd heard that the investigation over the cause had wrapped up.

"That was it."

"They came all that way only to say that? Wouldn't a simple phone call suffice?" She had a hard time believing their conversation had been so brief. Surely there'd been more to it. The drive from Sandpoint was almost two hours.

"Why is that so hard to believe?" TR's anger level was rising.

"I don't know. It just is. Maybe by dinnertime you'll remember more of what they said." It was a gesture, a way for him to recover his bad memory, or false story, or whatever it was he was attempting to hide behind.

"Yeah, sure."

Instead, he hid out most of the evening. Sara assumed he must have taken a decent dose of medication, because when she stuck her head into his room, he claimed he couldn't come out for dinner. She wound up leaving a tray of food at his bedside while he grumbled about requiring more sleep. It was exasperating, really, how good he was at withholding information.

~

She stood in front of the coffeemaker the next morning and rubbed at the spots of pain reverberating behind her eyelids. She'd been up half the night.

Sam shuffled in, dressed for school. Sara gave his T-shirt and thin soccer shorts the once-over and sent him back to his room.

"But, Mommm!" he groused. "I won't be cold!"

She was too tired to have this argument today. "No way, Sam. It's October. My phone says it's forty degrees outside and the forecast calls for rain. I don't care if all of your friends choose to freeze to death at recess. My son is not going to be one of them. Put on some jeans, and for the love of God, find a sweatshirt. We leave in ten minutes."

"In that?" he asked, aiming thorny sarcasm in her direction.

Sara looked down. A stretched-out nightshirt hung around her bare thighs. She yanked it down and grunted. "No, Mr. Smartmouth. Not in this. I'll be ready when you are."

She dashed down the hallway in search of yoga pants suitable for a quick car ride. Her dresser drawers were a mess. She'd done everyone else's laundry except for hers. All that was available was a too-tight pair of jeans with a button missing and an oversize pilled knit pullover. *Fantastic.*

This whole new driving-to-and-from-school thing was proving to be a failure. The point was to spend quality time with Sam. But as she snatched a pair of fuzzy slippers in lieu of socks, Sara realized her plan had officially imploded on her. This so-called quality time in the car had really just turned into a time for mother-son arguments.

Sam appeared in her bedroom wearing appropriate school attire and a substantial pout.

"I'm ready," he grumbled.

Sara glanced in a mirror and hastily dragged an index finger along smudges of mascara. It would have to do.

"Great, so am I."

She followed him out to the car, the tiny crack in her heart widening.

Was this where they were headed? Sam would be a tween soon, with rising hormones and opinions opposite of her own. Was that day arriving sooner than she thought? Or was her newly compiled stress permeating those around her? Inserting the key into the ignition, Sara silently promised to do better. Her relationship with Sam was too important.

After swinging through the elementary school drop-off and doing her best to pin Sam down for a hug, Sara drove off. She had every intention of returning home to check on TR and perhaps lure him from hibernation. But as the car eased down the next block, another thought occurred to her.

Passing a row of shops, a yellow-and-white-striped awning caught her eye. Her hands jerked at the last minute to make a hairpin turn. Angling the wheel, she parked in the last available spot.

The open door of a bakery beckoned her inside. Shiny windows revealing rows of flaky pastries practically sang her name.

It was a sign. She needed the morning off.

Once inside, a bell tinkled overhead. The intoxicating mix of rich coffee grounds and sticky baked breads swirled through the air. Sara's mouth salivated. A little hum played off her lips, and she nearly skipped to the counter.

After ordering a midmorning snack and scouting out a table in the corner, Sara settled in. Glancing around, she thankfully recognized no one. She wasn't exactly pulled together, but whatever. The early-morning-breakfast crowd had evidently filtered out. The place was now practically empty. She wouldn't be bothered.

After a minute, she flipped on her phone. Perhaps this opportunity could be used to do some more digging on TR. As soon as she entered the words *Sandpoint news* in the search prompt, a newly published headline popped up.

"Bingo," Sara said. She bit into an almond croissant with pleasure. She kicked her slipper in a circle and waited for the article to load.

Fast-Thinking Tenant Gives Detail on Burned House

UPDATE: Tenant comes forward, revealing details of coastal home fire.

Firefighters sprang into action earlier this month and attacked a house fire located on the Sandpoint coast. Luckily, the owner, celebrated artist Thomas Robert Harlow, was able to evacuate despite the lack of properly installed fire alarms.

When firefighters arrived, the fire at the Sandpiper Lane house, which started about 4:00 a.m., was still smoldering but had not yet moved below the upper level of the home.

Sandpoint police detective John Hernandez commended Harlow, who lived there, for apparently evading the larger flames and escaping. Although the man suffered burns, he was able to make it down the hillside to safety in the cove below.

"It was a very lucky escape [for the resident sleeping inside]," Hernandez said. "At this stage, we know the fire started on the upper level ... we're very thankful a tenant smelled the smoke and was quick enough to call the fire department before the house was fully engulfed."

The tenant declined to comment for the article.

Sara read it twice before leaning back in her chair. Who was this tenant? TR had never mentioned living with anyone. Did he have a groundskeeper or assistant? Or maybe he was out of money and renting out a room to cover his bills. The article gave little to go on, but the discovery of it bothered her. TR was continuing to omit personal information from her about his life. Why?

She nursed her foamy latte and stared out the window. What was so important that her father couldn't share? Rather, *wouldn't* share.

It was about time he started talking.

CHAPTER ELEVEN

SARA

"Who's living on your property, TR?" Sara stood in the doorway of the guest room and narrowed her eyes at her father, adrenaline and too much caffeine coursing through her system.

She'd caught him sitting on the edge of his bed, tying his shoes, when she'd burst into the room after leaving the coffee shop.

"Tenant?" he asked. She could tell by the way he paused before speaking that he was stalling.

"Stop playing games, TR! I'm tired of you acting as if I'm the crazy one looking for trouble where there isn't any. I've read the newspaper. I know someone was living with you!" Her breath was shallow. She hadn't realized she was panting.

"Ah."

"That's it? All you say is 'ah'? What the hell, TR?"

He eased from the bedspread, careful to secure his right arm against his side as he moved. Sara caught him wincing, but she didn't care. "I deserve an answer."

He shook his head. "You're making a mountain out of a molehill. It's just a maintenance man who works for me, that's all. I didn't realize I needed to disclose something so trivial to you. It's nothing. Just a worker." He lowered his eyes and began hobbling from the room. Sara had no choice but to step aside as he moved past her.

"So why is he still there? I thought the house wasn't livable."

"Guest quarters. Out back," TR called down the hallway.

Sara hustled to follow, her adrenaline only partially subsiding. She wondered how big these guest quarters really were and whether her father's worker might help speed up the process of returning TR to his house. "Can this person help you repair the damage? Fix the house?"

"Maybe. We'll see."

"When?"

He turned, the color in his worn features deepening. "Let me handle it! Right now I'd like to make some breakfast, if you don't mind. I will get around to talking to my worker later. Can't a man start his morning with a little peace, for crying out loud?"

"Fine." Sara stormed out.

Her father was done with the conversation, whether Sara liked it or not. God, he could be such a stubborn fool. Making any kind of progress with him was equivalent to rolling a large boulder up a very steep hill. Still wanting to talk with someone, she considered calling Charlie. He wasn't due home for a couple of days. She wondered if she could wait that long. But after their fight it was probably best to wait until they were in the same room before presenting him with further problems.

Going into her room, she sat down and dialed the one person who likely wouldn't judge—Birdie.

Her friend picked up after one ring. "Hey, stranger. What's going on?"

Instantly, the tension melted from Sara's shoulders. "Hi, Birdie. Sorry I haven't called. It's been chaotic around here. Did I catch you at a bad time?"

The distant sound of a radio sang in the background. "You caught me in my car, on the way to the restaurant."

Sara noted a hint of disdain in her voice. "Things not going well at work?"

Birdie exhaled. "Oh, you know. The usual. Big boss man thinks he knows what the customers want—which is a total joke considering he barely sets foot in the place for longer than five seconds anymore. He just needs to get out of the way. I'm the one on the front lines, making up the menus and talking to our regulars. Not him. Last night I had to explain why chicken marsala was tired. Go back to the 1980s, pal! My people want organic and deconstructed. Not conventional fare!"

Sara chuckled. Whenever Birdie talked food, she got overly passionate. She could only imagine the stink Birdie had raised with her boss. "Stick to your guns, girl! You are an amazing chef, and I love everything you make. Even if he does force you to make chicken marsala, I bet your version would be mind-blowing."

"Thanks. But you have far too much confidence in me."

"Nothing you don't deserve."

"What about you? What's all the chaos you mentioned? Is it Charlie?"

Sara sighed. "Yes and no. I mean, Charlie and I aren't doing great. He's overworked, and it's taking a toll. But that's not the only reason. My dad has been staying here. And it hasn't been good."

"Your dad? I've only heard you talk about your mom. Didn't you say you didn't know your father?"

Sara turned sheepish. "He left when I was about Sam's age. It's a long story. But he was recently hospitalized, and somehow I got roped into taking care of him until he gets back on his feet. Oh, Birdie, it's been awful. I think I've made a big mistake." She gulped back the salty taste at the back of her throat. Unloading her predicament to her friend felt good. She hadn't realized how much she'd kept pent up inside.

"Ah, kid. I'm so sorry. I had no idea. Listen, I have to get into work, but I want to talk about this more. Will you be around over the weekend?"

"Yes," Sara stammered, worried she might cry. "I'll be here."

"Okay, then. I'll come find you soon. Hang in there, kid. You've got this."

Sara closed her eyes. "Thanks, Birds."

"You bet. Stay strong."

~

Birdie arrived at Sara's house the next morning like a vision.

After the doorbell wakened her from another fitful night's rest, Sara emerged into the light and cracked the front door. She hiked up the waist of her baggy flannel pajama bottoms with one hand and smoothed her wrinkled top with the other. She'd recently given up caring what she wore. Maybe that was why Birdie met her with a strange expression.

"You're a sight for sore eyes," Sara replied, suddenly embarrassed at her appearance. She ran a tongue along a fuzzy set of teeth and blushed. She could stand to take a long, hot shower.

Birdie, on the other hand, stood before her as her usual upbeat, outdoorsy self in a Henley shirt, a down vest, and trademark red Converse, an impressive basket of assorted muffins cradled in her arms. The cold air had turned her cheeks rosy, and her smile was bright.

Birdie lifted the basket. "I thought you could use a little pick-me-up."

Sara spied large blueberries, gooey raisins, and crumbly toppings peeking out. Her stomach growled. Wedged just next to these treats was a chilled bottle of Sara's favorite chardonnay, tied with a yellow bow. Birdie had gotten up early to bake. Sara was most appreciative, especially knowing her friend's grueling schedule.

The locally owned eatery where Birdie worked was known for its organic Pacific Northwest fare with a twist of southern fusion. The most popular item on the menu was a scrummy barbeque shrimp and grits appetizer that made Sara's mouth water at its mere mention. The restaurant usually booked reservations three weeks out and, because of this, kept its prized chef on a ridiculous schedule. Having been there forever, Birdie was admired by her Portland patrons and had done well in her career.

She may have been five years Sara's senior—and had webbing lines of stress to prove it—but otherwise you'd never know it. To Sara, Birdie was a well of ceaseless energy and optimism; however, Sara knew her friend was finally growing fed up with having to tirelessly chase a carrot dangled by her boss. The restaurateur promised Birdie could take over as soon as he retired from the business. But no one seemed to know exactly when this would happen.

"Oh, Birdie!" Sara extended her arms as they hugged. "I seriously love you more than anyone I know right now."

Birdie chuckled, kicking off her damp sneakers just inside the entryway. Sara peered outside and noticed the sky was cloaked in a pale gray. It had started to drizzle. Having to continually leave one's wet shoes at the door was a small price to pay for living in the Pacific Northwest. The rain was what kept everything so intoxicatingly green.

Birdie tilted her head. "I'm glad to see you're in fairly good spirits, considering."

"You mean, considering I've become a bed-and-breakfast owner to a very needy guest?" She rolled her eyes to the ceiling.

"Eileen said she saw a couple of cops here talking to you on the front walk. Then she said you peeled out of here in a hurry," Birdie said.

"Oh yeah. That's true."

"I would have called, but I didn't hear about it until late last night, after my shift. Are you okay?" Birdie combed back a swoop of long bangs on her otherwise short hair. Her blue eyes held a piercing gaze as she waited for an answer.

Birdie was a no-bullshit kind of gal. Sara knew she couldn't sidestep this one.

She shrugged. "Yes. I'm fine, I guess. It's just my dad. I told you he was staying here. But I didn't tell you it was because his house burned down."

"What?" Her eyebrows shot into her hairline.

"Oh, Birdie. It's such a long story. We might need to wait until I uncork this wine before I'm ready to share it."

Birdie placed a steady hand on Sara's arm. "I'm here, anytime. Seriously. I may work a lot, but you know you can call me."

Sara bit her lip and nodded. It was all she could do to keep the tears at bay. She'd grown explicably emotional lately. The simplest of gestures were enough to make her weepy.

"Thank you. Can you hang out for a bit?"

"You got coffee?"

"Naturally."

Birdie stepped into the open living room, her colorful dog-printed socks adding a little spark of levity.

Sara grinned. This was what she admired most about Birdie. She was comfortable in her own skin. She always wore whatever she wanted and didn't give a damn about fashion trends. It suited her.

"Seriously, Birdie—these muffins smell amazing." The sweet aroma of brown sugar and cinnamon tickled her nose. Placing a palm underneath the basket, Sara realized the baked goods were still warm. "Did you just make all of this from scratch? On your day off?"

Birdie brought a hand over her heart and bowed. "Guilty as charged, ma'am." She drew out her mostly hidden southern drawl.

Sara marveled at her friend's generosity.

"You're a saint. Like Mother Theresa or something." Sara meant it. Birdie had some kind of an extra empathy microchip placed inside of her that most people didn't have. She worried she'd been a poor friend in return. When was the last time she invited her neighbors to dinner? Or brought them a gift?

Before she could recall, the sound of water running followed by several seconds of a hacking cough reverberated through the walls.

Sara tensed. For the briefest of moments, she'd forgotten all about TR.

Birdie threw her a look. "I take it that's not Sam?"

"I'm going to warn you right now," Sara grumbled, holding up a palm, "you're welcome to stay, but do so at your own risk. The old man is in rare form. There's no telling what you're about to encounter." She squeezed her eyes and tried to shoo the image of his open robe from her brain.

"Your dad? Really?" Birdie sounded amused.

"I'm serious."

"Well, now that you put it that way, I'm kind of excited."

"Don't be. He's a loose cannon. Anything can happen. He's lived alone for too long and now doesn't seem to know how to act appropriately in the civilized world."

"That sounds fantastic," Birdie mused. "But what does it mean? Has he been living out in the woods with a pack of wolves or something?"

Sara groaned. "Yeah, you've got the 'or something' part right."

Right on cue, her father emerged, cagey-eyed and rumpled, from the back bedroom. His mouth stretched into a gaping yawn as he dragged a sun-spotted hand along his jawline and raked over his day-old stubble. His eyes blinked a couple of times, adjusting to the light.

Thankfully, he'd learned his lesson and was now fully clothed. He wore an undershirt and gray sweatpants, which had been secured with a visible knot. And his mop of white-blond hair had been plastered down with a spritz of water.

Sara relaxed. Not too terrible for someone who spent the majority of his time loafing in bed.

Birdie cleared her throat.

"Hey, there, TR." Sara's voice cracked.

TR's head swiveled. A set of glassy eyes landed on the women, and then a flicker of something crossed his face.

Sara recognized that look. The old TR charm. A vine of dread began to creep along her skin.

He just can't resist.

For as long as she'd known her father, it was always the same. His default mode was flirting. Even when she was a small child, she'd come to recognize his change in attitude around women. It started with a look he reserved specifically for members of the opposite sex. He'd move in to press the flesh of their palm, lean in a little too close, and crack some kind of off-color joke. It didn't matter if the women he encountered were interested in reciprocating his amorous advances or not. As a child, she was confused but mostly annoyed. She liked it better when it was just them, one on one.

He didn't seem to care. TR was shameless.

Case in point, here he was, a washed-up old man sporting discolored Ace bandages down one side and a borrowed T-shirt that hugged too tightly around the middle. Up close, he smelled like the inside of a medicine cabinet. And his hair hadn't been trimmed in months. But none of this was going to stop TR's game. The swagger was still there.

After all, he was Thomas Robert Harlow. And in most circles that used to mean something.

Sara swallowed back a bitter mix of pity and disdain. Couldn't he cut the bravado and act his age? At least while he was in her house?

She shifted and tried to gauge Birdie's reaction. So far, her friend appeared entertained by the whole thing.

If only she knew, Sara thought.

"I thought I heard voices," TR announced, turning toward them.

Sara could tell by the added strut in his step that he'd miraculously bounced back. The evening before she couldn't even coax him from his room.

She snorted. How many pain pills had he taken?

TR crossed the room and reached for Birdie's hand. Birdie remained speechless—a rare sight.

As TR took over the room and began making boisterous introductions, Sam wandered in, bleary with sleep. It was unlike her son to rise so late, but perhaps all the recent activity had thrown him off his schedule. Mercifully, it was a bye week for soccer, so he was at liberty to be lazy.

Sara rushed over with a hug, simultaneously steering Sam back toward the kitchen. She was still intent on creating an invisible boundary between him and TR. Especially right now—instinct told her that her father was about to be inappropriate.

Setting a muffin and a glass of orange juice before him, she patted down Sam's sleep-induced cowlick and wished him a good morning. He smiled drowsily to the adults in the room, waved at Birdie, and zoomed in on his breakfast treat.

Once he was settled, Sara hurried to set down the rest of the goodie basket. Pivoting on her heel, she hustled back to join the twosome in the living room.

"Lesbian, huh?" TR's gruff voice thundered.

Sara cringed.

"You don't say!" It came out more like a declaration than a question.

"That's right, Mr. Harlow." Birdie's tone, bless her heart, remained cautiously polite, but she'd puffed out her chest ever so slightly.

So much for polite formalities.

"I knew a couple of lesbians once! Crazy broads!" He was still bellowing. "Where do you live?"

"My partner, Eileen, and I live next door."

"Sara!" TR roared, even though there wasn't any need. She was already propelling herself between them.

"What?" Sara's shoulders crept up around her ears. She was afraid of what was coming next.

"Get over here!" TR barked. He gripped her elbow and pulled her close. "I just learned your boring little neighborhood isn't so boring after all!"

That's when Sara realized her father was going to ruin not only her marriage but also the friendship that meant so much to her, all within the span of a single week.

CHAPTER TWELVE

TR

TR didn't know what the big deal was. He was merely making conversation with the neighbor gal. But the way his daughter was flapping about, blowing steam from her ears like an engine, you'd think he'd committed a crime against humanity or something.

Christ, she was uptight.

What was Sara so bothered about?

The other gal took it all in good fun. He merely let on that he'd once shared an artist's loft with a lesbian, way back in the day. If memory served, that chick had been some type of abstract painter. Lots of oil pastels—avant-garde, if you will. Large-scale canvases and such. Boy, that place was the scene of some wild parties. The things he saw! One time, he confessed, they'd all taken some particularly potent ecstasy. *And that drug can put everyone in a loving kind of mood, if you know what I mean. Man, those were the days.*

Sara's face nearly turned inside out at that one.

Too bad. It was a great story.

Apparently, he was offending his daughter's sensibilities. He could tell by how twitchy she'd turned. All red faced and glaring. So, on Sara's account, he downgraded the conversation to something a bit tamer. No need for anyone to get her knickers in a knot.

He asked Birdie from where she originated. When she claimed she hailed from the great state of Georgia, he gleefully inquired about her proclivity for whiskey. In his experience, every southerner he'd ever crossed paths with was a fan of Mr. Jack Daniel's. To his delight, so was this Birdie woman.

Things were looking up again!

He was about to suggest she might procure a little taste for him, something to wet his whistle, when Sara frantically batted them apart.

His daughter had grown up and turned into the fun police.

In the end, he'd been sequestered to the singular subject of the weather. The rain was mentioned, and that was about it.

The neighbor departed too soon, but at least she was considerate enough to leave behind a chilled bottle of wine. The glistening bottle caught TR's attention as soon as he entered the kitchen. Just the thought of popping the cork added a little perk to his stumbling step. But just like the case of the good coffee, Sara snatched it away with a frown and placed it high up in a cupboard to indicate it was off-limits.

Apparently, his punishment continued.

~

When TR awoke later from his afternoon nap, thanks to a fresh supply of meds placed on his bedside table, a hankering for something from the muffin basket lured him back into the light. He'd heard Sara announce she was going out earlier. Perhaps now he'd be free to bend the rules. He rose and set his intentions. Priority number one was to score a little alone time with a certain bottle of vino.

Thrusting his feet into a pair of wooly slippers Sara bought him, he heaved himself from the bed and navigated his way into the stillness of the house.

A faint clicking noise came from the main living area. He assumed it must be the dog. That thing was always gnawing on some kind of elaborate rubber toy. There was a whole basket full of them. TR shook his head. That animal was spoiled, if you asked him. Whatever happened to staying outside with a good old-fashioned bone? Apparently, his daughter's pet was too sophisticated for such a thing. Don't even get him started on the ridiculous fur-lined bed featured in the living room. Since when did dogs require designer furniture?

This yuppie lifestyle was beyond him.

Rounding the corner, he poked his head in to investigate.

To his surprise, he discovered the boy. Sara tended to keep the kid close by her side. But here he was, planted on the living room sofa, with his eyes glued to the television. Sara must have decided she trusted him around her son after all.

TR hovered in place for a moment, quietly observing his pint-size grandson. Up until a short time ago, he hadn't even known this boy existed—a lot of that going around lately. Now here he was, the next generation of TR's existence. It was remarkable, really.

The boy dangled his socked feet off the edge of the sofa, his spindly legs not yet long enough to reach the ground. Two worn sneakers and a half-opened book bag lay askew just below. Pens and papers had been spilled carelessly out onto the woven jute rug. A shiny white binder peeked out.

Something else caught TR's attention. Among the heap was a plastic sandwich bag containing a compact red-and-white asthma inhaler. His throat caught. He'd seen one of those before. A roommate of his in art school had suffered terrible breathing problems and carried one around religiously. A couple of times the guy had gotten himself into rather frightening situations. It had always unsettled TR.

Was his grandson sick?

He studied the boy a beat longer. The semi-interested dog beside him lifted an eyelid, his wiry tail twitching once, and then he was still.

The boy had a firm grip on some kind of gadget, the other hand buried in a bowl brimming with popcorn.

A buttery scent circled as TR approached.

"Hey, there, little fellow."

The boy broke his laser-sharp focus from a flat-screen television affixed to the far wall.

"Oh, hi." He briefly glanced back at the screen.

TR cleared a coating of stubborn phlegm from his throat and hobbled over to the edge of the couch. He silently cursed his body for not cooperating. Waking from sleep always required a reboot. TR's system was a lot slower than it used to be. Movement required effort; his limbs had taken on a significant stiffness lately.

TV was not something TR cared much about. Never had the use. (Too much propaganda and useless content, in his opinion.) But it must have been important in this household given the sheer size of the thing.

TR grunted. The ratio of art hanging on the walls compared to the technology showcased was disproportionate. Where was one's sense of self-expression? A higher sense of aesthetics?

"My mom said I wasn't supposed to wake you."

The boy crunched noisily on his snack as he spoke, his elfin jaw moving up and down. TR noticed his features were masked in caution.

TR nodded. "That's quite all right. I didn't hear you one bit. Just got a touch hungry, that's all." He patted his belly for effect. The pleasing aroma of popcorn caused him to salivate.

The boy nodded.

TR eased closer, hoping he wouldn't scare the boy off. There was something delicate and slightly skittish about this youngster, like the deer that lived in the woods beyond his property. Would this kid run off just as his father had?

Unfazed, the boy swiveled his head back to the screen.

TR squinted at what was so interesting. He had no idea what he was seeing. Textured 3-D cubes of varying size and color floated around and filled up the monstrous monitor. The frame changed several times. Mechanical clicks and clacks sounded as the boy deftly manipulated a controller in his lap. As a result, colorful boxes began stacking on top of one another to form a structure of sorts. More boxes popped up, and then what appeared to be an animated pickax came into view. Things were destroyed and reorganized, and the building resumed once more.

"What in Sam Hill is all that?" TR angled his chin toward the wall. The picture moved too fast for his taste. It was enough to make a person dizzy. Reaching out, he clung to the back of an upholstered chair and steadied himself.

"Minecraft." The boy kept building. It seemed nothing could break his concentration.

TR rubbed at his eyeballs. "Mind-what?"

The boy giggled under his breath. "Not Mind. *Minecraft.* It's a game. You know, on the Xbox?" His tone went up an octave, as if he were now addressing a very small child.

It sounded space-age.

TR didn't have the foggiest idea what this kid was talking about, but it intrigued him nonetheless. "Well, I've never handled an Xbox before. I'm more of an organic materials type of guy."

The boy paused and scrunched up his face. He was clearly not following.

TR took this as his opportunity to connect. "You know, paints and brushes and all that?"

"Oh."

With this small window, inspiration struck. Perhaps the two of them could speak some kind of common language if it involved the concept of creating.

"It looks to me like you're crafting some form of architecture. Is that right?" he asked.

"Uh, yeah."

Cubes moved at rapid-fire speed. He was going to have to look away soon. Either that or sit firmly in a chair for fear of falling over.

"How so?"

"The game lets you create worlds. See?" The kid pointed enthusiastically up at the screen. "In this world, I've made a couple of skyscrapers and a garden. There are some cows down there by a pond too."

"Cows and skyscrapers? Huh." TR didn't follow at all, but he was determined to try.

"Yeah, and I've got a bunch of tools too," the boy replied. "And fire. I've got fire."

This kid reminded him of how Sara used to be as a child. She was so clever and creative. Making little villages out of spare clay from his studio, fashioning farm animals and treetops from scraps. He used to adore this about her.

A pang of nostalgia seized him. Where had the time gone?

The boy's announcement broke his musing. "I've got other worlds too. I built an ice cave yesterday. Wanna see?"

A halo of warmth wrapped around TR's heart. His grandson liked to make things. Sara appeared to have given up her practice, but maybe there was hope with this boy.

"Yes, I'd love to see."

Just then, Sara burst through the back door. She was winded and overloaded. Balanced in her arms were bags of groceries. The crusty tail of a narrow baguette peeked over the top of one.

TR's stomach growled. He hoped the food was a sign that dinner would follow.

Sara set her things down with a huff. She placed her hands on her hips and zeroed in on the room distrustfully.

"What's going on in here, you two?"

"*Minecraft!*" TR boomed. His face broke into a proud smile. "I'm getting my first lesson!"

The boy giggled.

Sara glanced from TR to her son, an eyebrow raised. "I thought you were working on some overdue homework, Sam?" Her tone remained unimpressed.

The boy's face dropped. "I was. But it's Saturday, Mom. I need a break."

"Uh-huh." Sara scowled and went about putting the groceries away.

TR wondered if his daughter might be keeping too tight a grip on this kid. She held a keen eye on him wherever she went.

"I'm going to take a shower," Sara announced, seeming hesitant to leave them.

"Roger." TR threw a mock military salute in her direction.

Sara shot him a stormy expression and walked off. He watched her go, wondering how in the heck they might ever get on the same page. Even when he tried to lighten the mood, she took it as an offense. There was no winning.

Her bedroom door banged shut.

With a sigh TR returned his attention to his grandson. The tension in his lower back eased as he settled deeper into the living room chair.

"So, Sam," he said. "Let's see what else you got going on there."

"Okay, cool."

"Cool."

TR's heart swelled as this pleasantly imaginative boy chattered on at warp speed, happily regaling him with the intricacies of *Minecraft*. It didn't matter that every other word was completely foreign. What mattered was that he and the boy were connecting. This was something he'd missed out on with Sara after a certain point. There was so much he'd missed out on as a father.

For the next half hour TR was content. He was alive, despite his injuries, and was spending quality time with a grandson he never knew he had. After all this time, goodness still existed for him.

It reminded him of something else. Some*one* else. A ribbon of guilt wound its way into the room. And then suddenly TR was torn.

Was it wrong to be happy? Although he'd been determined not to admit it, he'd left things significantly unraveled back home. Things that were his fault. According to the cops who'd visited, careless use of cigarettes and paint supplies had sparked the fire. At first, TR had refuted the accusation that he could be so careless in his own home. It was preposterous, he told them. But deep down he knew they were right. He hadn't just been acting rashly the night of the fire; he'd been a damned fool. But he wasn't too keen on admitting this. He'd never live it down. With anyone.

Was it right to sit there in that living room and pretend? Not to tell Sara so much? To pick up and start fresh without looking back—again?

Because that was exactly what he'd done. There was so much left up in the air between him and Marie. She'd had enough and planned to leave him. This he knew. But he hadn't even tried to patch things up with her, let alone to bridge the divide with Bo. He hadn't even tried to reach out since leaving the hospital. Instead he let his pride stand in the way of all of it. He'd simply left.

Ever since the fire, he'd tried to dismiss these shameful realities from his mind. But doubt had a way of creeping in. On top of this, he feared Sara could only be held off for so long. Something was eventually going to have to give.

TR watched Sam move things around on the screen, manipulating worlds and rearranging the landscape as he liked. He witnessed his grandson partially build something up, only to abandon it and move on to something else when this no longer suited him. He moved on without giving it a second thought.

Cold reality began to settle over TR. This game was starting to feel a bit too familiar.

What had he done? He was no longer sure.

CHAPTER THIRTEEN

SARA

Guilt eventually got the better of her. That, and mainly she was just too tired to give a damn.

By dinnertime Sara went for the wine. At first she'd only meant to have a few sips, something to take the jagged edge off her week. But two glasses in, her resolve loosened. Tired of policing TR, she threw caution to the wind and slid the delicate bottle in his forlorn direction.

"Ah, I see we're having a French wine this evening." Her father feigned an air of surprise and reached across the table. *As if he hadn't been lusting after the bottle all evening.* She caught a flash of his true desire as his fingers swiftly coiled around the stem of a glass. Seizing the bottle, he helped himself to a hefty pour. "*Merci*, madam." He sat opposite her and tipped his chin graciously.

"Pace yourself," Sara cautioned.

"*Oui,*" TR replied solemnly.

"You speak French?" Sam asked.

"*Oui. Un petit peu.*" He winked across the table at her son. "Yes. Just a little. You know, I lived in Paris for a stint. Lovely country. Beautiful landscape. But the Parisians didn't quite get my art. *L'américain*, they called me. It didn't work out." His gaze turned distant.

"Uh-huh." Sara rolled her eyes and took a long pull of chardonnay. She could only imagine what he really meant. TR had probably pissed off some French father by courting his much younger daughter, or he'd drunk too much French wine and offended someone important in the Parisian art community. Meanwhile, she and her mother had been back at home, heartbroken and struggling to pay the bills.

Sara regarded him now. Did he even care?

Sam picked up the drop in conversation as he pierced a forkful of roast chicken and urged his grandfather to continue. "Cool! What other languages can you speak?"

Witnessing her son's eagerness, the crack in Sara's heart deepened a little. Sam would likely get burned if he got too close to TR's orbit.

"Well, I can speak a little Spanish—and some Italian too," TR said. "But only enough to order at a restaurant." He rambled on, inhaling large portions of his dinner. Oblivious to her discomfort, he continued. "Oh, and I know a lot of curse words in other languages! They're the easiest to learn."

"Ha!" Sam tipped forward, thrilled.

Sara banged her knife loudly against her plate. It was like dealing with a disruptive child. She shot TR a disapproving glare.

Her father shrugged as if to say, *I'm only telling the truth.*

"I know tacos and enchiladas!" Sam interjected, midbite. His excitement defused a sliver of tension.

"*Bueno!*" TR brightened and swung out his glass in a lively salute. Golden liquid threatened to spill over the rim.

Sara held her breath and silently thanked her son for innocently shifting the direction of the conversation.

The two continued to chatter on, listing all the Mexican dishes they could think of. Each congratulated the other as they did.

She pushed the food around on her plate and listened quietly to her father recall a world in which she never got to be a part. An alternate universe where she and her mother were never allowed. But in a small way, TR's enthusiasm toward Sam reminded her of times she and her father had spent together. TR used to take on that same sparkling demeanor, happy to engage in a little fun with her as a child. She only wished it had lasted.

She knew TR had moved to Spain at one point, thanks to Joanne's constant tracking of her ex-husband. It had made Sara sick, the way her mother was so obsessed with the man who had left them both.

Living with her mother had been like living with a pendulum. Joanne would be seething with rage one minute, tearing up TR's mysterious letters that Sara never got to read, and promptly lighting a match to the papers at the bottom of the bin. And the next minute she would be pining for the "one true love" she'd let slip from her life, tearfully running her finger over old photographs and pasting up clippings of press releases from the art section. Sara could never keep up.

They were always changing addresses, switching friends and sources of income. Sara did her best to be the responsible one, but it had been difficult when the rug was constantly being pulled out from under her. For the majority of their lives, they were two lost souls twisting in the wind.

TR's absence had left them both untethered.

That was why finding Charlie had been like a lifeline for Sara. When a mutual girlfriend introduced them at a party, Sara was enamored right from the start. At a mature twenty-seven to her twenty-three, Charlie was kind yet driven. He impressed her with his lofty aspirations and shiny aviation degree. Getting to know him, Sara was struck by how cool Charlie could be under pressure, methodical and steady handed. He was everything her parents were not. And that was wildly attractive.

But despite their different backgrounds, Sara found they had so much in common. They enjoyed all the same dramatic films, shared a love of Thai food, and even bought a pair of road bikes together. She also liked to think they shared the same worldview on most things. They both dreamed of having one or two children and a beautiful Craftsman home in a community that was small, but not too small, where they could bike with their kids to a neighborhood park but still find plenty of good restaurants and cultural events. Once Sam was born, Sara promised herself that she and Charlie would be the exact opposite of her parents. They would be good, steadfast, and whole. They'd be the kind of people who could be depended upon. And for a time they were.

Much later, when Joanne got sick with cancer, it was Charlie who stepped in and provided Sara with a foundation of strength. He cooked meals on the nights when she was too depleted from the hours spent at hospice with her mother. He looked after Sam and chaperoned school field trips. He lent a nonjudgmental ear when Sara complained about her mother's poor choices and deteriorating condition.

Being with Charlie felt like being offered a giant umbrella in the middle of a tumultuous rainstorm. He provided a place to stand still. A quiet place of shelter.

But not anymore, Sara thought.

These days, Charlie had apparently hooked his umbrella to something—or someone—else and was leaving Sara exposed to the elements. Overcome with emotion, she got up before the others could notice her damp eyes.

"Excuse me for a minute." Her chair scraped backward as Sara left the table. Sam and TR popped their heads up in unison, pausing their spirited conversation. "I'll be right back."

Sluggishness overcame her as she moved toward the solace of her bedroom. She was feeling lightheaded and needed a moment to gather her thoughts. She must have consumed more wine than she was used to having, because a gauzy haze settled over her. The sight of her unmade bed, with its inviting linen sheets, caused Sara to feel instantly drowsy. If she could just crawl under the covers for a respite, it might help.

Reaching her bedside table, she picked up her phone. She pressed the "Home" button, and the screen illuminated. No messages. Her heart darkened. Charlie hadn't even tried.

Without hesitating, she typed out a text message asking if they might talk. Doubt crept in as to whether he'd respond. Sara knew she was low on the totem pole when Charlie was away. Apparently, this was becoming the case when he was at home too.

Her mind ran through a list of female coworkers she'd heard Charlie mention over the years. There were Christy and Geneva. Someone else whose name sounded exotic, but she couldn't recall. Charlie had assured her he didn't really socialize with these women, but still, Sara would be lying to herself if she didn't admit the sharp tang of jealousy over them. Was her husband with one of them right now, having drinks and laughing around a bar with the other pilots and flight attendants? Please let the answer be no. She rubbed her forehead, trying to erase the image.

Keeping up with the men in her life was eating away at her.

Weary from anguish, she gazed longingly at her pillow. *Just for a minute,* she mused. The lids of her eyes slipped down.

She was wrenched back into reality with a literal crash. Slowly pulling herself from the clutches of sleep, Sara tried to shake free her funk and decipher the noise. She'd heard enough to know it had come from the main part of the house. But what was it?

A secondary crash sounded. Sara instantly recognized the shattering of glass. Bolting upright, she scampered across the sheets and in the direction of the ruckus. Adrenaline coursed through her as she thought of Sam. How long had she been asleep?

Arriving in the main living area, Sara felt her heart drumming hard against her rib cage. Where was he?

A head peeked around the corner.

"Oh, thank goodness." Sara exhaled as Sam emerged, unscratched, from his cowering position at the nearby broom closet.

"Mom?"

"You're not hurt?" Giving her son the once-over, she saw he looked afraid. She took a measured step forward and surveyed the scene.

"No. But he is." Sam gripped a dustpan and pointed a shaky finger beyond the kitchen table.

Blood was the first thing she saw. Blood on the floor, blood on the side of the counter, and the tile was littered with shards of pale-green glass.

More remnants of the wine bottle, along with what used to be a glass stemware, created a pattern of knife-edged fragments around the table legs. A chair had been knocked sideways. Damp footprints outlined a puddle. At the epicenter of this disaster was TR, tipsy and rather ashen. Sara's eyes darted to his left hand, which hung limply at his side. A scarlet gash ran from the base of TR's thumb up to the inside of his wrist. A river of blood descended.

"Shit!" Sara leaped into action. If TR's wound was as serious as the blood clotting onto the floor, he was going to need medical attention. And fast.

Acer added to the chaos by dashing haphazardly back and forth amid the confusion. He pushed his nose down to the spill, sniffing and whining nervously. His tail was tucked securely between his legs. TR swatted drunkenly in his path. Acer pinned his ears flat and growled.

"Shoo!" Sara crossed the room, the glass making a sickening crunching under the weight of her shoes. She managed to reach the middle and push the dog away impatiently.

"Sorry about the mess." TR's words were slurry. He didn't seem to focus. "I don't know what happened. Must have slipped right out my hand." His hooded gaze frightened Sara.

What had she been thinking, letting a senior citizen freely mix alcohol with pills? And in front of her son? What must Sam have thought? Surely the mishap had frightened him. Her gut somersaulted. The effects of her earlier buzz having worn off, she scolded herself. She'd known better but let it happen anyway. Sam had been placed in potential danger because of her neglect.

"Quick, Sam! Grab Mommy's car keys and fetch me a big towel from the laundry room!" She swiftly moved to TR's side and yanked his elbow high over his head. She knew enough from watching medical dramas on TV. If an artery was nicked, the bleeding had to be stopped.

TR leaned hard against her, feeling frighteningly like a felled tree. Sara braced herself. Being this close to her father, she could feel the heat of his uneven breath.

"Just need to lie down . . ." he mumbled.

Sara jostled his arm to keep him awake. "I know the feeling."

God, what if they'd both passed out and left Sam alone with this kind of disaster? Sara would never be able to forgive herself. She squeezed against the dampness filling her eyes. *Keep it together.*

A startled-looking Sam raced back into the room, his small feet nimbly avoiding the debris. He thrust a pristine Egyptian cotton bath towel at her, the price tag still dangling from its corner. Sara wavered and then seized it. This was no time to be picky.

"Okay, you two." She nodded first at Sam and then her father. "Let's get to the emergency room."

$\sim$

Three excruciatingly long hours later, after going through gobs of paper towels and Band-Aids and pleading with the hospital's overworked and ill-mannered intake nurse, TR was finally seen. Poor Sam had gone from frightened to exhausted, being a dutiful helper and making runs to the bathroom for supplies. He'd put on a brave face, but Sara was wrought with angst, wondering if the scene had been too much for him. After all, it was practically too much for her, and she was the adult.

Thankfully, TR was going to be all right. The cut was deep, and it was unfortunately (or ironically, depending how you looked at it) on his remaining good hand. But the doctor was able to stitch TR's split skin back together and treat it for infection.

Having slipped from the exam room for fear of passing out, Sara found an empty chair out in the hallway and collapsed. Mercifully, Birdie had driven over and retrieved Sam a couple of hours earlier. Her friend had assured Sara she would stay with him as long as needed. Sara only hoped this incident with his grandfather wouldn't scar her son for life.

What a disaster of a week it had been. Two hospitals in only a matter of days. Reuniting with her estranged father, setting him up as a houseguest, and having a near miss with a dangerous dose of medication and booze all under her nose.

The attending doctor had given Sara a ration of shit for this last one. She'd cowered against the flimsy hospital curtain while the physician plugged TR into an IV for hydration and laid out all the reasons why patients weren't supposed to mix anything with prescription medication. Period.

In the hallway, she dropped her head into her hands. Folding in half, she shuddered and then released a choking sob, crushed under the weight of her failure.

It was all too much.

Her head throbbed, her back ached, and her gut was wrenched in two over the conditions of her deteriorating family. Guilt hung around her shoulders like a two-ton gorilla.

Orderlies and nurses trudged by in a steady stream as Sara hugged her knees and cried. If this was what unraveling felt like, she was undeniably undone.

"Mrs. Harlow?" A gentle voice hovered just above her.

Sara glanced up, dragging the sleeve of her sweatshirt under her nose. She sniffled. "It's actually Mrs. Young, but yes, I'm who you're looking for. I'm Mr. Harlow's daughter."

It struck her then, with the force of blunt gravity, that for the first time in decades she was able to admit this out loud. So much of her life was spent trying to slough off the title, like it was a disease. There was no denying it now. Sara was TR's daughter, for better or for worse.

But this situation of theirs wasn't working out. If she and TR were to have a fighting chance, he was going to have to move out. She couldn't keep up with his antics, acting as both police and caregiver, all while trying to patch their relationship. Otherwise they might both find themselves circling the drain. And she'd be damned if she was going to let that happen. Sara was determined to understand her father.

The nurse handed her a stack of dispatch forms. "Your father can go home now."

Sara thanked her and stood. Could TR really go home? To his own place?

Just how bad was the fire damage anyway? Maybe the police had merely wanted TR to stay away so they could finish their investigation. Maybe now something could be done in terms of repairs.

The wheels of a plan began to turn, rolling over the possibilities. TR had a follow-up appointment at Pacific Memorial coming up. A chance to return to the coast. Maybe she'd even pay a visit to the property herself.

She needed an option B, because option A clearly wasn't working out.

CHAPTER FOURTEEN
SARA

When Charlie returned from his trip the next afternoon, he urged Sara outside and offered her a seat in a weathered teak patio chair. His face was twisted with worry.

"I'm here. Let's talk. I'm concerned, honey. Your texts worried me. And now that I'm here, you don't seem yourself."

Funny. Lately, Sara could've said the same thing about him.

"You look exhausted, hon." Charlie squinted under the glare of the sun. He'd positioned their chairs just so, the corners of the arms forming a point, their knees practically touching. TR was in his room napping, and Sam was inside constructing a Lego spaceship. The way Charlie had brought her out there, she felt weirdly as if it were an intervention.

"You're right; I am exhausted." She stretched her legs out and took in the sight of her own dirt-caked sneakers. Acer trotted over and occupied the space between them like a referee.

Charlie readjusted, and Acer took this as a sign and wagged his tail as he dropped a soggy tennis ball near his master's feet. Annoyed, Charlie kicked it away. Sara noticed how clean the soles of his shoes were. How perfectly ironed the pleats of his khakis looked. Her husband suddenly seemed terribly out of place in their overgrown backyard.

"What's going on, Sara?" he said, his face soft, his eyes warm and concerned in a way she hadn't seen in so long it tugged at her heart. "Is taking care of your dad overwhelming you?"

"Ha!" Sara slapped a hand over her mouth. That was an understatement.

Charlie's brow dipped. "Did I say something funny?"

She brushed back wisps of loose hair and snorted. Was he serious? Sara couldn't help it; she tipped her head back and emitted a cackle. It sounded deranged, and the volume cut through the still space. She didn't care. A ray of afternoon sun glinted off a nearby window and warmed her cheeks. She lingered there for a moment. It felt good to loosen her grip on the world for just a minute.

Charlie regarded her as if she were crazy.

Maybe she was losing it, but his statement was absurd. Of course TR was overwhelming her. It didn't take a rocket scientist to figure that one out. But the ludicrous notion was that Charlie didn't seem to take into account his own part in her breakdown. Was he really denying all responsibility? The fact that he'd practically abandoned her? Yes, Sara wasn't free of guilt. She wasn't the world's perfect wife; she knew this. Her rigid ways and unwillingness to bend, in order to be so very different from her own parents, could irk Charlie. But still. She was the one who always wound up staying, not him.

"Sara, talk to me." His tone was pleading.

She huffed. So much had happened, she didn't know where to start. No matter what she said, Charlie probably wouldn't understand. One had to witness TR's actions to fully grasp the drain they'd taken on her.

"Do you know," she began as she gazed out across the yard, "that human skin cannot survive without oxygen? For a successful skin graft to heal, it must grow and activate new blood vessels. Did you know that?"

"Uh, no."

"And did you know that if you don't reapply the bandages and topical ointments just so, it inhibits this process and you have to start all over again?"

"Sara, what exactly is your point?" His voice was laced with fresh concern.

Sara leaned in. Her eyes narrowed. "My point is, Charlie, that I've had to learn these things on the fly. A trapeze act without a net, so to speak. No backup, no support. Just me."

"Sara—"

She cut him off, anger bubbling its way to the surface. "Do you know I've been to the hospital more than once since you've been gone? That I've paced the halls of the ER in the wee hours of the morning and been lectured by doctors? That your son witnessed a near-fatal accident in our kitchen, a pair of detectives was snooping around at our front door, and my good friend Birdie was nearly run off by my father's vulgarity? Did you also know Sam had a geology project that he needed help with, but his parents were too preoccupied to give him a hand? That our dog hasn't been walked in days, and I'm pretty sure that milk in your coffee has gone bad?"

Charlie's eyes widened. He waved the mug of reheated coffee under his nose and made a face. Sara watched him deposit the mug on the ground and then purposefully suck in a couple of audible breaths.

Good old Charlie, always calm. Sara swallowed back her sarcasm.

"That's a lot to throw at a guy," Charlie said.

"This isn't working. I can't go on like this."

"Like what, exactly?"

"Like *this*, Charlie." Sara exhaled and rubbed at a knot in her neck. The quality of her sleep had been poor lately. She could use a massage. "Both of us are existing in two entirely separate worlds. I'm desperately trying to hold things together while you obliviously flit around the globe!"

He threw his hands up, his complexion coloring.

"Really, Sara? That's a bit unfair, don't you think? You can't possibly refer to my job as 'flitting around the globe.' Do you even know how hard I've worked? How many hours I've clocked in shitty hotels and overrun airports? It isn't all one big vacation, you know."

"Well, you could've fooled me."

"What's that supposed to mean?"

She spun in her chair to face him. "It means that every time I turn around, you're running out the door. It seems to me you'd rather be anywhere but here. Flying is just an excuse to get away."

"Oh brother, here we go. I'm here right now, aren't I?" The calming breaths hadn't helped. He was seething now.

The whir of a lawnmower started up somewhere on the other side of the fence. Sara could almost taste the cloud of diesel gas that followed. The machine's motor bumped along, muting out their surroundings.

Terrific. At least one of her many neighbors had overheard them arguing. It was blatantly clear there was no longer any privacy to be had inside nor outside of the house. There wasn't any peace.

She thrust her chair backward.

"Where are you going?" Charlie half stood, his mouth agape.

"I don't know." She spat the words at his feet. His concern was too late. Her anger bubbled over. Charlie was finally paying attention now that he decided to show up. But where had he been when she'd really needed him? He'd chosen to be away.

The lawn mower was deafening, ratcheting up her anger by the minute. Adrenaline coursed. It wasn't possible to sit there a minute more and listen to Charlie's excuses. She had to get out of there.

"Well, you can't just run away. What about—"

"Actually, I *can* run away. You do it all the time. Why shouldn't I?" She stood over him, jamming a finger into the air. "Why don't you stay home and take care of Sam for a change? It's the weekend. Spend time with your kid. I'm going out."

"Wait, what if your dad needs something? What am I supposed to do?"

Sara slipped through the sliding glass door and called over her shoulder. "Figure it out. That's what I've had to do."

∼

The quiet solace of her car felt like a gift. Locking herself inside, Sara started up the engine and then idled in the driveway. The sun had drifted behind a patch of clouds, darkening the sky to slate gray. A smattering of light raindrops fell outside. Sara noticed her ragged breaths begin to fog the windshield. The Indian summer was on its way out, the chill of October moving swiftly into its place.

Cranking on the defrost, she wondered where to go. It was Sunday. The day most people reserved for spending time with family. But right then, that was the furthest thing from her mind. She craved alone time. A chance to gather her thoughts.

It was strange to think that all she'd wanted yesterday was for Charlie to return. And now that he was back, attentive and ready for interaction, Sara couldn't stand to be in the same room. What did she even want?

She needed some kind of direction.

Inserting her thumb between her front teeth, she nibbled on a rough cuticle and deliberated.

Think.

It was crucial to be somewhere quiet. Preferably somewhere she'd have anonymity. Pampering sounded nice, but she couldn't exactly walk in and check in to a spa. For one thing, she didn't have an appointment. Going for a run wasn't an option either. Her street attire wasn't optimal, and she had no intention of walking back into the house to get a change of clothes. Letting the car idle a second longer, she did her best to gather her thoughts. Where did she used to go to be alone, before Charlie and

Sam? What place always had the ability to ground her in times of chaos? Someplace that would connect her to the joy she'd been missing.

An idea jiggled free. *Of course.*

Glimpsing the time, she calculated. It should still be open if she hurried. Angling the wheel, she headed the car north toward the city.

Pulling up to the two-and-a-half-block campus of the Portland Art Museum, Sara quickly scanned the streets for parking. The universe must have taken pity on her, because a spot opened up on the road ahead. As she eased alongside the curb, the coils of tension that ran down her back gave way and released.

She glanced at her phone. Four o'clock. She still had an hour until closing.

Climbing the short flight of stairs to the unassuming red brick entrance, she dug around in her purse for cash. A clump of coins jangled into her palm. At that moment, she was reminded of Joanne.

Back when Sara was young, and they didn't have much to live on, Joanne could sometimes scrape together enough for museum trips, no matter the city. For as wacky as her mother was, with often-unsound decision-making skills in other arenas, Joanne prided herself on being a faithful patron of the arts. And while Sara's father may not have been around any longer to lend his knowledge or further encourage Sara's sprouting artistic talents, Joanne at least made a sporadic effort to expose her to a small piece of this world.

Her mother had one good outfit reserved for such visits: a gauzy floral scarf draped around the shoulders of a burgundy dress. Sara closed her eyes for a flash and recalled it like it was yesterday. She used to think of it as her mother's museum outfit. Joanne would tilt a handful of coins in Sara's small grasp and tell her to purchase two passes. It was a treat of an outing, and they both knew it. The museum days would stretch from morning until night, not a single hour of rare indulgence wasted.

Sara would wander from room to room in awe. She'd sometimes linger in front of the bronze sculptures, glimpsing around before squeezing her eyes tightly shut, casting a silent wish that one day she'd work as an artist. That was her dream. Even if no one recognized her the way they did her dad, she wouldn't care. As long as she got to return to the clay creations she loved. That would have been enough.

But sadly, this dream was never realized. Not after TR left, taking his art supplies and Sara's hope right along with him. After that, the needs of Sara's fragile mother quickly became all consuming. Sara was forced to grow up too fast, to cast her childhood dreams aside as mere frivolity. More practical matters, like surviving with a depressed woman with spotty income, required her attention. And so the artist's dream quietly faded away.

Sara paid for her ticket and walked through the cool marbled lobby. Not growing up with any one religion, she imagined this was what church might be like for many people. A warm hug.

She'd been here before with Sam. And while most people came to this particular venue for Monet's *Water Lilies* and the vast collection of Native American art, she had other favorites.

The museum was small but had been known to feature an extensive variety of works. Years ago, before Sam, Sara had come two days in a row just to stare at the traveling Degas exhibit. She'd been particularly mesmerized by Degas's *Dancer Adjusting Her Dress*, an arresting pastel-on-paper profile of a skirted ballerina. The sketch was of a young girl unaware, her focus cast off in the distance while the artist surreptitiously captured her thoughtful reflection. It had taken Sara to places deeply personal.

She knew that girl. She loved that girl.

The similarities between Degas's dancer and the *Girl Rising* sculpture created by her father branded a mark on Sara's heart. A piece of both of their lives had been stolen and put on display for the world to see.

Sara wondered if anyone else noticed. But she never asked.

TR's art didn't ever show anywhere in Portland. And perhaps it was just as well. Despite the fact that he'd spent his later years living a mere stone's throw away, his creations remained housed in larger metropolitan areas. No, this museum was left for Sara's exploration without the overbearing presence of her father.

Sara strolled the rooms, wandering from exhibit to exhibit, taking in the strange beauty of twisted sculptures and moody paintings. Each corner held a different mystery: a photo here and an inkblot there. Each had its own narrative.

She drifted into a lower room: cool as a basement and still as a tomb. It was filled with serene music that beckoned her to sit awhile. She obliged her senses, choosing an upholstered bench; she absorbed the subdued aura of it all and imagined what it might be like to let go temporarily.

A dreamy state overcame her. This was what she needed to feel whole again. Whatever anger she'd arrived with had melted away at the door.

Instead of her life constantly being interrupted by others, she could find freedom here, integrating herself into someone else's reality.

Today was just for her, to leisurely hold an indulgence.

If only for a little while.

CHAPTER FIFTEEN

SARA

"Where have you been?" Charlie questioned Sara when she came home after their spat.

The corners of his mouth were pulled down; a glint of fear shone behind his expression. Sara noted, for the first time, that Charlie was genuinely troubled. Her so-called disappearing act, as he put it, had disconcerted him.

"I needed a minute to myself. You get that luxury all the time when you travel. I don't. I'm always here, taking care of people. You don't know what that's like day in and day out without a moment's peace for yourself. How could you?" Her tone was sharp and self-justifying, and she regretted the response almost as soon as it left her lips. She'd wanted to attempt to explain her need to run away. But on reflex, it came out as a heated defense for her actions.

"Right, it's all just paradise on my end," Charlie spat, not taking any punches. "I only have an entire flight, crew, copilot, and passengers to care for. No responsibilities at all! No problems whatsoever! My job is inconsequential compared to yours, is that it? That's pretty narrow of you, Sara." The pulsing vein in Charlie's neck confirmed she'd gone too far.

Their conversation had escalated once again, resentment and misunderstanding brewing on both of their ends. It wasn't the shape Sara hoped their marriage would take. She wanted to tell Charlie this, but stubbornness got in the way. He stalked off, leaving her sad and depleted.

It wasn't right to fight when their son was in shouting distance; poor Sam kept to his room, likely to avoid friction. Comforting himself with his Legos and books. Sara forced herself to push her marital strife to the side and focus on the other men in her house.

With all four of them under one roof, the house was now suddenly bursting with needs, all of which shared a common denominator—Sara.

~

Despite their arguing, Charlie made a pronounced effort all week to stick around and be involved. Sara supposed that through his anger he'd heard Sara on some level. She was afraid he was removing himself from their lives. Charlie must have realized that right now she needed backup. She thawed a little, thanking him for his helpfulness.

Charlie shuttled Sam places, made small talk with TR, and even dragged the rusty lawn mower out from the depths of the garage to tidy up the yard. Sara was grateful. But also confused and disappointed. All of this self-induced busy work brought him back into the family, but it managed to once again inch out space for everything else.

A palpable absence existed.

Charlie and Sara slept in the same bed, ate at the same dinner table, and shared polite conversation around Sam and an albeit dubious TR. But they hadn't addressed anything deeper. The activities of a full household kept interrupting them.

Sara quietly agonized. She did her best to compartmentalize her fears—a honed skill she'd taught herself when living with Joanne. Instead, her energy was thrust into a different mission: TR's departure.

In this regard, her research was proving futile.

For one thing, the police detectives she'd left messages for were hesitant to share their findings. Even when she'd informed them she was TR's daughter and primary caregiver, they claimed the investigation did not involve her. All findings were kept tightly under wraps. And when she'd asked TR, he snipped that he'd already told her all her knew. It was beyond maddening.

With so little to go on, Sara was even more resolute to get to the bottom of the issue. Her plan to make a change had been simmering for days.

It was now Thursday, and TR's next doctor's appointment was scheduled for the following Monday. Nurses from the burn unit had made sporadic phone check-ins since he'd arrived, but the doctor wanted to lay eyes on the wounds and make sure his patient was healing properly. Sara couldn't agree more. She'd been flying blind. It would be a relief to have a professional opinion.

Sandpoint wasn't very big; she didn't foresee any trouble once she got there. It was just a matter of delivering TR to his doctor's appointment and utilizing her time wisely. She didn't yet feel ready to share the plan with TR. He'd been cagey at best, and she needed to decipher why without him getting in the way.

Packing up Sam's lunch, Sara went over a list of ideas for her trip.

"Getting the boy off to school, are you?"

Lost in thought, she hadn't heard TR come up behind her, and she started. "Oh, good morning," she stammered. It was silly to blush. It wasn't as if he could read her thoughts. "Yes, just packing up some food."

Still in his robe, TR bellied up to the counter and eyed the colorful bento box full of carrot sticks, broccoli, and hummus. He screwed up his face. "Whatever happened to peanut butter and jelly? Or a solid egg-salad sandwich? Now, those are the best!"

Sara shook her head. "Uh, no. Those may have been the best when you were younger, but not these days. Peanuts are out, for one thing. Too many kids with allergies. And mushy egg salad? Gross. Sam would rather die."

TR parked himself on a stool and slapped a palm onto the counter in rebuttal.

"Nonsense! That kind of food builds fortitude! Besides"—he waggled his fingers over the lunch items—"how's he going to get excited about a box stuffed with cold vegetables?"

Sara snapped the container shut and shoved it alongside a bag of bagel chips. "Oh, he'll do just fine. You'd be surprised at the stuff his friends bring to school. Some kid always brings cartons of Thai food, another one is strictly Paleo . . ."

"Why do people like that kind of food? Even the name sounds unappetizing, like a disease!"

Sara rolled her eyes. Her father was an out-of-touch caveman. "It's a healthy diet that cuts out grains, dairy, and sugar. Among other things. Good, clean nutrition."

TR's eyes bulged. "No dairy! What the hell is this world coming to? I don't understand you Portland yuppies one bit. Too many excuses not to eat regular food. What's wrong with cheese?"

Her lips pressed together. Criticizing her was never a habit of his when she'd been younger. Why was he so disapproving now? She wanted to inform her father no one had used the term "yuppie" since the 1980s but thought better of it. He clearly held a firm distaste for new concepts.

Reaching for a box of cookies, she responded. "Nothing's wrong with cheese. It's just some people have figured out ways to eat that make them feel better. That's all. You should try cutting some things from your diet. You might be surprised." *Like grain alcohol and five spoonfuls of sugar in your morning coffee.*

"Humph."

"If it makes you feel better, he's getting dessert with his lunch." She held out the cookie box and rattled. "See?"

"Someday I'll take the boy out to lunch, and we'll eat a man's meal. None of this vegetarian bullshit."

Sara checked her periphery to make sure Sam hadn't emerged from his bedroom yet. TR's volume was rising.

Was he claiming her son didn't have the makings to be a man? What defined that anyway? She could only imagine what his remark meant. Consuming bloody steaks and fried potatoes, likely. That and bottomless snifters of bourbon.

"Okay, TR. You get yourself better, and we'll see about that. And by the way, stop calling him 'the boy.' He has a name, you know. It's Sam."

"I know that!" TR groused. Avoiding eye contact, he got up and prepared his black coffee with sugar.

Sara wasn't sure he *did* know this. If she didn't know better, her father was having trouble remembering new things. Information in his brain was sticking, refusing to be shaken free. Was it stubbornness or the early onset of dementia? It shouldn't surprise her that, at sixty-nine, TR had become set in his ways. But how hard was it to learn her son's name? It was his only grandson, after all.

And come to think of it, he hadn't really referred to Charlie by name either. Currently, Charlie was out for a run. She'd have to see how TR addressed him when he got back. So far, it had been mostly "that husband of yours."

Was this a result of her father's memory escaping him or TR simply not caring? Were these people considered inconsequential? The thought made her heart sink.

There were others TR refused to acknowledge as well. Like Joanne. Surely he hadn't forgotten Sara's mother. But he hadn't even broached the subject. Had he blocked his ex-wife from his memory like something unpleasant, a topic never to be discussed again? Sara tried to tamp down the hurt feelings that came with this notion. If she dwelled on it too long, the stinging behind her eyes would return.

Didn't TR even want to know the details about Joanne's passing? Up until now, he'd yet to utter her name. That was the biggest affront.

It was as if her mother hadn't existed at all.

She supposed TR and her mother were opposite in this respect. Where Joanne would let her messy feelings tumble out without a filter, never bothering to worry how they might affect others, TR held his opinions close to his chest. Perhaps this was one of the reasons they'd split. They were two vastly different human beings.

Was this how she and Charlie were perceived? She shook the notion from her head.

"So, TR," she began. "How's it going with changing your own bandages?"

Silence.

"TR?" The week prior, Sara had handed over the reins of wound care to her father. He wasn't hobbling as much anymore, and his full range of motion had almost completely returned. On top of this, the unsettling seeping of fluids had all but dried up. Things had progressed quite nicely, if she did say so herself. It seemed like the appropriate time to turn over the daily responsibility.

TR shifted in his seat. He fiddled with a spoon.

"Haven't had a chance to check them yet."

Sara's mouth popped open.

Haven't had a chance? It had been days. He'd had nothing but chances. Between slurping down her cooking and forever lounging on her living room sofa, what else had there been?

"You've got to change those things!" she blurted out. This stubborn bastard was undoing all her good work. Didn't he know this?

"Humph."

"You're not so infirm that you can't handle your own dressing. We were doing so well!" A bundle of carrots cascaded onto the floor as she jerked her arm across the counter. Bending at the knees, she scooped up the spill and shoved everything back into the refrigerator. "What is the doctor going to say when he sees you next week?"

"I'll be fine. Nothing a little ointment and some gauze can't fix." He pushed from his seat, turning to leave.

What was it with the men in this family? At the first sign of confrontation, they took off. She could nearly set her clock to it.

"I'm going to do it right now!" he hollered. "Stop being so goddamned bossy!"

Sara squeezed a tea towel and clenched her jaw until it hurt. She very much wanted to hurl something at the wall. How was she going to get her father to live on his own when he couldn't perform the simplest of tasks?

She was about to spit out a retort when Sam entered.

"What was Grandpa yelling about now?"

Sara's gut twisted. Her sweet, beautiful boy was already referring to TR as Grandpa, when the man couldn't even be bothered to learn his grandchild's name. Every ounce of Sara wanted to swoop Sam into a mama bear hug and shield him from the heartbreaking relationship he was entering. But she feared it might be too late for that. And she had no one to blame but herself.

"Oh, he's just extra grumpy in the mornings. Comes with old age. That's all. Here, sit down and eat some breakfast. We have to leave in a few minutes. If you hurry, you'll have time."

Placated by this answer, Sam shrugged and helped himself to a bowl of cereal. Sara watched as he tipped a jug of milk precariously close to the edge. A warning hung on her lips, but then TR's words rang in her ears. *Stop being so goddamned bossy.*

She held her tongue.

Charlie and Acer came bounding in through the back sliding door, the stench of sweat preceding them.

"I came back to take Sam to school," Charlie panted. He mopped his forehead with his arm.

"Okay, great." He was being considerate. "I wasn't expecting that. But thank you."

Charlie bent low and tipped his head under the chrome faucet. Letting the water run, he plunged his mouth into the stream and made giant gulping noises. Sara wrinkled her nose.

"No glass?"

"Nope! Haven't got time." He popped up and grinned. He was awfully happy all of a sudden. Must be the exercise. She told herself it was, because considering anything else, like perhaps another woman, was too much to take on at the moment. Allowing herself to follow that train of thought would surely send her spiraling. *No,* she told herself. *Don't let your head go there.* Charlie was not her father. He didn't make a habit of collecting women. But that still didn't mean he hadn't met someone special. Sara was too afraid to ask outright. It might be worse to know than to not.

"You ready to go, Sam-the-Man?"

"Yes!" Sam jumped from his chair and grabbed his bag. Scrambling out the door, Acer followed him out to the car.

Charlie turned to go.

"Maybe when you get back we can have breakfast together?" Sara hadn't intended it to sound so much like a question.

"Oh shoot. I can't," he said. A sheepish look overcame him. "I actually got a call from my boss while I was out. Seems some kind of flu has spread among the pilots traveling in the Northwest. They need me to come in. Just for a quick trip. Shouldn't be more than a few days."

Sara swiveled, her face smarting as if she'd been slapped. "You're flying this week?"

"Yeah, I depart in a few hours, actually. Crazy, I know."

She hoped Charlie would take time off. What happened to his concern about their relationship?

And then another thought dawned on her. Was this why he'd returned from his run so happy? He knew he got to run off and meet someone else? A trace of nausea materialized.

She'd been a complete fool.

"Charlie—"

"I know, I know," he said, backing from the room. "Terrible timing and all that. Truly. It sucks. But what can I do? Work needs me, and I said I'd go. Three days. I promise. Then we'll sit down and talk. You're pretty busy with your dad anyway. You won't miss me at all."

She had a sinking feeling it might be the other way around.

CHAPTER SIXTEEN

TR

On Monday morning, four days later, TR found himself being hustled through Sara's house and deposited into the front seat of her metallic-colored SUV. Doors slammed and the motor roared to life before TR could even get his bearings. What about coffee?

But he knew better than to ask. Sara was in a snit.

For one thing, the husband was back. Charlie had arrived the previous night, dropping his bags in the entryway and padding on stocking feet down the hall. Unable to sleep, TR listened as the master bedroom door clicked shut. Low murmurs and an exchange of a few harsh words followed. The door squeaked open and shut several more times before the house was finally silent.

Rolling over to glance at the time, TR had read 11:00 p.m. He'd lain on his back, studying the creamy stucco pattern of the guest room's small ceiling, and guessed at what was going on at the opposite end of the house. Sara must have given Charlie hell. She'd been pacing the floor since dinner, expecting him to surface. It had taken hours.

Now they were all paying for it.

He overheard Sara curtly informing Charlie she'd be gone for the day. Arranging for their son to get to school on time was her husband's responsibility. There was some bitter back and forth, but TR pretended not to eavesdrop while he searched around for a jacket. The dog followed anxiously at his heels, as if he, too, wanted to avoid the tension.

"Everything all right?" TR tried to quell his uneasy feeling as he asked, having a hard time adjusting his seat belt. Silently cursing, he tried to ignore the uncontrollable flaring pain in his right hand.

"Mm-hmm." Sara pressed her lips into a thin line and nodded. She tossed her purse into the back seat and thrust on a pair of sunglasses. Clearly, she was pissed off. Faster than he could blink, her foot pressed down on the accelerator, sending suburbia into a distant memory in the rearview mirror.

TR wondered if he should be afraid.

"Do you want to talk about it?" He didn't particularly want to do this, but it seemed like the proper thing to say. The way his daughter's chin trembled, he sensed she was about ten seconds from losing it. His eyes skimmed the road. The car sped up. For good measure, TR tightened his seat belt even though it aggravated his still-healing wounds. There'd been too many emergency room visits already.

A wise person would offer something sage to comfort his anxious daughter. It was bothersome to see her so upset. If she wanted to aim the anger in his direction, he could take it. He was a grown-up. He knew the part he'd played in her unhappiness. But then something dawned on him. The actions of his past were disturbingly familiar to those of Sara's husband. With a sickening feeling, he realized they'd both left.

Did Sara see things through the same jaded lens? Did she now group Charlie and TR together as the type of fellows who abandoned their families?

TR swallowed against rising shame.

"You know, sweetheart," he ventured cautiously. "Sometimes folks don't know what they're doing until it's too late."

Silence.

"What I mean is, sometimes the choices people make are about themselves, and they forget for a minute how it's going to affect those around them." His own guilt over leaving his family came to mind. But he continued an attempt at an explanation. "The harm isn't intentional. Am I making any sense?" He cast her a sidelong glance to check if she was listening. A threadlike vein pulsed at her temple. Her jaw visibly tightened.

Shifting, he made another attempt. "What I'm trying to say—"

"I know exactly what you're trying to say, TR!" she spat. The narrowing green of her eyes bore down on him. The car pitched forward.

TR's hand instinctively shot out to the dashboard, bracing as she carelessly ignored the road. "You want me to give permission to Charlie for disappearing all the time. You want me to understand that men are lured out into some great temptation, some big wild adventure, while the women have no choice other than to stay home and wait around. You want me to be okay with my predicament. You've always wanted me to be okay with this. Well, to hell with you, TR. Because I'm not!"

The car veered erratically across the yellow line. TR jolted in his seat as the tires edged over the median. Sara snuffled and swiped angrily at tears. TR sucked in his breath. She was losing control. His heart hammered. This frantic daughter of his was going to be the end of him.

"Sara!" His voice cracked as he hollered.

It felt like eons before she reacted, like she couldn't see beyond the fury. He gulped and delivered a pleading glance. Thankfully, she corrected the wheel just as an oncoming truck laid on the horn.

"Sorry."

TR exhaled. But his muscles remained rigid.

"Do you want to kill me? Is that it?" Agitation pulsed as two bandaged palms flapped in the air. "The fire didn't do your old man in, so now you're going to finish me off with the car?" A fragment of fear jarred itself loose along with the accusation. TR instantly wanted to take it back. The fire wasn't Sara's fault. He knew this.

Sara snorted. "Oh my God, TR."

Her face screwed up, and then she let out some kind of howl. *Was she laughing or crying?* He couldn't tell. Maybe she was losing her mind. "It's all about you, isn't it? The world revolves around the great *Thomas Robert Harlow!* God forbid something threaten your perfect party of one."

He realized now she was mocking him. He dropped his hands into his lap and pivoted away, offended. "I never said that."

"You didn't have to."

TR pushed his nose in the other direction and tried to conceal his wounded feelings. His daughter clearly didn't understand.

The car bumped along. Both of them refused to acknowledge one another.

A band of greenery stretched along outside. The road began to taper and bend. Buildings gave way to miles of coniferous trees mixed with mustard-colored aspens and an occasional meandering stream. He'd missed this, being out in nature. Being inspired by his surroundings. The ability to walk into his studio on a whim and freely paint or mold something, the freedom to create what moved him.

But despite his inability to connect with her, he'd given it all up to be with his daughter. Despite the painful struggle of relying on her care, despite the awkward reunion and having to continually eat crow, he was grateful to be near his long-lost child again. It was a gift.

Especially after the sins he'd committed. And the truths he had yet to tell her.

TR hadn't meant to cut Sara from his life. In fact, at the time, he didn't believe that was what he was doing. But he'd been a restless father, and at thirty-nine years old his creative spirit had summoned, and so had the high-end art consigners with large checkbooks. Joanne was growing too clingy, sucking the wind from his sails. He'd thought if he could just go away for a short while to focus on his newly important career, things could be realigned.

But he'd been weak. A charmed lifestyle had opened up for him, and he couldn't deny its glittering invitation. TR had run willingly right into the center of the spotlight. As time marched on, he neglected to look back. And Sara, he sadly realized, had suffered deeply.

Like a cruel twist of fate, here was Sara's own husband slipping from her too. It was tragic, really. History was repeating itself without her consent. And did that little boy, Sam, feel now as his mother did then? That the men in their lives left them behind?

It was difficult to swallow past the tightness in his throat. *Deal with it,* he told himself. *You deserve to feel sick. Just think of how Sara must feel.*

But there was something else too. The nearer they got to the coast, the worse it became. Because as much as TR yearned for his oceanfront home, he had no intention of facing Marie's wrath and the heavy disappointment of Bo. Things had ended on such a hurtful note: Marie intended to leave the relationship, claiming she was unhappy. Bo closing off, sadly embittered by one too many disagreements with TR over the past four years. The fire had been a mistake, a giant one. But TR didn't like to admit his mistakes.

Not yet anyway.

He stole a glance at his unsuspecting daughter. *Now was not the time.*

~

TR must have dozed off while deep in thought, because the next thing he knew, they'd arrived at the red-and-white-striped drop-off zone of the hospital.

Right, my checkup. He grumbled at the thought of more doctors. Too many prying clinicians for his taste. He was beginning to feel like a specimen in a lab.

"TR?" Sara said gently. His shoulders relaxed a little. He liked it when she softened.

"Yes?"

"Everything all right?"

"Sure. Fine." He traded a lie for the sake of peace.

She nodded only once. Her features remained neutral. "Okay. Well, we're here now. We made good time. I have some errands I need to run. I thought maybe you could do this appointment on your own?" She was asking permission, but TR knew she'd do what she wanted anyway.

"Sure, fine. Whatever you want." He readjusted himself and reached for the handle.

"TR?" A note of concern could be heard over his clumsy exit.

"Yes?"

"I, um . . . Nothing." She shook her head. A strand of strawberry hair fell from the loop of her hair band. Miniature lines around her eyes suddenly appeared more prominent than he remembered. Darkened half moons hung below them. She must not be sleeping.

Whatever sentiment was about to cross her lips fell away. "Your appointment is on the second floor. There will be a check-in desk when you get there. I'll be back in an hour. How about you find a seat in the lobby until I return?"

"All right, then." He signaled a goodbye and hobbled through the entrance. The car's motor hummed and faded behind him.

Once he was inside, a fluorescent corridor resembling a long tunnel stretched out before him. Why were the walls in these places always painted an unappealing shade of green? He'd never been a fan of hospitals, and look how many he'd visited lately. All the sights, sounds, and smells of it made him jumpy. It was the last place he'd wanted to be. But seeing as Sara dropped him with no other means of transportation, he currently had little choice in the matter.

Scanning the area, he located color-coded signs for the various medical wings. It appeared he was standing in the yellow section of the building. His doctor worked in the blue section. He was on the entirely wrong end of the building.

"Great," he muttered. "Drop a guy off as far away from his destination as possible, why don't you?"

As he wound his way through the labyrinth in search of the correct elevators, fresh pain spiked, and perspiration clung to his brow. TR thought of Sara. Instead of being there to support his arm and guide him in the right direction, she'd left him to his own devices. On purpose.

He dabbed at his hairline and trudged onward. A shaky hand reached over to slide along the wooden handrails that ran the length of the walls. With every new step, his legs took on the sensation of heavy ropes. Winded, he paused to catch his breath. He hoped he hadn't much farther to go.

A young woman ambled by. TR released his grip from the railing and nodded. No need to appear completely helpless. He wondered if he seemed this way to Sara. Probably not, considering she'd been encouraging him to do more for himself lately.

A light flickered in his head.

Of course, the evidence had been there all along. It was obvious. Why was he just putting it together? First, Sara had stopped changing the dressing on his injuries several days ago. She'd casually mentioned over extra refills of coffee that perhaps it was time TR attempted to do this for himself.

You're in much better shape than when I found you, she'd pointed out. The sudden suggestion had bewildered him. Was he?

In addition to this, she'd started to leave out a depressing bag of cold bagels and a jar of peanut butter in place of the enjoyable hot breakfasts to which he'd grown accustomed. *Feel free to help yourself* was her flippant remark as she breezed in and out of the room. Looking back on it now, TR was pretty sure she'd put an emphasis on the words "help yourself."

At long last, he arrived at a bank of metal elevators. Taking a minute to quell his hacking, he punched the "Up" button and frowned. Several seconds went by without the glowing numbers ever changing floors.

TR grunted.

As he waited, a hunched-over woman in a ratty orange wheelchair appeared. Did she, too, have a daughter who'd ditched her in the parking lot with the car still running? The woman must have felt him staring, because she somberly acknowledged him over a pair of bottle-thick glasses. He opened his mouth to offer assistance, only to clam up when a harried gal rounded the corner and hung a paper pharmacy bag over the wheelchair handle.

He glowered. Apparently, TR was the only one alone in this scenario.

His index finger jammed the "Up" button as his thoughts went back to Sara. With rising panic, he understood that his daughter was preparing to kick him out.

But this, TR thought, was a much more complicated proposition than Sara realized.

CHAPTER SEVENTEEN

SARA

She'd lingered out front until TR got himself through the hospital doors. The worrier in her wanted to jump out, to secure her father's shaky arm in hers and guide him to safety. Instead, she'd forced herself to stay put. This was hard. It wasn't in her nature to leave people in the lurch. Doing so supplied her with an acute sense of failure.

But she'd needed to get out of there. For more reasons than one.

Aside from encouraging TR to go it alone, Sara wanted a break. The drive over had been harrowing. She hadn't expected that.

TR had spent the better part seeking forgiveness; he'd even tried smoothing things out on behalf of Charlie. That was ironic. She assumed this was her father's way of offering a mea culpa. And she supposed that she should be grateful he was acknowledging his mistakes, even in his bumbling way. How long had she ached for such an admission?

But that wasn't quite it.

What TR didn't know—and what she couldn't bring herself to admit—was that Sara was afraid. She wasn't merely afraid the men in her life were leaving. She'd weathered that storm before. She could probably do it again. The thing that terrified her most was that, as a result, she would turn into her mother.

For Sara's entire life she had never wanted to be Joanne. When TR vanished, her mother lost her identity. What took its place was a frightening range of bewilderment, confusion, and rage. A single event had disoriented Joanne forever. She'd placed so much emphasis on her partnership, her marriage to a larger-than-life personality, that when it dissolved, so did her sense of self.

Sara swore she'd never let that happen to her, no matter the circumstance. Joanne had relied on men to make her whole. Never mind she had a young daughter to look after or the need to put food on the table. The sands of time stopped for Joanne when she ceased being someone's wife. She'd given up on discovering her own aspirations, allowing whatever dreams she may have had to fall by the wayside. She'd transformed into a person Sara found difficult to respect, let alone love.

But here Sara was anyway, despite everything she promised herself. At forty years old, she had a young child and a shaky marriage, and she had failed to follow through with her desire to someday become an artist. She wasn't succeeding at anything. She was a wreck. Instead of staying home to look after Sam, she'd chosen to run. And just like Joanne, she was losing her marbles. The car had nearly gone off the road, for one thing. And her outburst with TR came from somewhere so deeply buried even she didn't recognize it. What would come next? A complete emotional breakdown just like her mother?

Sara shuddered.

In the meantime, she had other matters on her mind. Namely, locating TR's house. She was currently traveling on a snaking surface road, following the navigation on her smartphone. Hopefully, there'd be time to travel to and from TR's place without arousing suspicion.

She'd researched the area before they'd left. The town of Sandpoint was comparatively large for Oregon's seaside, but it was nothing like the bustling city of Portland. Still, Sara had to squint at road signs to keep from getting lost.

Rain spit down on her windshield, partially obstructing the visibility. A clinging film of wet fog blanketed the town, wrapping everything in a lazy, pallid hue. To one side of the car was a precarious, rocky hillside that bordered the road. Its muted browns and greens colored the landscape like a rough oil painting. On the other side of this was the endless blue ocean.

The view from the road was impressive. Beyond the cliffs and past the rolling sand dunes, great outcroppings of rock launched themselves up from the churning seawater. These sea stacks dotted the coastline, resembling mini islands set adrift in the choppy waves. Sara peered up to see teams of milky seabirds circling above the tall formations.

Cracking the window, she inhaled. Salty humidity touched the back of her throat. The air was alive, surprisingly invigorating. She began to appreciate the appeal this place held for TR.

Her cell pinged, indicating the turnoff was near. Only a few cars passed as she made her way. TR wasn't kidding when he said his home was secluded.

A cluster of run-down-looking mailboxes marked the turnoff for an unpaved road. Sara veered right as a marker indicated the start of Sandpiper Lane. The road considerably narrowed then, leaving her nervous on a strip of lane barely meant for a single car. Almost immediately a steep drop-off materialized. If another car came at her, she would have nowhere to go. And the slightest error might send her plummeting into the ocean below.

No wonder TR didn't have any friends left. Who would want to risk coming here?

On the left, a wooden sign jutted out from the thick bushes. Spiky weeds and overgrown shrubs obscured its message. Sara slowed to read it. CAUTION: STEEP AND NARROW TRAIL. EXPERIENCED HIKERS ONLY.

She swallowed hard. Tightening her grip with moist palms, she drove along the path. Where in the heck was she going? Maybe this was a terrible idea.

After she'd sweated it out for several minutes, this portion of the road mercifully widened again. Someone must have recently maintained the road, because the landscape had been cut back in sections, allowing for a car to pass. Mossy trees and twisty vines lined a shaded stretch of packed dirt. It reminded Sara of *The Hobbit*, a book Sam never tired of reading. A secret forest. Any minute now, a band of elves might spring out from the undergrowth.

Reaching over, Sara studied her phone. She was nearly at her destination. Her father really lived this far out of the way? It was a marvel he hadn't died out there during the fire. How had anyone even known where to find him? The smoke must have been the thing that saved him. A distress signal from his island of isolation.

The dirt ended as the wheels crunched over a gravel drive. She was finally here. Sara let the car idle and took in the sight, her breath slipping between her lips. She released her grip and pushed her sunglasses back.

It was astonishing: TR had been so close to Sara yet completely inaccessible. He'd built a hidden life and chosen not to share it.

Stepping from the car, Sara pocketed the keys and leaned against the warm hood. She needed a moment to recalibrate.

Her first assumption was that there'd be stillness. She'd been wrong. Instead, the atmosphere was charged with a symphony of bird chirps and frog croaks. She cocked her head. Perhaps there was creek nearby. In the background, a faint buzzing of insects whirred in the treetops. They gave the air an almost electric feel. Beyond all of this, way off in the distance was the unmistakable power of crashing waves.

She moved cautiously along the gravel in her ankle-high boots. Whatever worker TR employed didn't seem to be around at the moment. Still, she was afraid to make any noise.

The property itself was expansive. On the perimeter, nestled against a dense backdrop, were two small structures. Each had a crudely shingled roof; years of damp weather had covered them in slick moss. The exteriors were encased in wood siding, with peeling paint and windowed doors. With the buildings in the middle of all that nature, the elements had clearly had their way with things.

Sara assumed these small cottages to be the tenant's room and TR's art studio. She recalled her father enjoyed a quiet space to work. Remarkably, neither building appeared to have been touched by fire.

On the right of the two smaller buildings loomed the main house. It was expansive, stately, and badly damaged.

Sara's breath caught. Hearing about the accident was one thing, but seeing the remnants up close was nothing short of haunting.

The singed wood siding reminded her of a box of matches that had been lit and then blown out. A crumbling frame propped up an obvious lack of a roof; the upper third of the home was unmistakably destroyed. The authorities weren't kidding when they said it was uninhabitable.

As she approached the bricked front walk, an odor of smoke permeated her mouth and lungs. Everything had a distinct tinge of charcoal. Sara reflexively brought a hand over her mouth.

Scanning the front, she noticed the cement foundation and an apron of stone facade were mostly intact. Save for what looked like soaked and trampled landscaping around the front porch, there appeared to be no damage to the entry. This must have been how TR escaped the flames. He'd miraculously had a way out.

Higher, the scene was entirely different. The upper level consisted of a wooden skeleton, a charred black frame. A brick chimney remained erect amid crumbling walls. Empty openings gaped like hollow eye sockets where doors and windows once were. Scorch marks, melted flooring, and decay could be seen without even going inside. The roof was all but gone, reduced to piles of ash.

The hair on Sara's arm rose. An eerie feeling washed over her. This fire had been no joke. Her father had cheated death.

Common sense told her not to try to enter. She didn't know what she'd be getting into if she did. And besides, if something were to happen, no one knew where she was. She thought of Sam waiting back at home. She couldn't afford to put herself in harm's way. Instead, she opted to walk the perimeter.

Picking her way through the grassy overgrowth, Sara arrived at the back of the property. Once more, the scene gave her pause. It was a strange and startlingly beautiful view. A source of inspiration.

The two-story home balanced on the edge of a craggy cliff that spilled out and over, dramatically diving into the Pacific Ocean. The setting was wild and untamed, with winds whipping up from the deep waters below. A salty spray misted the air. Everything out there felt raw and refreshing.

Sara's eye caught a worn footpath, where the grasses had been beaten down and matted. Craning her neck to see, she followed it as far as she could without moving. It trailed sharply off to the right and then progressed down a more gradual grade to what appeared to be a cove below. A mass of rocks hugged a spit of sand on either end, making it completely private.

She shaded her eyes and studied the trail. Hadn't the police report said TR had been found down there? Face-first in the sand? It seemed treacherous, but he must have been trying to get as far from the fire and as close to water as possible. It was a wonder anyone found him at all.

In her mind's eye, she could envision him careening down the path, a fiery blaze at his back.

Something loud sounded behind her. Sara startled and spun on her heels, scanning one end of the house to the other. Only the stony facade looked back at her.

What was that?

Someone or something was moving around, dragging across the gravel. But she wasn't entirely sure. Perhaps it was an animal from the woods. Or maybe she was imagining things. Spooked, she hustled back the way she came.

Rounding the corner, she nearly tripped over the metal bucket of an empty wheelbarrow. She caught herself and cursed. Where in the heck did that come from? Had it been there before? She saw no trace of movement.

She continued on the path, careful to avoid the spiky weeds that poked her from all directions. Maybe she hadn't heard anything at all. This panic was merely self-induced.

A flash of white darted in her periphery, and her thoughts slowed. Was that the worker after all? A shape moved behind one of the smaller buildings. Someone was out there.

Whoever it was, he or she was hiding.

Sara tensed. Oh God, was she going to get murdered way out there in the woods? Maybe TR hadn't shared much about his maintenance man because the guy was some kind of wacko, someone too unstable to secure a real job, living way out in the middle of nowhere in order to hide from society. Maybe he wouldn't be so welcoming to a stranger who'd wandered onto the property uninvited. And she'd failed to tell anyone where she was going.

With a jittery hand, she fumbled in her pocket. Her car was within sight. Retrieving her key, she jammed the sharp point through her knuckles and prepared to defend herself against an attacker.

Blood pumped in her ears as she strained to listen. She just had to make it across the driveway. Detecting nothing, she broke out into a sprint. The soles of her boots pounded across the loose rocks.

"Hey!" a male voice shouted.

The toe of her boot caught as Sara stumbled forward. She swayed and then lost her balance. Bracing, she shot her hands out to catch her fall. Both knees went down first. The impact was jarring. A cloud of dust and dirt flew up, impairing her vision. Sharp rocks pierced her skin, stinging on contact. Footsteps closed in on her, and every muscle contracted as Sara desperately groped for her car key weapon.

The voice shouted again.

The car was only a few steps away. She could make it. Gathering herself up, she readied to flee. But it was too late. A figure was now standing over her, casting a long shadow across the dusty drive.

"Are you all right?"

Sucking in the pain, Sara sprang to her feet and wheeled around. She was wired with adrenaline and ready to fight.

"Stay away!" she cried out. Her warning was shrill and weak sounding.

"Whoa, hang on a second." A hand went up.

Sara drew herself together and fisted the key at her side.

A set of hazel eyes studied her suspiciously. He wasn't particularly tall, but he might still be able to overpower her. Her gaze flicked to where his muscles flexed under a dirty white T-shirt. His hands went to his sides. Thankfully, he wasn't brandishing any kind of weapon. And he had a young face, probably around twenty years old or so.

"You're trespassing on private property," he said.

"No, I'm not. I have a right to be here."

"And why is that? You don't live here."

"Do you?"

He arched a brow. "Um, yes. As a matter of fact I do. And now I'm going to have to ask you to leave, or I'll be forced to call the cops."

"Hang on," she said, standing her ground and giving him the once-over. "So you're TR's worker?"

Miniature creases around his eyes gathered as he smirked. He scratched his unkempt pile of bleached hair, taking a moment to likely size her up. "Uh, not really. But I suppose that's what you'd see. You must be one of his fans. Came to take some photos for your blog or something like that. Well, I got news for you, lady. He took off. Doesn't live here. And even if he did, he wouldn't agree to see you anyway. The old man's not into visitors of any kind."

What the hell was happening? This kid wasn't at all what she'd expected. And why was he so protective of TR? She eased off a bit and unclenched the key.

"I know he doesn't live here. He currently lives with me."

The smirk disappeared as a wave of disgust twisted his face into a grimace. "Fuck. That's so typical! You're telling me that the old codger is somewhere else, shacking up with you now? You a girlfriend or something?"

Sara reared back, the idea obscene. "No. God, no! I'm definitely not a girlfriend."

"Then who are you?"

She rolled the truth around on her tongue. She wasn't sure she could trust this guy. But what could she say? She didn't want to be forced to leave just yet. She still had questions.

"If you must know, I'm his daughter."

His face dropped.

Crickets chirped in the background.

"And you are?" Sara waited for a reply. For someone so cocky, this guy seemed to have suddenly lost his voice. His jaw clenched and released. A hand rubbed at his freckled forehead.

"I'm Bo."

"That tells me nothing," Sara said. "If you aren't an employee, then who exactly are you?"

"I'm his son."

Sara's keys slipped between her fingers and plunged into the dirt, right along with her heart.

CHAPTER EIGHTEEN

SARA

Before she had a chance to shore up her shock, a screen door attached to one of the cottages whined open and then banged forcefully, rattling in its frame. Following this, a female voice rang out. Sara straightened.

At first glance, it seemed as if a volatile cyclone were fast approaching. Sara watched, mouth agape, as a flurry of dark hair and intensity flew in her direction. Tied to the tangle of long, flowing hair was a green scarf that trailed behind, twisting dramatically in the wind. From what Sara could see, this woman was all hair and eyebrows. That, and a curvy figure worthy of an old Hollywood movie. She watched motionless as a cloud of dust moved in, kicking up around Western boots and the hem of a long, floral dress. A set of tempestuous black eyes zeroed in on them.

Sara could tell, even amid her fury, that this woman was beautiful and exotic—a rare bird whose nest had been unpleasantly disturbed. And she was striking out.

Backing up cautiously, Sara retreated. She had the distinct impression she was not welcome.

Preceding the woman came a long slew of declarations delivered in a rapid-fire language Sara could not understand. But the tone of the words was as clear as day. This woman was livid.

At that moment, something glinted in the sun. Sara's eyes widened as she tracked an object in the woman's right hand—something dark and metallic.

A gun!

Cold terror shot through her veins, and every fiber of her being told her to run.

"Shit!"

Scrambling, Sara made for the car. Tiny fragments of loose gravel rolled under her feet and impeded her momentum. Her limbs jellied, causing her to feel like a frantic character in a ridiculous cartoon. Fear fired on all cylinders as she willed herself to move faster, her heart charging in her chest.

A scuffling sound of shoes and urgent breath closed in on her. There were more yells in the background.

Someone reached out and grabbed her, and Sara nearly collapsed with fear.

"Whoa, whoa." Bo dropped his voice next to her ear, as if he were coaxing a frightened pony. His fingers tightened on her arm. "Hang on there."

"She's got a gun!" Sara screamed.

"What?"

Sara thrashed against Bo's grip, stinging tears obscuring her view of the car. With a burst of energy, she writhed around and delivered a solid shove to Bo's chest.

He stumbled backward but still held his grasp.

Footfalls rushed in, and then a heated conversation in a foreign language unfurled around her in what sounded like intense arguing. A scolding even. Blood pumped loudly in her ears, and it took Sara a second to understand what was being repeated. Something was being said in English over the woman's crazed voice. Something calm and steady.

"You're okay. You're okay. See, it is only a camera. No gun. Just a camera."

A camera?

The grasp on her jacket loosened. Sara slowly angled around. Both the red-faced woman and Bo stood together, side by side, staring. Cautiously, Sara's eyes moved to the woman's hand. Poking out from the long sleeve of a cardigan sweater was the long, shiny black lens of a camera.

"See? No gun. Just my crazy mother. She is a photographer. Always with a camera. Nothing more." Bo's eyebrows hovered above his inquisitive features. As her heartbeat slowed to normal, Sara noticed the gentleness in his eyes. She was momentarily reminded of Sam.

This Bo person might be her brother, and that would make him Sam's *uncle*. She blinked hard, absorbing the possibility.

The woman paused and cleared her throat. To Sara, it sounded like something of a growl.

Bo gestured. "Mamma, you're scaring her. She thought you had a gun."

The woman snorted, followed by a disparaging glance at Bo.

"Silly child," she sneered in what Sara could now tell was a throaty Italian accent and waved the Canon in the air like a peace flag. "What would I want with a gun?"

"I, uh—"

"You Americans are all the same. You think in Italy we'd go around swinging guns from our holsters?"

Bo dropped his head in frustration. "Mamma! *I'm* an American. And you've lived here for years. This is not the Wild West."

The woman barked a response in Italian. Bo spat back something equally terse, and for the next minute Sara found herself in the strange position of witnessing a mother-son feud. Only she didn't know these people.

"Excuse me," she broke in. "Could someone please tell me what the hell is going on?"

They stared back at her.

Sara saw it now, the similarity. Both had heads of thick hair and matching unruly eyebrows. Their skin was creamy yet of differing complexions—one olive and one peach. Mother and son stood squarely, of equal size and stature. And their lips were unmistakably full.

But the woman had a fierceness about her that the son—TR's son—lacked. A sort of razor's edge. Sara had no doubt this woman could easily bring someone to her knees if she wanted. It was written all over her disapproving face.

"You said you are TR's daughter?" Bo began. His expression was one of genuine confusion.

Did TR have another family hidden out here all this time? She and Joanne hadn't been enough, so he went and started over with someone else? The bitter taste of old rejection surfaced. Her father's betrayals ran much deeper than she'd known.

"Merda," the woman uttered under her breath. Both hands flew up and then smacked back down at her sides. Her proud shoulders sagged into what Sara detected as defeat.

"English, Mamma!" Bo cast a watchful glance at his mother.

"We've already been visited many times by the police. Too much spying around. We don't need more of this from you! You cannot just show up now. It isn't right!"

"Mamma!"

The woman looked away.

Bo studied her. "Why do you say that?"

Anger flashed in the downturned corners of her mouth. "Because this girl shows up only to cause trouble. That's why. She has no business here. Don't you see?"

Sara flinched. Had her father told this woman something about her?

"She says she's TR's daughter, Mamma. But something tells me you already knew that."

Dark eyes raked over Sara's still-wobbly frame. "Yes, I know who she is. Just look at her. She's the image of her father." The woman's large knuckles dug into her wool cardigan, yanking it tightly across her floral dress. Both arms locked over her large bosom.

Under such scrutiny, Sara had the urge to cover herself.

"And you still want to run her off?" Bo asked.

His mother jutted out her chin and glared. Sara recoiled. She planted her feet, however, and held her ground. She had a few burning questions of her own, namely why this woman thought she had dibs on TR and his place when his own daughter did not. Who was she to run Sara off?

"Oh my God, Mamma!" Bo let out a heavy exhale and stomped in a circle. Puffs of gravelly dust kicked up. "What the hell?"

My sentiments exactly, Sara thought.

She did the math. If what he said was true, that he belonged to TR, then he would have been born when Sara was in her late teens—roughly around the same time as her catastrophic encounter with TR at the Los Angeles art studio. Had this feral woman been in the picture way back then? Had she been standing in the room all those years ago when Sara's mother thrust her into the crowd of partygoers? A recollection of her teenage humiliation crept in.

The night she'd agreed to go see TR, it was solely because her mother led her to believe he'd asked for her. But when they arrived at the gallery party, they'd taken him totally by surprise. Her father had been celebrating with a roomful of strangers, and Sara instantly sensed that their entrance was being treated like some kind of unplanned entertainment. People pointed and whispered at Joanne's garish dress and exaggerated antics, while all Sara wanted to do was melt into the walls. TR acted as if he'd been thrown off balance, tripping over himself and his words, like he didn't know what to do with her. Of course, this sent her mother into a bigger fit. Sara had run from the room with her mother in tow, the night and her memory of her father ruined.

As she stood on TR's property now, once again feeling unexpected and unwanted, Sara began to shake. Had this always been the case with her father? Had TR not been interested in getting his old family together because he was busy playing house with this woman and her son?

The realization was a hard blow. Sara's anguish quickly shifted into rage.

"This isn't right!" Repulsion for her father's callous actions overwhelmed her. Adrenaline coursed, and she very badly wanted to hit something. Wildly glancing around, she threw up her arms. "I came here to check on my father's house. He never mentioned details about other people living here . . . nothing about a family!"

Her throat burned as she said the words. TR had this whole other family, including a grown son. And he'd kept it from her, his only daughter.

If I am his only daughter, Sara wondered. The idea served as a fresh dagger plunging into the deepest parts of her.

TR didn't really like children, nor did he care to be tied down to convention. So why—or rather how—was it possible a woman and her child were standing there, claiming TR and his house as their own?

The hot flare of fury that had started in the base of her gut continued to build. Her father had been keeping monumental secrets. She'd cared for him, and he'd lied to her. He'd gone out and made another family to replace her. And here she'd been, all this time since his accident, assuming they might be getting closer. But it was all a sham. The people standing in front of her were proof of that.

Bo had backed up a few inches after her outburst. He looked unsure of what she might do next. "The fact he didn't tell you about us is pretty messed up," he said to Sara. His hand went to the back of his neck and rubbed. "But my dad can be messed up. Like, a lot of the time."

"You can say that again." She balled her fists and glared into the distance, blinking back her lament.

How many more times would her father break her heart? How many times would she let him? TR had sunk to a new low and pulled Sara's faith right down with him.

"He never mentioned me? Like ever?" Sara noticed Bo's gaze drop to the ground. She recognized the awful feeling of dejection in his face. For a brief instant she empathized with him.

"Humph!" Bo's mother spit forcefully into the dust near her feet. Sara flinched. It felt oddly as if it were some kind of curse. Only whom was the woman cursing? Sara hoped it wasn't her. But by the way the woman's eyes landed softly back on her son, Sara understood TR was to blame.

"Are you his wife?" Sara was almost afraid to ask, but a hundred questions were pushing their way forward.

"Ha!" The woman's face tightened, and she folded her arms. "No. I'm not married to that idiot!"

Bo shook his head. Sara wasn't sure what to make of it.

"Oh. Well, then how long have you two been living here?" she asked.

"Four years," Bo answered. "Four long years." His mother nodded once and then looked as if she might spit again.

Why only four years? She was on the verge of asking when Bo continued.

"I don't know where to go from here," Bo announced. "Obviously, TR didn't want you to know about us, or he would have told you. I'm not sure why." He swallowed. Sara returned his gaze and detected a hint of grief.

"I guess so." Sara felt the hollowness of her own voice. Her father had played them all for fools.

Bo's mother huffed out audible exasperation in the background, as if she were growing weary of the conversation. It angered Sara that she'd kept silent, even though she knew Sara existed. Had she discouraged TR from attempting to reconnect with his daughter, or had he made that decision all on his own?

"So, you say he's living with you?" Bo asked. "We thought he'd come back by now. But then again . . ." Bo's words drifted off. He bit down on his lower lip, looking as if he were afraid he'd said too much.

Sara's ears pricked. "Then again what?"

Bo shook his head. "Never mind. It's a long story. Maybe you could come inside, and we can talk for a minute."

Sara hesitated. A big part of her yearned to sit down and ply Bo with all her burning questions, and to process what it all meant. She wanted to find out as much as she could about this other family that had been hidden from her. But another part of her simply needed to go. Unearthing TR's massive well of secrets had set something off inside her. Something irate and powerful. She had an urgent desire to confront her father—with everything.

"I'd better go," she blurted.

"Goodbye, then," the woman said. She clapped her hands together as if to say *that's that*.

"Ma!" Bo glared. He turned to Sara, his face crumpled. "Go where?"

"I just have to go. I need to be somewhere." She had no intention of telling them her plan. Sara wanted TR to know her fury, to demand answers. These people would have to wait.

She glanced beyond Bo to the remains of the charred house. Blackened ash stood like pillars of the past. And TR had left it all behind. Just as he'd left her. She was going to find out why.

"I have to go!" Sara turned on her heel and sprinted to the car. No one was going to stop her this time.

CHAPTER NINETEEN
SARA

Sara wrapped a pair of trembling hands around the steering wheel and tried not to hyperventilate. Hot tears of rejection streamed down her cheeks as she drove back to the hospital, clouding her vision, but she didn't bother wiping them away.

How could TR keep something so big from her? There was another woman and a son. Living with him. Existing this whole time just hours from Sara's world. And yet they'd been hidden. Sara had been ignorantly caregiving for TR as if he had no other options. They'd spent hours alone, she and her father. There'd been so many quiet times when confessions could have been made. When they should have been made. She'd started each morning by intimately tending to his wounds, for God's sake.

And TR chose to cruelly withhold the truth.

Another child existed. In place of her. Had TR been a great and present father for this Bo person? Had he held this boy in his arms and invited him to be his muse? Had he been there, steadfast during the difficult adolescent years, offering the guidance and consoling she so desperately could have used but never received? The very image sickened her.

Accompanying her anguish was the intensifying wrath that came from being duped. Despite all of Sara's reservations, she'd brought TR into her life anyway. He had been invited into her home, and yet he'd violated her trust. He'd been absent from Sara's life not because he was too proud to admit his mistakes and return, but because he'd been playing house with a new family. Her sorrow and fury were almost crippling.

There was a whole bevy of reasons to be livid with TR, deceit being high up on the list. But she was also furious with herself.

She'd been such a fool. For beginning to soften toward her father, for trusting him, and for never considering he might have another family.

Cranking the radio dial to "Off," she navigated through pelting rain. The day had morphed into a depressing shade of gloom, with dense coastal fog and heavy precipitation assaulting the tiny town. It was as if the onslaught of dreadful weather were somehow trying to run her out of town.

She squinted at the road ahead. A slick layer of rain flooded the pavement, causing her to grip the wheel even tighter for fear of hydroplaning. The last thing Sara wanted to do was lose control. But she feared that had pretty much happened anyway.

What she would do when she got to TR, she wasn't quite sure. Tossing him out of her life came to mind.

So far, Sara had uncovered far too many questions and not enough answers.

What on earth had TR been thinking? That he'd get away with so much deception? He was back in his hometown for the day, just minutes from where people were evidently awaiting his return, and he'd chosen to say nothing. He'd let Sara believe that without her, he was utterly alone. That he had nowhere to turn, nobody to help out in his hour of need. And she'd stupidly bought it. Hook, line, and sinker.

Sara groaned.

At that moment, she could almost sense Joanne's ghostly spirit hovering over her shoulder, clucking her tongue in disapproval. Her mother would have known better. And her daughter should have too.

Arriving back in the hospital parking lot, Sara aimed her car for the farthest spot and parked. She pulled in a couple of deep breaths, steeling herself. Dropping her hands into her lap, she noticed they were still shaky. Her reflection in the rearview mirror revealed an inky stream of mascara had marked her face. She crouched low in her seat, hiding from passersby. She wasn't in any shape to go inside.

Maybe the best thing to do would be to leave. To turn the car for home and desert TR altogether. The idea was tempting. But then a second thought followed. If she left now, she'd rob herself of the opportunity to confront him. And she wanted to see the look on his face when that happened.

Snatching her cell, she dialed hospital reception. As it rang, she blotted her cheeks and attempted to mask the emotion in her voice. After a minute, she was patched through to the office of TR's doctor.

"Hi, I'm looking for Thomas Harlow. Do you know if he's left yet?"

Clicks of a computer keyboard could be heard through the line. The receptionist emitted a couple of "hmms" as Sara waited. Finally, the girl informed her TR was just recently taken back. There'd been some kind of mix-up with his appointment, and he'd probably be another thirty minutes or so before he was finished.

"Thank you." She hit "End." One more thing to add to the list of screw-ups for the day. No doubt TR would be in a foul mood because of it.

Let him stew, she thought. He deserved a little discomfort. And then some.

Sara deliberated all the ways to go after her father. God, did she really have a brother out there this whole time and didn't know it? Someone who'd gotten the fatherly parts of TR that were never offered to her?

157

She absorbed the thought with a fresh dose of resentment.

The woman, with her inhospitality toward Sara, was another story. Judging by the looks of her, with crevices bracketing a set mouth and protruding knuckles jutting up from weathered hands, Sara guesstimated the woman to be in the vicinity of sixty years old. This made sense, given that his girlfriends had always been younger. All except Joanne.

Sara squeezed her eyes at the thought of her mother. Someone else who'd been replaced.

She checked the time. TR was sure to be finished with his checkup. Turning her key, she set the car into reverse and backed from her hiding spot. The rain had faded. A layer of smokelike mist rose up from the blackened asphalt.

His familiar shock of bright hair could be seen as she rounded the corner. TR spied her and flagged impatiently. His self-regard made her anger flare all over again. The sleeves of his blue-and-red windbreaker were pushed high above his elbows. A single ball of cotton was taped to the inside of one arm. The doctor had taken a blood sample.

Surprisingly, TR's usual swath of bandaging was absent. The doctors must have noted an improvement and removed the protective dressing. Sara lightened slightly with relief. She was over her role of playing nursemaid. Especially now.

"It's about damned time!" TR snapped as she opened the car door.

Her molars ground together. He was lucky she even showed up. "I'm here, aren't I?"

"What a disaster that was!" TR grunted and landed with a thud in his seat. "I was an entire hour too early! Did you know that? And no one in that godforsaken joint knew what to do with me!"

"Just don't, TR," Sara growled. She was ready to unleash. When she was through with him, being late for an appointment was going to be the least of TR's problems.

He scowled.

"Do you have something to tell me?" Sara bored into him with her gaze, barely containing her mounting rage.

"I'm not sure. Do I?" Something resembling panic flashed across his face.

"Stop with the lies, TR!"

Her father's mouth hung open with bewilderment.

"I'm waiting."

TR needed to start confessing. Fast.

CHAPTER TWENTY

TR

It was a test of some sort. He realized that. But TR didn't know the answer. Whatever it was, he had the distinct feeling that everything was at stake. He searched her face and wondered what to say. What was his daughter after? This was the angriest he'd ever seen her. Her nostrils flared as her breath pushed out through her nose. Her lips disappeared into that familiar thin line of disdain. Oh God, she hadn't run into Marie or Bo in town, had she? Fear seized him. How would that even be possible? He instantly regretted not telling her about them sooner.

As he debated over what to say, his daughter fumed. Her expectant gaze hardened, and she threw the car into gear. They began to drive out of town swiftly. Too swiftly. Sara's anger seemed to double as she waited for him to respond, racing the SUV back along coastal roads and out onto the main highway, cutting through the soggy marine layer on a dangerous course.

His throat tightened. He might be losing his chance.

He considered asking her if they could make a stop, to put an end to all the secrets. But he quickly buried the notion. Thrusting an unwitting Sara into meeting a sibling she didn't even know existed might hurt both of his children. Sara and Bo hadn't asked to be a part of their father's mess. Putting them together before they were ready would further fragment his delicate relationships with them. He didn't know how he'd tell her, but surely Sara would be upset when she learned he'd been keeping something so big from her. And Marie did not like surprises. Showing up unannounced after severed communication would likely send the two of them back into hostile territory. How would it look if he appeared with his long-lost daughter and admitted he had preferred to spend the past weeks living with her and avoiding them? Yes, Marie had talked of leaving, of breaking up. But she'd also tried to reach out while he'd been hospitalized, and TR had stubbornly refused for fear of facing backlash from the fire. Now he realized he'd been wrong. But he wasn't sure how to fix things.

There was so much he needed to explain to Sara. Confessions played on his tongue, hiding behind his teeth, yearning to escape. This was it; he just needed to tell her the truth. *It's now or never,* he told himself.

Before he could speak, a high-pitched ringing reverberated from the center console of the car. Both he and Sara jumped. Three more chimes rung out, their urgency echoing from inside the compartment. Sara flung open the cover and thrashed around with a free hand to locate the phone. On instinct, he reached across the seats in case he was required to grab the wheel.

The severe point of an elbow stopped him.

"I got it," she barked. Retrieving the phone, she cradled it between her chin and shoulder.

"Yes?" Her tone was short. "What? When?" Sara eased her foot off the gas, slowing to listen.

TR picked up her change in tone and was concerned.

"Where is he now?" Her face pinched into a tight question.

A muffled voice escalated on the other end as TR strained to listen. It belonged to a male; he could tell that much. It must have been Charlie. Sara's husband had been left back at home, in charge of the boy and the dog. A red flag of worry popped up.

"Did you plug in his nebulizer and connect the mask?" she inquired, the immediacy in her voice climbing. "And how long did that last?"

TR's chest tightened. Had something bad happened?

More muted responses on the other end could be heard. Sara appeared as if she were running through a list of procedures as she responded to the information being fed to her. Toward the end of the conversation, he heard a vague trickle of relief in her voice. She spouted off a few more instructions and nodded.

"Okay. Tell him I love him and I'll be home in less than an hour. Let him watch TV or play the Xbox or something calm. Read a book. And please don't leave the house with him, Charlie. I mean it. Sometimes the medicine makes him shaky, like he's had too much caffeine. You need to watch for that and cut back on the Albuterol if this happens. He doesn't like to feel that way; it scares him. Okay?"

A few more head nods.

"Okay. See you then. Bye." She pressed the screen and dropped the phone into her lap. He noticed her hands were shaking. The car continued to speed past others. Sara leaned forward and frowned. TR noticed the tight lines in her forehead and the determined clench of her jaw. He felt for his daughter at that moment; she bore so much on her own. He supposed she always had. The realization saddened him.

"Everything okay at home?" TR ventured. He couldn't bear to think of anything happening to that beautiful boy.

"What?" She did a double take like she'd forgotten he was in the car with her. He could tell her anger was still lurking, but she had temporarily set it aside because of the phone call. "Yeah, it's going to be. Sam suffered an asthma attack. Charlie is just not that well equipped to handle things sometimes."

"You mean he's not equipped because he's the father, or he's not equipped because he's just not around to have enough practice?" he asked carefully.

"Yes."

"Yes to which part?"

Sara tossed him a look of sheer exasperation. "Yes to both, okay? You fathers have the luxury of coming and going when you please. Leading secret lives. It's the mothers who stick around and make sure the family doesn't fall apart."

TR felt himself bristle.

"Sara," he began. "I know you think all husbands, all fathers run out and ditch their families."

"Don't they?" she snarled, her anger returning.

TR scratched at his jawline, choosing to ignore the jab. It hurt nonetheless.

"There are things you don't always know about. Extenuating circumstances that prevent one from—"

Sara snorted. *"Extenuating circumstances."* There was fresh venom in her delivery.

"Let me finish—"

"I met him." His daughter's exclamation came out in a whimper. Her eyes were suddenly wet. It caught him off guard.

"Who?" he asked, afraid of the answer that might come.

"Do I have to spell it out for you? Can't you just come clean for once?"

"Sara, I—"

"The other factor. Your extenuating circumstance."

The racing in his mind came to a grinding halt.

"Oh." TR's lips went numb. It was too late. She'd found out before he'd had the chance to explain. And he understood, before she said another word, it was going to be hell trying to repair the damage.

CHAPTER TWENTY-ONE

SARA

Why couldn't life only deal her one disaster at a time? Why did it instead have to rain down on her all at once? At the moment, all she wanted to do was magically time travel back to her house and hold her son. Sam needed her, and she wasn't there. She was with her father instead, who had deceived her and wasted her time. It wasn't fair.

And then TR had to go and shoot his mouth off about men and their legitimate excuses. It was all Sara could do not to swerve the car off the road and boot him out. How dare he?

"Start talking, TR," Sara snapped. What did her father have to say for himself? She wanted to know.

"Ah, Christ. This wasn't how I wanted things to play out. I was going to tell you." Her father squirmed in his seat.

Fury reverberated up the back of her spine. "When? When were you going to share the little tidbit that there's another family—living on your property! My God, TR, it's not like informing me you're out of fresh laundry! I went there to check on your house, and instead I find some guy named Bo and his crazy mother confronting me!"

He flinched, and she wondered if he'd ever planned to tell her the truth.

"It's complicated," he said. "And what business did you have tromping around on my property?" He banged a fist down on the center console.

The nerve of him attacking her about trespassing was outrageous. "Well, maybe if you'd been more open with me, then I wouldn't have had to resort to sneaking behind your back. This relationship is pretty one-sided, TR."

"What does that mean?"

"It means that I've opened up my entire life to you—you're living in my *home*! And you haven't given me anything in return. Do you know what it was like for me to stand there, completely unprepared, and have some stranger tell me he was your son? A sibling I knew nothing about? It felt like shit, TR!" She shuddered as she held back a sob, the salty burn of tears collecting at the back of her throat. How could he have done this to her? The mix of humiliation and heartache twisted inside her chest. "You lied to me. You're still lying to me. Why is it so difficult to understand this?" She batted the tears away and couldn't believe she was crying. Again. He'd walked out on her and Joanne, only to go off and create some kind of replacement family without ever looking back.

A heavy sigh passed between TR's lips. "I'm sorry you had to find out that way. But like I said, it's complicated. I was going to tell you. I swear. I just have some things I need to figure out first. Trust me, you don't want my own damn worries stacked up on top of yours right now. Let's just get home so you can see Sam."

It was useless. He simply didn't know how to open up. Sara didn't particularly know how to do this either, especially with someone who'd disappointed her so desperately. But she was trying. What had TR done to bridge the divide? Absolutely nothing. She stared straight ahead and seethed.

At last, after many agonizing miles of TR's stalling and stammering, Sara gave up. She was emotionally spent from it all, and she just wanted to go home. It was a relief to finally return to the familiar tall fir and cedar trees that dotted the street corner of her neighborhood. The homey sight served as a pleasant welcome-home banner to Sara's inflamed state.

Charlie's car sat parked in the driveway, and some of Sam's things were strewn across the front lawn. Her heart dropped. Had Sam been in such distress that they'd left belongings scattered carelessly outside?

The front door flung open, and Sam's expectant face emerged. Even from a distance she could tell his color looked a little pallid. But he was smiling, and that was a huge relief. Sara grinned and waggled her fingers from her spot inside the car.

"Your boy there looks to be in one piece." TR ducked his head and peered through her side window. Even in her anger toward him, she could detect the concern in TR's voice. He cared for his grandson, if for no one else.

"Yep." She nearly responded with a snarky retort about *his* boy, now that she knew he had one, but she stopped herself. She pushed out of the car, and her feet sped up the brick walkway, leaving TR behind.

"Hi, Mom!" Sam called out. A ring of bright orange rimmed his mouth. Must be the sports drinks Charlie was forever buying for Sam. The amount of artificial dye used in them made her cringe, but it was better than a lot of the other sugary drinks many of his friends enjoyed, and she let it go.

"Hi, babe. How's it going?" Her smile widened. She told herself to keep her resolve, for Sam's sake. She didn't want him to see her break down.

"Oh, you know. Pretty good." He shrugged as she approached.

Sara's heart expanded. Here he'd been pulled from school, had been made to suffer through breathing treatments, and still managed to greet her without a complaint. He really was a great kid.

For the last half of the drive, she'd yearned to inhale his little-boy smell of strawberry shampoo and frozen waffles. This was what she needed right now, to wrap her arms around the one sure thing in her world and hold on tight.

Everything else could take a back seat.

~

As she entered the house and deposited her coat in the front hall, Charlie came to greet her. Acer also appeared and wedged himself into the entryway, not wanting to be forgotten. His tail thumped happily against Sara's leg. Out of habit, Sara picked up a nearby rubber dog toy and tossed it into the living room to get him out of the way. He went trotting off in search of it.

"Hey," Charlie said. The corners of his mouth were turned down, but he offered a small smile nonetheless. He looked tired.

"Hi. No more complications?" Sara asked. She first looked at Charlie and then Sam, who was still at her side.

"No. He's okay now." Charlie's hand reached over and ruffled the top of Sam's head. "He handled it like a champ."

"Thanks, Dad," Sam said.

Sara nodded and met his gaze. "That's good."

Charlie's eyebrow rose. "What about you? You okay? You look like you've been—"

Sara's eyes quickly darted toward Sam, and she shook her head for Charlie to stop. Her son didn't need to hear what had gone on in the car. Not when she was still so raw and might easily fold over into a heap of emotion.

"I was just worried about Sam, that's all. But it sounds like you guys had it handled. If you two will excuse me for just a second. I need to go to the bathroom."

Charlie cocked his head and watched her walk past them. "Why don't you go back to resting on the sofa, buddy?" she heard him ask Sam. "I'll make you something to eat in a bit."

Sara made it to the back of the house just as the tears came cascading forward. Blurry eyed, she slipped into the bathroom and hunched over on the edge of the tub. Grabbing a giant wad of toilet paper, she pressed it to her face and wept.

Charlie knocked softly on the door and asked to be let in. Still sobbing, Sara leaned over and released the lock. Her husband entered and knelt down on the mosaic-tiled floor beside her. A comforting hand lifted to meet the small of her back.

"Sara, honey, what's the matter? Is it Sam? Because he's okay now; he really is." After so much distance between them, the tenderness of his touch weakened her.

"No." She blew into the toilet paper wad and then dropped it into her lap. "I mean, yes, I was worried about him. But that's not it. It's TR." A fresh wave of sobs shuddered through her as she slumped over her knees and tried not to wail.

The gentle hand that had been placed on her back stiffened. "What did he do now?" A rising irritation trailed Charlie's question.

Sara wanted to explain. Her first impulse was to confide in him, to lean on her spouse for support. But then she remembered what lay between them. The distrust, the distance. The confusing way her husband kept leaving. And because of this, she found herself clamming back up. On top of that she couldn't stop crying. Every time she paused to take a breath, more jags followed, making it impossible to speak. She pressed more toilet paper to her face and let Charlie know she was too broken up to talk. She'd reveal the root of her distress later. He looked confused.

"I'll be right outside if you need me," he said.

"Thank you," Sara said, his soothing words enveloping her before he clicked the door shut and exited into the hall. And for the briefest of seconds, she didn't feel so alone.

Charlie followed her lead throughout the dinner that followed, yo-yoing between casting bewildered glances at her and shrugging on an air of false normalcy in front of Sam. His expression, however, remained doubtful. Sara didn't have the energy to do anything other than push her food around. She hadn't any interest in keeping up the pretense of dialogue.

Afterward, while Charlie and TR awkwardly attempted to make small talk over the task of clearing the table, Sara quickly retreated. Sneaking into the shelter of Sam's room was the only thing that sounded good to her. She sought solitude with her sweet son, to be among his boyish things that reminded her of happier times, to wrap him in her arms and forget about the problems with her father for a while.

As she settled onto the mattress of his low bed, the distress from her long day sank down with her. Her stocking feet kicked over the end of Sam's striped comforter as she watched him get ready for bed. In drawn-out movements, he crossed the room and retrieved a pair of pajamas from a pine dresser. A listless hand closed the drawer. He operated as if underwater.

"Feeling sluggish, pal?" She eyed him closely. His breathing had thankfully returned to normal, no longer forcing his chest to rise and fall in rushed actions. For this, she was truly grateful. Watching Sam suffer was the worst kind of agony.

"Yeah, just tired," Sam replied. A yawn escaped.

Sara had the urge to reach out to stroke his soft face. He was still her baby in a certain sense, sweet and big eyed. But little indications that he was indeed changing had begun to morph his features. Like the crop of fresh freckles skimming the bridge of his nose. The summer sun had left its imprint on him, and Sara knew there was more to come. His once-minuscule set of baby teeth had all but given way to large permanent ones, widening his jawline and sculpting the places where baby fat once resided. And his shoulders were broadening, shaping his torso into a small V that reminded Sara too much of a teenager's body.

These were all minor changes that likely no one noticed but her. And still, each new development was like a tiny arrow to her heart.

This was her only child. There wouldn't be any more babies to hold. She and Charlie had agreed Sam was all they needed to round out their little family. He was it, and she desperately wished this time with him could last forever.

As much as she craved to smother Sam in affection, she also knew enough to respect his space. He'd be transforming into a hormonal tween any day now, seeking privacy without the irritation of his mother hovering around. Time was going to march on whether Sara was ready for it or not. It was important to cherish the little moments. They wouldn't last. So she lingered on the edge of his bed and chose to keep him company as he went about his bedtime routine.

"I've been tired all day," Sam said, ambling over to switch off the light on his shoebox-size goldfish tank. A solitary fish, which had lived for three curious years, swam in a circle as if to flap good night to his owner. Sara wondered how a thing so small had managed to last so long.

"That's just the medicine," she reassured him. "You're always tired after that stuff makes its way through your system. Your lungs had to work overtime today. Your body has been through a lot."

"Uh-huh."

"You're going to be okay; you know that, right?" Her voice inched up an octave. She knew she was stating this more for her benefit than his. Sam didn't get fazed by these types of episodes the way that she did. He'd been experiencing them his whole life; however, it was her job to comfort her son. This was the best way she knew how—by reiterating his strength.

Sam mumbled a sleepy response and wandered down the hall to change his clothes and brush his teeth. Sara reclined onto the downy bedding and waited for him to return. The clinking sound of silverware being rinsed in the sink and then placed back into a drawer drifted through the house. A faint murmur of male voices followed. Sara closed her eyes and guessed at what her husband and her father were discussing.

Had her father spent time like this with his own son? Had he tucked Bo into bed as a child, maybe read a book aloud and sat in his room to cherish the little-boy moments? Had TR been a better father to his other child than he had to Sara?

The image was piercing. Her nose stung a little with the welling of fresh hurt. Shifting, she blotted at her watery eyes. The painful idea of being replaced lodged itself in her heart. Why hadn't she been enough?

She tortured herself imagining her father whiling the years away with another child. A child that maybe was more like TR than she was. Did Bo pick up where Sara had been so cruelly left off? Had he been invited into TR's studio, just as Sara had, when he was younger?

Just thinking of this left an acrid taste in her mouth. She'd naively believed this singular aspect of TR's world belonged only to her. The memories of her childhood spent squirreled away in TR's workspace had been the one solid thing she could still claim in their twisted history as authentic.

What was real anymore? Had her whole life been a lie?

"Sam?" she asked as her son came back into the room.

"Yeah?"

"What do you think of your grandfather so far?"

Sam shrugged. "I dunno. He's cool, I guess."

Sara peered at him, cautious. "Cool how?"

"Well, for one thing, he makes funny jokes. And he plays video games with me. That's pretty cool. I mean, for an old guy."

Sara chuckled. "Yes, I suppose you're right. Most old guys don't play video games. Unless you count Dad." She winked.

"Ha! That's true. Dad's old too." He laughed and scampered onto the bed beside her. "Why did you ask?"

"Just wondering." She held her breath, forcing herself not to say anything. Sam scooped a cluster of stuffed animals onto the floor.

"I'm fine with Grandpa," he added as he slid under the sheets. "I kind of like having him around. It's like getting a surprise package in the mail. You don't know it's coming, but it's fun anyway."

"You're right. Your grandpa is definitely a surprise, all right. I'll give you that."

Sara hoped her smile didn't look as sad as it felt.

CHAPTER TWENTY-TWO
SARA

Sara and Charlie had stayed up late into the night as she tearfully shared the day's events with him. It was good to talk to him, to have him warm and attentive—almost like old times. And she yearned to ask him about his recent distance, why he'd chosen to travel and not be with her. But her blubbering got in the way. She was already unglued over TR. Her findings deeply tormented her. Recalling the story caused her voice to quaver and mournful sobs to once again roll forward. She was a wreck. How many tears had she shed over her father? The grief inflicted by TR had become like a boomerang that kept coming back to hurt anew.

It was a small relief, however, to share her feelings with someone else. For his part, Charlie intently listened to the details of the encounter with Bo and Bo's mother, shaking his head and being appropriately outraged. He seemed genuinely upset for Sara.

"Unbelievable! I can't imagine what that must feel like to suddenly know you have a sibling," he said. "And I also can't believe your dad kept something so big from you all this time. You must be in a state of shock."

"I am," Sara sniffled.

"I'm so sorry, hon." The tenderness, as Charlie reached across the pillows to hold her hand, had taken her slightly off guard. There'd been so little intimacy between the two of them lately. This change was a rare but welcome one. They'd lain that way, fingers intertwined, until Sara fell asleep on a dampened cheek.

With daylight came fresh sorrow. A pair of fuzzy slippers on her feet, she snuck outdoors at dawn, leaving Charlie snoring softly, and curled into a backyard lawn chair with a blanket. The way the sun was just pushing over the horizon told her it would be hours before the rest of her household would wake. She welcomed the cold air and solitude.

When Sam was an infant, this had been her favorite time of day. With the rest of the world still shrouded in heavy slumber, she'd rise, tucking her hungry baby into the crook of her arm and feeding him as the sun came up. It had been a ritual she'd cherished. Peacefulness in their private sanctuary. That was years ago, of course, before the hurdles of caring for her sick mother, parenting a young child, and fretting over a splintering marriage protruded up at her in every which way. She hugged her knees and looked across the yard. She missed those days.

The banging of a screen door on the other side of the fence caught her attention. Unfolding from her seat, Sara craned her neck. The outline of a woman could be seen in the neighboring yard. Sara smiled. She'd know that profile anywhere.

"Hello, over there." Sara cupped her hands and called to Birdie, then reflexively shrank back. She hoped her louder-than-intended volume hadn't woken the entire neighborhood.

A hand popped up from the next yard over. A rustling of feet tromped through thick grass. After a second, a blonde head of disheveled hair poked up over the fence line.

"Sara? You're up awfully early." Birdie's voice was still thick with sleep.

Sara shuffled over and pressed her face up to the one-inch spacing between the fence's wooden slats. A wisp of steam rose up from the mug in Birdie's right hand. She'd clearly been up before Sara if she'd already made coffee.

"I could say the same thing of you," Sara said.

"That's true. But you know me; I have no choice on weekdays. I gotta get into the restaurant before one of my staff gets in there and screws up my delivery for tonight's specials. You should have seen what one of those fools did last week to my Wagyu skirt steak. Marinated the entire thing in some ridiculously spicy crap before I could even save it." She clucked her tongue. "What's your excuse, lady? Insomnia?"

"Yeah, something like that. I'm sorry about work. Anything I can do to help?"

"Nah, but thank you. I appreciate the offer."

"Well, I'm here if you need moral support or anything else. Clearly, all I have to do is wake up early and wander around my backyard."

Birdie laughed and pushed up on her toes. The bright red of her Converse could be detected at the fence line. Two blinking eyes appeared over the top.

"What's going on over there with your dad and Charlie, etcetera?" Birdie's mouth was up against the fence, reminding Sara of a game of telephone she used to play as a girl. It was tempting to stick her ear through the slats just to give her friend a laugh.

Instead, she rotated around and propped her shoulder against the wood post. One ankle kicked across the other. She tugged her sweatshirt a little tighter across her middle. The sun was beginning to warm the yard, but a formidable morning chill still clung to the air.

"Oh, you know," she said. "Just the usual mess." Sara wasn't sure she had the strength to unspool her whole drama from the day before. If she did, she might transform into a soggy heap right there in the backyard.

"Uh-huh. Like what? Last time I was over there, Charlie was MIA and your dad was, well . . ."

"Oh, I know what he was. My dad is the opposite of politically correct. I hope he didn't offend you too much."

Birdie slurped her coffee and let out a grunt. "Honey, I've been offended a lot in my day. Your dad was no big deal. Honestly."

"We haven't had a real chance to talk since then, and I'm sorry about that." The realization troubled her.

"No sweat."

Sara breathed a sigh of relief. "I'm lucky to have you as a friend. If I haven't said that enough, I'm saying it now."

A few fingers wiggled through the gap in the fence, followed by a hand. Before Sara could ask, Birdie latched onto her free hand and gripped.

"I'm right here, kid. Anytime." She squeezed twice.

A pooling gathered in the corners of Sara's eyes. With overflowing gratitude she squeezed Birdie's fingers right back. God, she was lucky for such a friendship.

After a few more minutes of chatting, they said goodbye, and she slipped back through the kitchen slider. Inside, she nearly smacked into a robe-clad TR.

"I didn't expect anyone else to be up yet," she said stiffly.

"Good morning to you too," TR boomed. The raspiness still lingered, but Sara noted the smoke damage in her father's lungs had been clearing up lately. That was a good sign, she supposed.

TR squinted at the backyard. Sara sidestepped around him, very much wanting to combat her weariness with a shot of caffeine.

"Who were you talking to out there? One of your neighbors?"

Opening a cupboard, she brought down a mug. *Let him get his own coffee,* she thought.

"That was my friend Birdie. You know, the one you insulted the other day?" She wasn't going to let him forget his sins.

"Ah yes, the lesbian! She seems like a decent gal!"

Her fingers fumbled around in agitation as a box of coffee pods toppled, spilling out all over the floor. She jumped back as one exploded. Tiny black grains scattered around her feet.

"Damn it!"

"You okay there?" TR made his way around to help. With a dramatic groan, he bent at the waist and pinched a couple of pods between his arthritic fingers before placing them on the counter.

"Yes," Sara snapped. Why did he have to make everything so difficult? "And can you please stop referring to my friends and family by their pronouns? My friend has a name. It's Birdie. You don't need to call her out by her sexual orientation all the time. She has an identity, you know."

TR stopped cleaning up and straightened. This time he was the one who looked hurt. "I didn't mean anything by it. That's just how she was introduced to me, that's all."

Sara jaw tightened. "No, that's not how she was introduced. I believe I introduced her as my neighbor. Besides, she's more than that."

"Okay, okay." He put his hands up as if to indicate she should calm down. Sara hated when people told her to relax. It just made her more uptight. "Like what?"

"What?"

"You said she was more than just a friend. So enlighten me."

She cast him a wary look. Clutching a plastic pod, she jammed it into the coffeemaker and deliberated while hot water hissed through the filter. "Well, for one thing, Birdie is a hardworking chef at a popular restaurant downtown. She's been reviewed like a dozen times, and her food gets really good ratings. Some guy from the Travel Channel even did part of his show there last year. Sent flocks of tourists in the door for months."

TR traded places with her at the coffee machine and pressed a button to fill a questionably clean mug he'd plucked from the sink. Sometimes his carelessness astounded her. Sara noticed the skin of his bare forearm sticking out from the terry cloth robe. It was still red and angry but nowhere near the weepy burn wound she'd come to know in his days after the hospital.

"Excellent!" TR announced. "What's she make over there at this fabulous eatery of hers? Anything I would like?"

Sara thought for a moment. When had she been to Birdie's restaurant last? It had been a while since she and Charlie had made a point to eat downtown at all. Lately, all they did was order subpar take out and then dine separately. At first it happened gradually, Sara sometimes consuming a plateful of dinner over the kitchen sink while Charlie was away and Sam was off at soccer. Then Charlie started going for evening runs once he was home, claiming he was out of shape from sitting in the cockpit for hours on end, instructing his family to go ahead and eat without him if they got hungry. One day, family dinners just sort of ceased altogether.

Sara was ashamed she'd let so much of their lives fall by the wayside, even before TR surfaced. A change was in order. Maybe she and Charlie could make reservations at Birdie's place after things settled down.

"Well, Birdie did mention some kind of special this week that involved Wagyu beef. Do you know what that is? It's pretty great. Expensive but great."

TR's eyes sparkled. "I like the sound of that. She must be a talented person, that Birdie."

He's trying, she thought. It wasn't amazing. But it was a step.

"We should go check it out sometime."

"Check what out?" she asked.

"The restaurant. Go see what this Birdie gal can do. Sounds interesting!"

"Oh yeah. Right. Sometime."

The last thing Birdie needed was her father barging into a public place, the place Birdie took so much pride in and hung her reputation on, and shooting off his big mouth. And Sara didn't trust herself not to have a cataclysmic outburst of emotion in his presence, no matter where they were. TR still owed her an explanation. And she was going to get it.

"Wait here," she said and retreated to her bedroom. Her bare feet crept softly across the rug as she came to the edge of the bed and stood over Charlie. Her heart snagged. He'd been good to her the night before. She wanted to return the kindness. But right now she needed his help.

She stared a second longer and marveled at his unburdened peacefulness. Her husband lay unmoving, the rhythmic rumbling of his low snores filling the room. Refracted light cast dim shadows along the floor. Window shades were drawn, a tumble of clothes from the night before spilled across the arm of a chair, and Acer had taken up residence in her empty spot on the bed. It was as if time had stood still in that room while the rest of the house went about the activities of the day.

Sara placed a gentle hand on the lump under the covers and shook. "Charlie?" she murmured. "Do you mind getting up?"

His eyes flitted open and shut several times, as if the lids were too heavy to operate.

"Charlie?"

"Hmm?"

"Can you please take Sam to school? I need to talk to my father."

"You're already up. Can't you take him?" The words came out sticky, like molasses.

Even when Sam was a baby and crying bloody murder in the middle of the night, Charlie's reaction time had always been painfully sluggish. He slept like the dead. Always had.

Sara moved to the shades and gave a slight yank. Daylight spilled in. Charlie rolled over and grimaced.

"No," she said. "I can't take Sam today. I need you to do it. Please get up and do this for me. It's important."

"Okay," he conceded, peeling back the duvet. She could tell he was still groggy. "I'll take him."

"Thank you. I wouldn't be asking if it wasn't really important." He nodded. The dog, who now yawned and stretched languidly from his position on Sara's pillow, eyed her suspiciously.

"Traitor," she whispered at Acer. Two fuzzy ears popped up and then lay back down. Sara rolled her eyes at the lazy animal and left the room.

Charlie was set to leave again that evening, and after their first tentative steps toward each other last night, she felt torn over where to place her priorities. But there just never was enough time.

Sam was up and dressed, pouring himself a bowl of cereal in the kitchen. Sara found him chattering away with TR, who poked a finger into Sam's bowl and plucked out a single Cheerio. She observed as her son enthusiastically hopped around, retrieving a second bowl for his grandfather and preparing two identical breakfasts. In return, TR clapped his grandson on the back, and the two clinked spoons before settling down at the table.

An outside observer might think they'd been close all their lives.

A bit of Sara's tension dislodged and fell away. Accidental trips to the ER aside, TR's presence might very well be making a positive impression on Sam.

"Hi, there," Sara said.

Both of them looked up at her. Sam chomped on a spoonful of breakfast and swallowed. A dribble of milk remained at the corner of his mouth. Sara made a wiping motion. He grinned.

"Guess what, Mom?"

"What?"

"Grandpa's going to help me with my art report after school today."

The excitement in his voice pierced Sara's heart like a sword. "Is that so?" She didn't know why the statement made her nervous. "Is this a new project?"

TR followed Sam's lead and pumped his head in the background.

"Yeah, I have to write two pages on a famous artist by Friday. My teacher says we can pick the medium," Sam said.

Sara raised an eyebrow. While she'd taken Sam to the museum on occasion and encouraged him to take in what he observed, she wasn't aware he comprehended the definition of such terms. But he was ten years old and could organize the apps on her smartphone better than she could, so why wouldn't he know such a thing? He really was growing up.

Sam took another bite and then continued. "Grandpa said I could do it on him."

"Do what on him?"

His face scrunched. "Mom. Are you listening? The project. He's famous. His stuff was in a museum in New York City!" Sara was aware, not that her father ever took her to see any of his work himself. He'd been long gone by then. The reminder felt like a punch to the gut.

"And I once met the president." TR's chest puffed.

Sara forced her eyes not to roll.

"Did you hear that? He met the president!"

The two clinked spoons again, as if congratulating one another on a small victory. Was she ready for this? For TR to expound on his life with Sam?

Sam knew the origin of TR's fame; Sara had shared the basics when her son had expressed curiosity about the man he'd never before met. Erring on the side of caution, she'd downplayed the details a bit. He'd been told about the creation of the bronzed sculpture of her and TR's notoriety in the art world. But so much had been omitted, partially to protect her son and partially to protect her own feelings. Was she a bad parent for shielding this from Sam? Not informing him more of his family history?

"Yeah, buddy. I did know that." She glanced at TR, wondering how much he'd told Sam about the sculpture. "Your grandpa is talented."

A cluster of crinkles formed at the edges of TR's eyes. "Your mom here used to have a knack for sculpting too."

Sara flushed, caught off guard.

"She did?"

TR nodded. "Yes, you should have seen her when she was just about your age. She'd spend hours with me in my studio, crafting little animals and fairytale creatures out of clay. A little girl lost in her own fantasy world, your mother was."

Sara wasn't aware TR so clearly recalled this portion of her childhood. Since arriving, he hadn't broached the subject of her art, so she assumed it meant nothing to him. But hearing him acknowledge this now caused her insides to crumble. She missed that part of her life so much; she could almost taste the loss. The piece of her she'd chosen to set aside when responsibilities for those who couldn't care for themselves, like her mother and Sam, came along. At some point there didn't seem to be extra room for frivolity—at least that's what Sara told herself at the time. But now she wasn't so sure.

TR's face dropped abruptly, turning solemn. He extended a finger in Sam's direction and narrowed his gaze. "Never give up your sense of creativity, son! It's a terrible thing to waste."

Was this a barb at her? Sara wondered.

At the moment, however, it wasn't about her. This was about Sam and his grandfather wanting to make an impression.

Considering his grandfather's warning, Sam cocked his head. "Um, okay."

Sara moved to the pantry and stuck her face inside, pretending to root around for lunch items. She no longer wanted to engage in this particular conversation. It felt too much like picking at an old wound. And she couldn't really discourage Sam from finding out about his grandfather. That didn't seem fair.

Charlie suddenly emerged with Acer trotting right behind. Sara noticed he'd run a wet comb through his hair and pulled on a pair of relaxed jeans. His face, however, was anything but.

"Good morning," she offered tentatively.

"Hi." He averted TR's gaze and planted a brief kiss on Sara's cheek.

"Hello, there, Chuck!" TR saluted from the table. "No piloting today?"

Charlie visibly stiffened and turned around. "Hi, TR. No, not today. I'm sticking around to take Sam here to school. But come this afternoon, I'm off again."

"So soon? The airlines must be pretty busy for not ever giving you a break," TR said.

Sara felt and twinge of gratitude toward her father for pointing this out. True, Charlie's plans had already been set earlier, but he'd witnessed the meltdown she'd had the day before. Couldn't he tell she needed support? That flying away wasn't the compassionate thing to do to his fragile spouse? Watching him hustle around the kitchen, she supposed not. She felt a crack in her heart expand once again.

Charlie clutched a stainless steel to-go mug and eased toward the back door. "Yup, pretty busy," he responded to TR. Switching gears, he tipped his head in Sam's direction. "You ready for school, pal?"

It was clear Charlie had no intention of engaging.

The only flicker of light in the situation was that Sara and TR were finally alone again. And while Sara's head was swirling with mixed emotions over Charlie, she was also keen on continuing a conversation with her father.

"So," she began, coming up beside him and scooting out a chair. "It's just us for now."

"Yep."

TR readjusted himself in his seat. Sara thought she caught a strained expression cross his face. Her eyes went to his burned side. His pain must have been flaring up again. It had been days since he'd touched his pills, or so he told her. Perhaps his recovery was going more slowly than she'd realized. She'd been so eager to sleuth out his faraway secrets that she'd neglected to inquire about the actual person sitting right in front of her.

She contemplated what to say next.

TR must have sensed her studying him because he changed the subject. "That kid of yours is something special. Clever little guy."

Sara warmed. "Yes, he is special. That's nice of you to say."

"Well, I mean it. I enjoy spending time with him."

"I'm glad to hear it. I'm pretty sure he likes spending time with you too. Charlie's dad, Sam's other grandpa, he can be well, kind of austere."

"Oh? And what do Charlie's parents think of their son marrying the daughter of an artist?"

"You mean do they approve of my wild upbringing? Uh, that's doubtful. I didn't come with a pedigree. But then again, Charlie didn't become the doctor they'd hoped for either, so whatever. Their expectations have always been distorted. I try not to pay too much attention."

This wasn't the direction she'd wanted their discussion to go. TR was the one who was supposed to be spilling his guts. Not her.

But unexpectedly, it felt cathartic to share some of her life with TR She'd waited so long for a parent to come around and pay a little attention to something other than themselves. Sitting there, confiding her situation to her father filled her with a warmth she'd never anticipated.

"Well," TR said, breaking through her contemplation. "Charlie's parents must be crazy. Because from what I can tell, you're a terrific mother, and that's the most important job of all, is it not?"

This stunned her. Was her father actually offering praise? Was he congratulating her on a job well done where both he and Joanne had failed? Whatever his perspective, she was going to take it. She'd waited forty years for validation.

But she refused to be deterred. "We need to talk."

"Right." She noticed him bristle, his fingers going rigid around the cup.

"We should discuss what's going on at your house. You have a son. And I knew nothing about him." Her voice caught. "When I first picked you up from Pacific Memorial, you said there was no one else who could take you in. That you couldn't return home. And for whatever reason, I believed you. Obviously, or you wouldn't be here right now, sitting in my kitchen and wearing my husband's bathrobe." Her volume was rising.

TR lowered his eyes. An index finger dragged across a veinlike crack in the wooden table. Sara saw his Adam's apple undulate as he swallowed several times, appearing to search for the right words.

"TR, don't you have anything to say?" *Please,* she thought.

TR rumbled, clearing his throat. His chest rose, filling with a labored inhale. After a moment, he dropped his chin. "Believe me or not, I didn't share certain details of my life because I wanted to spare you. I know it doesn't feel like it, but I was protecting you from being hurt, to a certain degree."

Sara felt a surge of heat at his deflection. He was protecting her from his blatant abandonment, she assumed.

"But I can see this is all bothering you quite a bit."

The idea that a newly discovered sibling was merely "bothering" her, like it was some trivial inconvenience, filled her with hot indignation. But Sara held her tongue, too afraid if she said this, it might stop her father from sharing more.

TR continued. "I'll tell you about Bo. You're my kid. You have a right to know about your brother."

My brother. The words rang in her ears. *I actually have a brother.*

As mad as she was over Bo's existence, she couldn't wait to learn more.

CHAPTER TWENTY-THREE
TR

"Yes, he's my kid," TR said. "And he's Marie's kid too. But that doesn't mean he 'belongs' to me. Bo belongs to no one. He's a nomad, just like his mother—spends most of his time wandering the earth, in search of better things."

"What does that mean?" Sara asked, her face contorting. She had suggested to TR that she wouldn't judge, but they both knew this wasn't true. TR could tell by the bewilderment that was splashed across her face that at the moment his daughter was far from objective.

He reached for the sugar jar and tipped a generous amount into his mug. Stirring, he bided his time. It was important to proceed carefully. Dredging up the recollections of certain events was unsettling him. With a fidgety hand, he tapped a spoon against the tabletop.

Sara squirmed with impatience. The dog got up from his spot by the door and came to rest supportively at her feet. TR marveled at how an animal could instinctively sense so much about his owner.

If TR had his druthers, they wouldn't be doing this at all. This sort of interrogation really went against the grain of what he believed. A man's business was his and his alone, was it not? And yet, there was

Sara, looking raw and exposed and desperate for more. He had to tell her something. He just worried doing so wouldn't be as satisfying as she might've hoped.

Such information might be too painful for his upset daughter to handle. It was one reason that he'd kept this portion of his life from her in the first place. That and his mounting shame over leaving her. The realities of TR's world had understandably upset her.

What could he do? She'd begged to know the truth, and so he was telling her. But they hadn't even gotten to the heart of things, and already he detected a brimming of emotion threatening to spill forward.

What's more, Sara's appearance at the property meant something else equally ruinous: Bo had met her. Marie too. But Marie had, at a very minimum, been aware all these years of his history with Sara and Joanne.

Bo, on the other hand, was an entirely different story. Surely meeting Sara, who probably admitted she'd never known a son existed, was one more reason for Bo to hate his father. In his son's eyes, TR did everything wrong. Especially parenting.

"TR?" Sara balanced on the edge of her seat, searching his face. "What does that mean, exactly? Don't Bo and his mother live with you?"

"Yes and no."

"I'm not following."

TR shook his head. "They do and they don't. But you're jumping ahead. I thought you wanted me to start at the beginning."

Her mouth shut. TR could tell it was taking everything his anxious daughter had to hold herself back.

He scratched his head and continued.

"I met Marie a long time ago. When you were probably a teenager. And that's the truth. She and I didn't know one other when I was with your mother."

"Okay." A whisper of relief escaped.

He knew what she must've been thinking: that he'd left her to go make another family. It wasn't true, but his compassion toward her grew regardless.

"Marie was a photographer—still is, actually. My manager at the time had set up a photo shoot of me and some of my work in a gallery out on the West Coast. I'd just flown in from Europe, and I wasn't particularly thrilled about returning to the States just yet. But the work demanded it; there was a gallery tour and parties for the press and what have you. It was all arranged. All I had to do was show up."

Sara frowned. "Why bother if you weren't interested?"

"Never underestimate the power of the almighty dollar. I'd made a decent amount up until that point, but really, it was never enough." He stopped and pointed at her. "Money does something to a person. It awakens a greed you never knew you had. I wouldn't wish that on anyone."

His daughter leaned back in her chair with a flat expression. TR couldn't tell what she was thinking, but he meant what he'd said. Money had been like a drug to him back in those days, luring him deeper into the void, never quite enough to satisfy his newfound cravings for wealth and fame.

"Marie arrived on the scene and distracted me from all of that material garbage. She was the real deal. *Is* the real deal, rather. You should see her photographs. She has the ability to see actualities in things that no one else ever notices. Little details that get amplified once they're pointed out, you know what I mean?"

Sara cocked her head.

"Well, I'll show you sometime. Some of her images could move a person to tears. Marie was the one who introduced me to the idea that it was the artist's job to shine the light on the unseen." He hooked two fingers into the air to make quotes. He remembered Marie saying this to him. So much of his artistic education was owed to her. Marie wasn't a sculptor, but she'd given him a whole new set of metaphorical tools with which to work. In a sense, she'd been both a lover and a mentor. Meeting her had been everything.

Thinking out loud, he continued. "Marie gave me a fresh perspective on my art. It elevated me, if you will." He stopped and rubbed at the stubble of his beard. It had been a long time since he'd reflected on this part, the earlier version of Marie.

Sara remained still, taking it all in. TR suddenly wished he could make his perplexed daughter understand what he saw in Marie. How she so wholeheartedly captivated him. But this would of course inflict pain. Marie wasn't Sara's mother. She was the new love in his life. TR had moved on with this woman.

"Anyhow, she's an artist of another genre who is so gorgeously committed. A real believer in the craft, you know? And what's more," he added with a sly smile, "if you hadn't noticed, Marie's a beautiful Italian goddess to boot. I was a goner from the moment I met her."

Sara blinked, and he immediately wished he could take this comment back. He'd stupidly gone too far once again. He was trying not to hurt his daughter but was doing a terrible job of it anyway.

Sara seemed to read his thoughts and dropped her wounded look to jut out her chin. "More like beautiful and dangerous, if you ask me. The woman practically attacked me when I showed up. She has a bite to her, that one."

TR sighed. If only Sara knew the half of it. He twisted his mouth, trying to find the right words. "Yes, Marie is a passionate woman. She has reason, I suppose." He thought about their fighting and Marie's constant exasperation with him.

"Meaning?" Sara asked.

"Never mind." He waved a hand. He wasn't prepared to go into it. "We're getting off track."

Sara didn't look convinced. "So why all the secrecy if you were so enamored with her?"

"Marie was married."

"Oh." Sara flinched, clearly distraught by this development. He'd broken up two marriages for the sake of his own happiness. He tried to warn Sara this would be unpleasant, but she'd wanted him to tell her everything. So that's what he was attempting to do. Regardless of how it made him look.

He pressed his palms into the table and remembered having a similar reaction after he'd found out Marie had been committed to another man. When she'd so heartlessly tossed the bit of information across the bed after their first night together, TR's heart had already begun to crack wide open for a woman who didn't plan to stay. Marie's soul had been like an impossible lock, and all TR desired was to find the key.

"The affair carried on for some time, but she had a husband she wasn't prepared to leave."

"So that's why you were photographed with a different girl on your arm every other night."

TR colored. He was unexpectedly ashamed to see himself through the eyes of his daughter. Somewhere out there a child had been watching. What must Sara have thought? It was one thing to leave Joanne, to move on because his first marriage simply didn't work. But it was another to publicly trot out a parade of pretty birds who were half his age and far too beautiful for someone like him. Sure, he'd had his fun. Oftentimes too much fun. His thirties and forties were one never-ending party. But he'd left carnage in his wake. Namely his poor daughter. All-encompassing remorse filled him.

"I'm not going to lie. I was a fool. I tried to make myself forget Marie by climbing into bed with many other women," he said.

"Gross."

He frowned. He was oversharing again. He didn't know how to do this.

"I know. You're not the first person to accuse me of being a scoundrel. It's true. I was lonely and stupid and self-centered. Be glad you didn't know me during that period of my life, Sara. Honestly. I was spinning out of control and consumed with my own mixed-up priorities. I suppose Marie took my mind off my losses and represented some kind of love I might still be able to attain. Does that make any sense at all?

"Yes." Sara's response was barely audible.

"In any case, I got fixated on what I might be able to control. I hoped the photos in the gossip rags would snag Marie's attention. I believed making her jealous might be the answer."

"And what better way to do that than flaunt dopey supermodels in her face?"

"Exactly."

Sara rested her elbows on the table, cradling her chin on the heel of a hand. "Wow, TR, you really are petty."

He threw her a self-conscious smile. "Thanks, kid."

"So then what? Marie keeps you around for her own amusement for a stretch and then returns home to her husband? You go off and drown your sorrows in women and booze? That can't be the end of the story. I've met Marie and Bo at your house, so I know it's not."

"Right."

She shook her head. "Here you had all this fame, this great art that the industry was falling all over itself to get their hands on, and you're supposedly too caught up with making your ex-girlfriend—or whatever she was—jealous. It just sounds sort of, I don't know, high school."

"I see." He knew he should be offended, but he wasn't. In truth, it was a surprising relief to share this hidden slice of himself with Sara. It actually was quite therapeutic to have his grown daughter sit across from him, face open and attentive regardless of what she may have thought, and still willing to listen. He appreciated that. There was still so much to explain. And while he wasn't ready to delve into everything quite yet, the sole act of sharing some of his shame with Sara was beginning to dislodge the boulderlike weight that had resided on his heart for too long.

"So," Sara ventured. "Then what? When did Bo come into the picture?"

"Ah yes. Bo. He's a predicament I wasn't expecting to have."

Sara pulled back. "You're calling your son a 'predicament'?"

He ran a hand over his face, wiping back the weariness. This next confession would take some finessing. "It's complicated."

"So you keep telling me."

He considered where to begin. "Bo hasn't been in my life for very long."

"Okay . . ."

"For starters, his name is short for Robert."

"Okay . . ." He could tell Sara was calling up her best reserves to be patient.

"And I didn't name him."

"Who did?"

"Marie's husband."

Her mouth dropped. "I'm starting to understand why it's complicated."

"Exactly."

"Don't tell me Robert is the name of Marie's husband?" She winced as if to brace against bad news.

"Bingo."

"Shit." His daughter was markedly at a loss.

A pregnant pause filled the space between them, pushing out any room for words. TR slumped back against the frame of the wood chair. He knew it was a lot for his daughter to absorb and piece together.

TR recalled the bittersweet event of meeting his son, and he treated it as if it were a tender bruise. Having Marie walk back into his life, after years of him trying to snuff out the pain of her leaving, was a shock. But never in a million years had he expected she'd come calling with a boy at her side: a child she claimed belonged to TR but had raised with another man. A stranger. It was a cruel blow, and TR had regretfully not handled it well.

It was this part he most feared sharing with Sara. And by the ashen look on his daughter's face, she'd had about all she could handle for one day. Would this be the thing that shut her off from him for good? He wasn't sure.

CHAPTER TWENTY-FOUR

SARA

Sara's head was ready to explode. Her father had lived this whole other life beyond the art galleries and constant stream of parties and superfluous girlfriends. He'd had a second family of sorts, only it wasn't what she'd expected. In some ways, TR had gotten a taste of his own medicine—a child kept from him, the way he had kept himself from Sara all those years. The mixture of satisfaction and bewilderment ebbed and flowed in her mind as she tried to slot it all into place.

At some point she was vaguely aware Charlie had returned from dropping off Sam. The back slider had squeaked on its tracks as Charlie and the dog slipped through and then retreated to the far end of the house. Sara could tell, from the bumping around in the master bedroom, her husband was performing the all-too-familiar task of packing an overnight bag.

But Charlie and his unavoidable departure were the least of her concerns at the moment. She was too busy unwinding the tangled string of information being fed to her by TR.

"So you're telling me Marie just returned, with your son, and didn't have some kind of ulterior motive?"

"It's not as easy as you make it sound."

"Why not?" Sara wanted to shake him. Her father was willfully ignoring what was potentially one of the biggest developments in his life. "You said you met Bo nearly four years ago, when he was seventeen, right? That seems like an awfully long time for someone to keep a secret."

"I know." TR fiddled with a placemat.

"Maybe she thought you had money. Did you ever think of that?" Sara was aware of the rise in her voice. She wanted her father to take this seriously. Why did she always have to be the adult when it came to her parents? Couldn't someone besides her be the mature one in the situation?

"I don't think Marie was after my money."

With his words Sara recalled that TR was broke. But if Marie had been gone for so long, she would have had no way of knowing that. And by then, it may have been too late for her to turn around.

"Then why was she back?" *And why were you able to eagerly reunite with her and not able to put that kind of energy into reuniting with your own daughter?*

TR pushed out a puff of air. Sara's eyes flicked to the robe pulled tight, shrouding his tender burn wounds. She could tell he was growing physically uncomfortable. They'd been huddled together in the kitchen for a long time now. Her father likely needed a break and probably wanted to change out of his pajamas. Even so, she pressed him to continue.

He begrudgingly went on to share how Marie had raised Bo with her husband, Robert, for the first half of Bo's life. TR had been left completely in the dark. But after a time, relations became rocky between Marie and Robert. Things deteriorated, and she left her husband to flee back to Italy.

TR was adamant he was utterly unaware of any son for the first seventeen years of the boy's life. "Seventeen years of oblivion," as TR put it. Then, one day four years ago, both Marie and Bo landed on his doorstep in Oregon. They'd taken TR completely by surprise. Marie claimed she still loved him. And the boy was a withdrawn teenager. While TR might have been pleased to see them, he wasn't. If anything, he was profoundly confused.

"So you invited them onto the property, and they unpacked their bags? Just like that?" How was it possible TR and Marie had picked up as if they'd never left off? The thought of him embracing this other family so easily caused a spark of Sara's envy to ignite.

TR shook his head. His eyes had grown weary. "No. Not just like that. There's been a lot of commotion, so to speak."

Commotion. Was he referring to the reunion with his ex-lover and her adult child, or the fire? Something in her gut told Sara the two events might be somehow linked.

"Does this have anything to do with what happened to your house?"

TR scratched at his head, tufts of his thick hair flopping every which way, reminding Sara of whitecaps in a choppy sea. He seemed to be debating something. Before she could press him further, he abruptly got to his feet.

She frowned. "Where are you going?"

He offered a half smile, pulled down at the corners with a trace of melancholy.

"Sorry, kid. I'm getting pretty stiff sitting here. I need to get up and stretch. Maybe take a hot shower to ease the muscles. Do you mind?"

She vacillated. It would be a setback to let him go. She urgently wanted him to keep going, but she could also tell he was visibly sore. His body was still healing, after all. "Maybe we can pick up right after your shower? We still have so many things to discuss."

He nodded, shuffling away. "Yeah, sure. Maybe."

Sara watched him leave. TR may have been forthcoming—finally—with elements of his past. Not necessarily about her, and why it had been so easy to walk away. But also he was disappointingly not willing to uncover much about his present circumstances.

She speculated why he didn't want to go back to his house. Was he perhaps content being back with Sara again? That despite a lack of apologies he wanted to somehow make things right with her?

The door to the guest room clicked shut. Sara remained in her chair and contemplated. There were too many holes in TR's story. The biggest mystery was why he'd led her to believe there was no one else, no other family to help him after the fire. There was clearly discord between him and Marie and Bo; otherwise he would have returned to be with them weeks ago. For some reason, he didn't want to speak to them or even let them know where he was staying. Bo had acted genuinely surprised when Sara informed him TR was living with her.

Why all the secrecy?

Reaching for her cell phone, she unlocked the screen and began scrolling through her calendar. As usual, boxes of bright red blinked up at her, indicating the list of appointments and obligations requiring her attention. With a hasty swipe of the finger, she brushed her responsibilities to the side. None of this mattered. Other than Sam's well-being, everything else would have to take the back seat. Even, she regretfully realized, her marriage. TR was like a forceful magnet, drawing her ever closer. It was too strong to ignore.

She must have been lost in thought, because Charlie was suddenly there, the shine of his polished work shoes snagging her attention as they crossed the tile floor. A lump formed in her throat. How long would he be gone this time?

"So I'm off." Trepidation hung in his voice. "You going to be okay?"

She turned to face him. "Yeah, I guess I'm going to have to be. Where are you headed?"

"East Coast and back again. I should be home in four days."

Sara straightened. That wasn't so bad. It was certainly a shorter trip than some of the recent ones.

"So what happened?" he asked, angling his head toward the guest room.

She sighed, standing up so they could talk more intimately. "He told me some stuff . . . He didn't even meet Bo until four years ago. But I still think he's hiding something."

Charlie frowned. "So he's got *two* kids he ignored all their lives? Nice. Honey, you don't owe someone like that anything, no matter who they are. When are you going to kick him out?"

Sara stiffened and pulled away. "He's still my father, Charlie."

"Does he know that?"

Resentment bit at her. "Whether he does or not, I do. And I still have questions. And . . . he needs me." Why was she defending him? A short time ago she'd been ready to kick her father out herself. It was like TR and Charlie had her so turned around she didn't know what she wanted anymore.

She felt the weight of his stare.

She supposed she didn't blame Charlie. It couldn't be easy for her husband to have a relative stranger living under the same roof, especially when there was no end date in sight. She would lose her mind if either of his parents ever chose to show up unannounced. They were judgmental and overbearing. She doubted she'd last two days in that scenario.

"I'm working on it," she said, not waiting for his response. Bending to brush invisible crumbs from the table, she debated whether or not to share more with Charlie. But he was leaving, so what was the point?

"Does *he* know that?" Charlie's head angled toward TR's room.

Sara pressed her lips together. He was closing off from her again.

In the old days, she would send Charlie off to work by throwing her arms around his neck and burying her face into the folds of his uniform. She'd wish him safe travels and request he call her at every free minute from the road. But standing there now, inches from her husband's clean-shaven face, his airline uniform starched and stiff, she sensed the returning of tension. Her heart sank.

Charlie's eyebrows arched as he waited for her to answer.

"No, not yet."

"I don't know if his staying here is healthy for you. In fact, I know it's not. Look at all the pain he's caused. I don't understand why you can't see that. I'm trying to help you if you'd just let me."

And you leaving this frequently is helping? she wanted to ask.

"I'll think about it."

"Don't get sucked back in, Sara. I don't think it's good for any of us." He planted a dry peck on her cheek before uttering his goodbyes. "I'll be back by the end of the week. We can talk later, but I hope you intend on making some changes."

Sara mumbled goodbye and did her best to gather up her discontent. She didn't necessarily like the thinly veiled ultimatum being given. Her situation with Charlie would have to be placed back into its compartment for just a little while longer. For the next four days, she had to focus on getting to the bottom of things with her father.

~

Sara sat at her computer and calculated. The steady stream of water from TR's shower could be heard in the background. She estimated she had about fifteen minutes of privacy. She needed to be quick if she were to make her list of calls without TR overhearing.

It was Tuesday. Sam would be at school for another few hours and then off to soccer practice. She had no intention of leaving town and her son when a potential asthma attack might rear its ugly head again. Glancing at her schedule, she noticed the next day was fairly empty. Without thinking, she picked up the phone and dialed the home of Sam's regular playdate. As the other end rang, she told herself that if this worked out easily, then it was meant to be. The idea had come to her last night when she'd lain in Sam's bed. Today, she was going see if she could pull it off.

Don't force anything, she thought. *If it happens naturally, then you're meant to go.*

Maggie picked up on the second ring. "Hello?"

"Oh, hi, Maggie. It's Sara."

"Hey, Sara. How are you? I haven't seen you in a while."

Sara cringed. She knew that was code for, "Why haven't you been present at the school meetings?" Maggie was the PTA secretary and caught every little thing. Sara supposed this was her job; Maggie did record the meeting minutes after all. But while her friend was generous with her time, Sara worried Maggie might be judging her.

All moms judged one another, didn't they? Sara envisioned the women at school keeping mental tallies on their peers: those who volunteered the most, those who left their kid with the nanny more often than not, and those who flaked out on carpool duty. Sara was suddenly ashamed to admit she was once one of these women on the righteous mommy brigade, tsking under her breath and holding others to a higher standard than even herself sometimes. Anyone who reminded her of Joanne's unreliable parenting had been silently scorned. The ugliness of her attitude was apparent now. Who was she to decide how another parent should spend their time?

A light shiver ran through her. Sara imagined she might be getting a taste of her own hypocritical medicine at that very moment, as she prepared to eat humble pie and ask Maggie to pull up the slack.

"Yeah, I know I've been kind of absent lately. I'm still dealing with some family matters. The situation has gotten more, er, complicated than I'd like." Her teeth snapped together. She immediately wished she had put her predicament another way.

"Oh no. I hope everything is all right?"

The excuse Sara had been using ever since TR arrived was that a family member had fallen ill, and she needed to help out. The PTA members reassured her they understood, and luckily another member stepped in to fill Sara's shoes. She hadn't realized it until now, while talking to her friend, but it had actually been a relief to hand over her obligations. Oddly, Sara didn't miss the part where she was required to run the show.

"I'm fine. Thanks for asking. But I'm actually calling with a favor. I have an especially crazy day tomorrow, and Charlie is out of town—"

"Want me to take Sam after school tomorrow? Adam would love to have him come over and play."

Sara exhaled. "That would be so great. Thank you! I think I should be done around dinnertime, and I could pick him up then. Does that work?" She'd calculated it all out in her head. If her drive to the coast took just under two hours each way, she should still have plenty of time to drop Sam at school, race to Sandpoint, do some digging around, and return by sundown.

"You bet," Maggie answered.

Sara closed her eyes. Maggie hadn't hesitated a beat with her offer of help. Perhaps Sara had merely been projecting her own disapproval back onto herself, and any negativity from the other moms had been in her own head.

"Thanks, Maggie. I owe you one."

Sara said goodbye and hung up the phone. She would make a point to be more grateful. Because as much as some of the women drove her nuts, she also acknowledged how many would step in to help when she requested it. She only hoped she could return the kindness.

The pipes in the walls let out a squeak that ended with a thunk, announcing the finish of TR's shower. Sara tensed. With quick hands she began straightening pillows and gathering up dog toys, pretending she'd been occupied with chores. Reaching the front room, she caught a glimpse of her panic-stricken features in the wall mirror. *Calm down, you fool.*

Pulling her shoulders back, she shook off her nervousness and told herself it was silly to feel as if she'd been caught doing something wrong. There was no reason for guilt.

But TR would be emerging from the bedroom soon. There wasn't any more time to plan her visit to the coast. She was just going to have to improvise. Shaking off the apprehension, Sara reassured herself she was a savvy person who could figure it out as she went. She'd lived for years with Joanne, for Christ's sake. Her life back then had been the very model of improvisation.

She'd become obsessed with uncovering TR's secrets. Whatever the cost, Sara was determined to get to the bottom of her father's story. The draw of knowing more about the fire, her father's apprehension to return home, and details of a newfound sibling was all too powerful to deny. She was going to find out. Even if that meant going it alone.

CHAPTER TWENTY-FIVE
SARA

Wednesday morning's departure to the coast took longer than she'd planned. What she'd thought would be a quick itinerary turned into over an hour of responsibilities. After depositing Sam at school with a hug and a wave, parking TR on the living room sofa with a tray full of snacks and a marathon of old movies, and fretfully changing her clothes twice, Sara finally aimed her car west.

She'd given the excuse of needing the whole day for personal appointments and felt fairly certain TR had zero idea where she was headed. After their disrupted conversation from earlier and the need to care for Sam in the evening, she was even more determined to get back to the coast.

TR had only offered a lazy nod as she left. He seemed more consumed with keeping Acer's nose away from his plate of food than inquiring about Sara's whereabouts for the day.

As the miles ticked by, Sara's mind ran over scenarios of what could possibly happen once she reached her destination. For one, she'd be getting there much later than anticipated. Second, and perhaps more troublesome, her arrival would once again be unannounced. But that was how she wanted it. It was a risk. Showing up and surprising Marie was most assuredly going to ruffle some feathers. But Sara feared any kind of advance warning might cause Marie and Bo to keep her off the property altogether.

She wanted to find out all she could about her half sibling. She'd believed she had no real family left anymore. Bo's existence had changed all of that.

She'd been psyching herself into donning an armor of bravery, but as her wheels crunched over the gravel drive of TR's home, her faux exterior cracked and threatened to crumble to the floor.

She'd been anxious from the start. Confronting one's potential half sibling could do that to a person. What if Bo didn't like her? What if she didn't like him? Given all that had happened, she wasn't sure she could take the regret of creating yet another bad family relationship. She cautiously held on to a small piece of hope. Being there was opening herself up to disappointment; she realized this, but she was there anyway.

Parking under the cover of shade, Sara cut the engine and waited. Her gaze darted from one end of the property to the other, her senses on high alert. She was keenly aware of her heart moving rapidly against her rib cage. The extra-large to-go cup, now drained of coffee, hadn't exactly calmed her nerves.

Pushing the driver door ajar, she paused. A chilly breeze seeped inside, causing her to shiver. Her hand shot to the back seat to retrieve a scarf. The coastline held a soggy quality—even more so than Portland. There was something brackish and raw lingering, the fall elements at their fullest exposure. A gust pushed her door, opening it farther. Sara crept out as the surrounding landscape rustled. Her pulse picked up. Hastily, she surveyed the front yard.

Relax, she told herself. *Quit being so jumpy.* It was only the wind, which had picked up, sending treetops to bend to and fro in a kind of a shuddering dance. Willing herself to move, Sara went in search of her brother.

She folded her arms across herself, steeled for another confrontation with either Marie or Bo. Surely they would've heard her pull up. There weren't any other vehicles around, but then again, nor had there been on the first day she'd visited. This was strange to her. How did anyone get around? Especially off the precarious dirt road that led to the main highway.

Taking two cautious steps forward, she approached the front of the house. Nothing had changed since her previous visit. The front walkway was still bordered by wilted flowers and broken shrubbery, no doubt trampled by firefighters. The windows appeared vacant. Charred wood and heaps of ash encased the second story. It was all untouched. From what Sara could tell, the main house had not been disturbed since the fire.

Turning on her heel, she opted for the outer buildings instead. As she made her way across the driveway, her boots beat down the rocky gravel surface. The wind picked up once more, producing a faint whistle. The tail of her cotton scarf whipped violently in front of her face, momentarily obscuring her view. The cold temperature was biting, and her nose began to drip. With an impatient hand, she snatched her scarf and secured it back into place. Moving faster, she closed in on the first of two miniature houses.

Rounding the corner, she was surprised how the otherwise rough and unkempt front landscape had now transformed rather nicely into a manicured garden of sorts. Piles of gravel now gave way to a carefully raked path, bordered by shrubs of green and purple that Sara recognized as sea lavender. In the center of all this sat a square, smoothly poured concrete slab. Balancing on top was a quaint wrought-iron patio table nestled with two matching chairs. If she didn't know better, Sara would have imagined it the scene of a charming little tea party.

Certainly TR hadn't been responsible for this sweet little vignette. Marie hadn't necessarily struck her as the tea party type either. But what did Sara know?

The path veered off into two directions. To the right was the building from which Marie had barged out. Sara peered at the small, paned window on the side of the structure. A gauzy window curtain was parted, but from what Sara could tell, no one was home.

The second building, to Sara's left, was a bit different. Rather than having the aesthetic of a guesthouse, it seemed more utilitarian. No delicate curtains hung in the window of this one. And instead of a trimming of lavender, its front entrance was lined by practical stone pavers. Sara went closer. A coiled-up hose accompanied a pile of wash buckets and a large, freestanding metal sink. They sat on the lip of two crude concrete steps. A plastic Tupperware containing used paintbrushes was tucked between the buckets. Everything was coated in a faint shade of powder gray.

Ah. Sara felt a warm shock of recognition. *Of course. The studio.*

Instinctively, she made for the door. Placing her hand on the rusty knob, she glanced over her shoulder. Other than the wind, she was alone. She hesitated. Perhaps she should begin at the guesthouse—she'd come here to find out more about Marie and Bo. But as she hovered on that top step of the additional building, every fiber of her being was being drawn inside.

It took some jimmying to get the door open, its splintering frame weathered and swollen. With a forceful shove, Sara was at once standing inside.

The first thing she noticed was the cold. It seemed to travel up from the stony concrete floor and into the center of her bones. The room's interior, no larger than her living room, had a cavelike quality. Hard, unforgiving surfaces and dank, dark temperatures blanketed everything. A slight hint of mildew wafted from something piled in the corner.

But another, stronger, and much more pleasing scent reached her nose next. The familiar smell of clay—so earthy, rich, and full.

Her fingertips grazed along the rough stucco wall until she located a light switch. When she flicked it upward, a fixture in the ceiling buzzed and came to life. Sara blinked. She took shallow breaths and allowed her sight to adapt.

The interior was a familiar shade of powder gray, muted and fine, and encasing everything. Reaching out, she ran a hand over a nearby surface, which produced a cakelike dust on the pads of her fingers. Curiosity pulled her farther inside. Her eyes, now fully adjusted, skipped around the room. A wooden stool. A tin of delicate carving tools. Giant gray slabs stacked along the walls. A pine table. The wrinkled canvas apron hanging from a single hook. Each object represented a carefully thought-out workspace.

And while this was the first time Sara was seeing these elements, one thing was for sure: she loved each of them instantly.

As she came into contact with the objects, the hairs on her arms stood on end. The room may have been cold, but her belly was warm. An inexplicable joy broke free and swam up from somewhere deeply rooted inside of her. Sara's eyes grew moist as a hundred happy childhood memories flashed before her.

She knew this place. And it felt like home.

Sara hadn't realized how much she'd missed this scene, an artist's sculpting studio chock-full of items from her past. But encountering it all now, she felt a familiar comfort come rushing back. It was like the reassuring hand of an old friend, coming to rest on her shoulder.

Just as she was about to peruse a rack of half-finished sculptures, a noise sounded behind her. She wheeled around just in time to catch Bo come thumping through the door. Sara froze.

Bo loitered at the threshold and seemed to be deciding what to do next. After a second, his features relaxed and he closed the door.

"It's you again."

Sara straightened. She would not run a second time. "Yes. It's me." She clapped her palms together, sending a cloud of chalky dust into the air.

Bo exhaled, the fabric of his nubby wool sweater deflating. A calloused hand combed through his light hair. "I saw your car out there. But still I wasn't totally sure what I was going to find in here." He gestured. "I saw the light was on."

Sara hunched. Suddenly sheepish about intruding, she could feel the heat rising in her cheeks. "Yeah, I searched but couldn't find anyone. So I thought I'd give myself the tour. You know, to check out my dad's stuff." She wondered if she should have said "our dad" instead. TR wasn't just hers anymore. The realization jolted her, but not in an unpleasant way.

Bo nodded, the explanation seeming to be enough.

A thought occurred to Sara. "This stuff is his, right? I mean it's not yours or your mother's?"

"Nah. I don't work out here. This is all TR. Although I did build him that wheel table." His thumb jerked in the direction of a rather modern-looking pottery wheel. Surrounding it was a tray and a smooth-yet-unfinished wood platform. It had been sanded down and notched out to form a wide horseshoe, allowing for the wheel to fit snugly up against it. Sara noticed how clean and new this particular piece of equipment looked. She wondered if it had even been used.

"You a woodworker?"

Bo shrugged, kicking at something on the ground with the toe of his boot. "Nah, I wouldn't say that exactly. I dabble. Sometimes TR asks me to build him things. So I do."

Sara could tell he was being modest. The craftsmanship of the table was pretty good. But as far back as she could recall, her father had been insistent on molding his art with his bare hands, kneading and manipulating his clay until it matched the vision in his head. And he certainly didn't construct vessels with the use of a potter's wheel. That just wasn't TR's style.

She looked around the room. There were few signs of anything other than sculpting. It was strange to think of TR attempting something new.

"I didn't know my dad threw pottery. He's always been a hand-build kind of guy. I noticed he's still sculpting." She indicated toward the metal rack of art.

"He doesn't throw, really. But one day he got a bug up his ass, saying his sculpting was crap, and ordered this thing from a catalog." His toe kicked toward the wheel. "Says he wants to try something different. But as you can see, his new purchase hasn't been touched."

"Huh."

Bo shoved his hands into the front pockets of his jeans and rocked back on his heels. It appeared neither knew how to keep the conversation going.

Sara looked beyond him, through the foggy window. "And your mother? Is she around too?"

Bo shook his head. "She took off. On a freelance job for some environmental magazine."

"Ah."

"You're scared of her, aren't you?"

Sara's brow arched. "Wouldn't you be? I mean, no offense or anything, but she seems kind of . . ."

"Crazy?"

"You said it, not me."

Bo chuckled. "Yeah, my mom can be a bit of a handful. But she's harmless. Really. All bark and no bite."

"If you say so." Sara was unconvinced. It was a considerable relief, however, to know the hostile woman who came at her once before wouldn't be charging out from her hiding place today. It gave Sara a moment to breathe. Spending time talking to Bo held a surprising ease. He clearly seemed more welcoming than his mother.

"So," she began cautiously. "My dad tells me you guys met when you were seventeen?" *And that you're my brother even though I'd never heard of you.*

"Yep." A veil of something mildly defensive drew across his face.

"And you've been living here ever since? For about four years?" She wanted to make sure TR had told her the truth.

"Yeah. I mean my mom and I travel some. We don't always stay here. But lately we have. I do some work in town. You know, some handyman stuff. Woodworking, as you put it." His fingers made quick air quotes and dove back into his pockets.

"That's cool," Sara said. She was desperately trying to act casual, pressing her tongue to the roof of her mouth to keep the onslaught of questions at bay. "So you live out in that guesthouse?"

The second building was no more than a few steps away, and Sara wondered if he'd been inside, watching her when she first arrived.

"Yep. That's where I sleep. Now my mom sleeps in there too. It's tight, but I guess it works. Because, you know, the fire sort of wrecked most of the big house."

"Can I go into the big house? Or is it not safe to walk around in there yet?" Her request came out in a rapid tumble. She was all too eager to see more of her father's world, and it showed. Her hands squeezed together as she waited for Bo to answer.

He studied her, his features softening. Maybe he felt sorry for her. Maybe he knew what it felt like to try to piece together clues about a father who hadn't always been around. For whatever reason, Bo agreed.

"Sure. You can look around. I'll come with you, because navigating all the damage can be tricky. But you can check out anything you want to."

"Thanks." Sara smiled.

"No problem." He smiled back as they trailed out the door together and along the path to the house.

CHAPTER TWENTY-SIX

SARA

The first thing Sara noticed was the stench of smoke. Its cloying potency, seeping from every fiber of the house, stung her eyes and nostrils. She coughed as she entered, detecting something electrical to the odor. And while the lower level seemed to have escaped the flames, the smoke had contaminated everything, from the paint on the walls to the heavy window curtains.

"Holy cow!" she exclaimed, tugging her scarf up over her mouth and nose.

Bo wound his way through a cluster of living room furniture, casting debris aside as he went. The chestnut floors were coated in ash, smaller chairs had been overturned, and a litter of loose papers was strewn about. Sara guessed the firefighters had dashed through this portion of the house in order to reach the upper level. They likely had to drag all kinds of equipment through the front door in time to spare the rest of the structure from the flames. She doubted keeping TR's things untouched had been a priority when doing so. The place looked as if it had been ransacked.

"Yeah, it's pretty bad," Bo said. He bent and plucked a couple of dusty books off the ground before depositing them onto a round coffee table. "There's no way someone could live here like it is now."

"Is there any insurance? Somebody to come out here and assess the damage?" Sara's voice was muffled behind the fabric of her shirt.

"Yes, believe it or not, the old man actually had homeowner's insurance. I don't know how good it is or anything, but an insurance adjuster came out a couple of weeks ago. He wore a paper mask and jotted down a bunch of notes on his clipboard. I don't know what happens next. Maybe the guy will call TR?"

"On what phone?" Sara almost laughed at the thought of TR being reachable to the modern world. As far as she knew, only a handful of people were privy to his whereabouts.

"Right." Bo pushed hair from his forehead. "He doesn't exactly carry a cell phone."

"I think he'd rather die."

"Well, the insurance guy mentioned something about a restoration company. You know, a service that comes out with fans and cleaners and possibly rebuilds part of the house?"

"Does TR's plan cover any of that?"

"Dunno."

Sara eyed the mess and nodded. "That would be good if it did. But how long would something like that even take, I wonder?" There was so much work to be done. At the rate events had been going, TR could be holed up in her guest room for another six months. She figured he must not have been getting along with Marie and Bo enough to take up residence in the small guesthouse. And how bad had things gotten to make TR seek her out?

A thought hit her. "Seems to me it might be helpful for some of this stuff"—she gestured at the furnishings—"to be dragged out of here and aired out in the yard. Either that or haul it to the town dump. What do you think?"

Bo's jaw opened and shut. No response.

"What is it?" Sara sensed he was hesitant to trust her.

"Well, that's really nice of you to think of ways to fix things. Especially since TR's not even here to do that himself. But . . . well . . . don't you think him not being here is a sign?"

Worry pulsed through her. "What kind of sign?"

"That he maybe isn't planning on moving back here."

"He's not?" Her scarf slipped from her grasp.

No way. TR could not take up residence in her guest room forever. Charlie had already indicated he wasn't thrilled about how long the situation had gone on. That would be the last straw in her marriage for sure.

"Do you really think that?" Sara searched Bo's face.

"I don't know, but he's sure making an effort to stay away. Remember that until I met you we didn't even know where he was staying. My mom sent ridiculously expensive flowers to the hospital; after she finally cooled off, she began to worry and tried to reach out. But the stubborn old codger wouldn't accept her calls or her visits. He's prideful to a fault . . ." Bo trailed off.

Sara startled. This was all news to her. Marie sent flowers? If this was true, it meant TR lied—no big shocker there—about his so-called manager sending that giant bouquet and balloons, inquiring after his best client. And while her father's evasiveness wasn't really a surprise, it was peculiar that he'd covered up Marie's efforts. The strangely *nice* efforts from what Sara considered a rather unkind woman. Clearly, TR hadn't wanted Sara to know any of this at the time. He'd wanted her to believe there was no one else.

"Bo," she said in a measured tone, careful not to press him too far. "Could you maybe tell me what exactly happened here on the night of the fire?"

It was very slight, but Sara noticed something pass behind his eyes.

"Didn't TR tell you?"

"No. Not in so many words."

"Maybe you should ask him first. He was the one inside."

The fact that Bo didn't come out with a straight answer was bothersome. Bo clearly was TR's son, because they both evaded pointed questions in the same agitating manner. Sara couldn't figure out what these men were hiding.

She'd expected to spend more time inside, to wander around and investigate, but her eyes were beginning to water from the sting of the toxic air.

"Can we go out back?" Sara pointed toward the ocean view.

Bo was already in motion, apparently glad for the diversion in their awkward conversation. "Sure. Let's go out the front door and walk around the side. It's easier to get to the backyard that way."

Sara followed him, casting a final glance. She wanted to carry home a mental inventory of the inside. Just in case she didn't return.

Reaching the strip of grass and overgrown bushes that bordered the back of the house just steps from the rocky cliffs, Sara shaded her eyes from the glare of the midday sun. Just as she'd done before, she located the trodden-down trail that led to the private cove. She tried to imagine TR's harrowing escape.

"Have you ever gone down there?" She cocked her chin toward the patch of sand below.

"To the beach?" he asked. "Yeah, a handful of times. I don't do it very often, only because it takes effort to hike back up here again. It's a workout for sure."

Sara moved closer to the cliff's edge, her shoes maneuvering around overgrown, craggy juniper branches. She tried to envision how her father, injured from the fire and likely jolted from the dead of sleep, had managed such a feat. "Good thing TR made it to safety down there. To the water, I mean."

"Yeah. He can be resourceful when needed. It's a matter of sheer will, I guess. And will is something he's got in spades."

The wind carried her laughter across the yard. "You can say that again. God, he really is stubborn, isn't he?"

Bo chuckled in agreement.

Sara backed away from the edge and came to stand next to Bo. Together, they gazed out over the current of dark blue waters. A bit of tension loosened. It was strangely serene being there with him. She was standing beside another person who actually knew what it felt like to be TR's child. They stood that way for a long time, contemplating.

Bo finally broke the peaceful silence. "Does TR know you're here? Talking to me?"

Sara shook her head. "No, he thinks I'm running errands. Right about now he's probably on my couch and—"

"Drinking your booze?"

Sara released a nervous laugh. "I hope not!" Pulling her phone from her back pocket, she pressed a button to check the time—three o'clock. "Shit!"

Bo swiveled to face her. "What? Did he call?"

"No," Sara replied, already running for the path that led to her car. "I got a late start today. I promised I'd be home to get my son. I gotta go!"

"You have a son?" Bo's rapid scuffle could be heard just behind her. He was jogging to keep up.

Sara reached the driveway and spun around. "Can I come back? You know, to talk some more?" She clutched her key and hoped he'd say yes. There was still so much more to know.

"Sure."

Sara grinned. "Thanks. Oh, and when exactly is your mom coming back?" Running into Marie wasn't something she was quite ready to do.

"I think she's gone for about three or four days. She took the train down to Northern California."

"The train?"

"Yeah, she doesn't like to drive. She usually phones me when she's on her way home."

Sara calculated her week in her brain. She'd need to return in the next day or so in order to be gone while Sam was in school and Charlie was away.

"I'll try to be here Friday. Is that okay?"

Bo's shoulders lifted, his face optimistic. "Fine by me."

"Okay, then. It's a plan."

"A plan." Something conspiratorial passed between them.

Reversing and then driving away from the house, Sara watched Bo get smaller in her rearview mirror. He just stood there in a cloud of gravel dust with his thumbs hitched through the belt loops of his jeans. For some inexplicable reason, Sara felt a tug of emotion catch in her throat as he faded away. As her car bumped along the rutted dirt road, she tried to identify the source of this feeling.

Before that afternoon, only a tiny piece of Sara had been holding out hope that she'd actually like her half brother. She probably wouldn't be blamed for holding a grudge. But she didn't want to hate TR's son. He might be the only extended family member left with whom she could have a relationship. Whether she and TR patched things up or not, Sara found herself wanting a connection with her sibling. And after spending the afternoon with this young guy, she cautiously realized that she did like him. There was still much to learn; she wasn't glossing over all the uncertainty. But Sara's instincts informed her Bo wasn't the disappointment she'd feared him to be. He was actually quite thoughtful.

The dirt road tapered off, spilling into the wider lanes of the coastal highway. Now successfully clear of the swirling dirt that accompanied TR's private lane, Sara let her windows descend as she welcomed the damp air. Scrounging around the center console for a hair band, she steered with her knees and secured back her weather-matted locks. She didn't care that her carefully blown-out hair had transformed into a frizzy mess. It was worth it. Peering out her window, she smiled out at the rugged terrain. The coast felt good. Like a shot of happiness to the soul.

Sara's mind hovered on the details of the inviting art studio. It was extraordinary to realize how the sole act of walking among stacks of clay blocks, various works in progress, and a collection of familiar tools brought back a powerful rushing of old feelings. And those feelings unbelievably didn't include bitterness.

She recalled how good the fine pottery dust felt against her fingertips, the deeply satisfying aroma of wet clay, and the beautiful sight of hand-sculpted objects. The entire essence of the place had a dreamy effect on her. A piece of her childhood adoration for her father, her propensity for art, and the possibilities of creating again were in that room.

And Sara suddenly knew she wanted all of this back: her sense of family, her artistic side, and the pleasure of creative fulfillment she somehow gave up along the way.

Two days was suddenly a very long time to wait.

CHAPTER TWENTY-SEVEN

TR

He supposed Sara's polite smile was the same that evening, as she greeted him briefly with bits of small talk and hustled Sam farther inside the house, requesting that everyone wash up for dinner. But TR noticed there was a slight alteration in the way his daughter regarded him. A kind of masked avoidance. It was unnerving, really. If TR didn't know better, he'd say his daughter was privy to something she wasn't sharing.

The day had been strange without anyone else around. There weren't any loud voices, no little boy playing, nor Sara's automatic check-ins. Sure, the curly-haired mutt with his wet nose and wagging tail had kept him company, winding up into a tight ball on the rug as TR attempted to recline. And the television had been kept at a high decibel, filling the room in an effort to drown out the insufferable silence. Still, TR found himself alone.

And the loneliness was unbearable.

All of this proved ridiculously ironic, of course, considering how deeply he'd once cherished solitude. He was an artist, for God's sake. Artists loved to be alone! TR grumbled. What was the matter with him if he couldn't even spend one measly day by himself?

Perhaps he was just getting old. This thought frightened him even more than the first. Too many things were changing. He was discovering he didn't like change. Not one bit. And his daughter's mysterious glances and excessive busyness weren't helping.

He wondered if Sara had been off somewhere, stewing over their previous conversation about Bo. TR hadn't necessarily wanted to discuss the intricacies of his other family with her: the fights, the dissatisfaction that masked Bo's face whenever TR tried to give constructive criticism about his work, the exasperated proclamations from Marie. But Sara had pressed him until he had no other choice but to oblige.

Now that things were out in the open, he fretted that the disclosure may have had a negative effect on his daughter. He'd confessed that not only had he been living in the same state as her, just hours away, but he'd failed to reconnect. He'd also been spending much of his time connecting with another child. He'd chosen to be with his son instead of Sara.

He'd chosen one child over another simply to avoid his own goddamned guilt.

It wasn't meant to hurt Sara. But TR could see how she might not see things that way. He was beginning to see things from his discarded daughter's point of view. And he felt downright lousy about what he saw.

"Need any help in there?" he called across the living room and into the kitchen, with an urge to be more helpful than he had been.

Sara was banging cupboards and murmuring instructions to Sam. "Nope, we're almost all set. Thanks."

TR heaved himself off the sofa, his arm acting as a brace. Righting himself, he stretched out the lingering stiffness in his limbs before ambling in her direction. Pinpricks of discomfort still flared up along his right side from time to time, but the majority of his pain had thankfully subsided. Even so, he hobbled at an uneven pace.

"How was your day?" Sara glanced up briefly as she prepared dinner.

"Fine. Fine." TR entered the warm kitchen and bellied up to the counter. The dog trotted past them and out the now-open sliding glass door. Damp air trailed inside, carrying with it a hint of pine. TR scratched away the tickle of his day-old beard. How long had it been since he'd let the animal relieve himself? he wondered. The hours of the day had somehow run together into one extended nap.

"Did you make yourself some lunch?" Sara asked, not breaking her concentration as she stacked plates and unwrapped a plastic clamshell containing a spiced rotisserie chicken. Premade food seemed to be a theme around there, especially roast bird. TR wasn't complaining. He appreciated a good hot meal as much as the next person. But still, a little variety might be nice from time to time. His stomach grumbled. For a flash he missed Marie's steaming pots of handmade pasta and buttery Dungeness crab.

He shrugged off the hunger. "I threw together a turkey sandwich earlier today."

"Hmm, hmm," Sara answered, distracted.

TR watched as she glopped spoonfuls of creamy microwaved mashed potatoes onto three plates and then shook out portions of prepackaged salad.

He shifted his attention to the boy, who was poking a finger into the side of the potatoes and licking. "How was your day at school, sir? Fill up that big brain of yours?"

Sam giggled. "School was good. You know, the usual."

"I see."

It struck TR how remarkable this kid could be at times, taking everything in stride. Must be from being around grown-ups so much. An only kid sort of thing. That's how Sara had been. The only child who, instead of staying home to play with dolls, was carted from one adult party to the next, staying up late and absorbing conversations on art and politics that floated in the rooms around her. TR was proud of this aspect of his daughter's upbringing. It made her a well-rounded person, able to adapt to new surroundings. And God only knew what new surroundings Joanne had subjected the girl to as they drifted from one town to the next. He'd heard rumors over the years. But he wasn't ever really sure. Joanne was all blame and no responsibility.

But the finger, he knew, should remain firmly pointed in his direction. He'd played the biggest role in his daughter's unhappiness. After the fire hit, he'd had time to lie in the hospital bed and look back on the offenses he'd caused in his lifetime. He didn't like what he saw. Realizing he'd been given a second chance, that he wasn't dying, he was injected with a driving desire to right his deepest wrongs. While he wasn't able to make amends with Joanne, he could certainly try with Sara. He very much wanted to make up for the pain he'd caused.

"So," he ventured. "Get all your errands done today, Sara?"

"Oh, um, not all of them." She set plates down as chairs were drawn away from the farm table. "I think I'll have to go back out and get some more things done on Friday. So you'll be on your own again."

"Oh yeah?"

She busied herself with adding food to a plate. "Yeah, I'll be around tomorrow—Sam's got school and then soccer. But Friday I'll kind of be out of pocket again. You don't mind, do you?" It came out more like a statement.

TR shooed the air with a hand. "Don't worry about me. Acer and I can hold down the fort." He searched around for the dog, who was now nowhere to be found.

He fumbled around with his fork and knife for a moment, clenching the flat stainless handles and willing away the discomfort before digging into his meal. He was determined to enjoy the night with his daughter and grandson, but something told him Sara was pulling away again. Who knew how much time he had left in her house? Better to take it all in while he could.

~

The following morning the absentee husband returned ahead of schedule.

Charlie came pushing through the door, bag in hand and pinched strain on his face. TR could tell right off the bat that this guy wasn't happy. His appearance was pretty much the worse for wear, with obvious displeasure stamped across his face as he noticed his father-in-law sitting on his sofa. Their eyes met and locked. The two men greeted one another with curt nods.

Brushing hastily past TR, Charlie gripped his travel case and retreated to the master bedroom. He heard Sara's voice next, mumbling something unintelligible from the other side of the wall. She'd been busy all morning, dropping Sam at school and leaving TR alone with his thoughts while she showered. He'd sought to continue their discussion about Bo and Marie, but she seemed to be giving him the brush off. And now that Charlie was back, he suspected plans might be thwarted once again.

Something was amiss. The air had an eerie stillness to it, like the atmosphere right before an earthquake hits.

He overheard Sara's clipped voice, followed by harsh whispers. Two seconds in the door, and those two were already fighting.

What a shame.

He wondered what the argument was about this time. He snatched one of the coffee table magazines he'd read a hundred times and pretended to be occupied while he eavesdropped. What exactly was going on back there?

After a moment, a deep barking cough rumbled down the hallway. Sara said something that ended with "medicine" and then stalked out from her room. She went to the kitchen and searched around for something. A box was retrieved from the high cupboard. She filled a water glass and then retreated again. The door shut and muted out more coughing.

TR reclined and waited. He'd liked it better when the colorful neighbor gal came over instead. That was more fun. The husband only tended to bring everything down. A real wet rag.

A short while later, Sara emerged into the living room.

"Well," she announced. "Charlie's apparently home sick. I think he might have the flu."

"You don't say?"

"Yeah, looks like it. His cough is pretty bad, and he says his throat's on fire. He called in another pilot to take over the rest of his shift. I think he just needs to rest. Quietly." There was an emphasis on that last part. TR got the hint loud and clear.

"Roger." He kicked his stocking feet onto the coffee table and crossed them at the ankles.

"So"—she looked around the room, picking at her cuticles— "Charlie's the type of person who, well, when he gets sick, he gets, um, agitated easily. Doesn't act like himself, you know?"

"Okay . . ." Where was this going? TR already understood he was to be quiet, as she had so bluntly put it.

"I think Charlie was hoping to come home and have the place to himself."

"Ah."

She glanced at his socks. TR thought he caught her nose wrinkle.

"So, maybe you should . . ."

"You mean get out and make myself scarce."

Sara shifted. "Yeah. Pretty much."

TR dropped his feet. Yanking at the drawstring waist of his seat pants, he rose. He knew a hint when it was dropped in his lap. He wasn't a moron.

"Your husband isn't thrilled that I'm still hanging around, is that it?" He understood perfectly, but he wanted to hear Sara say it out loud.

She exhaled. "Yes."

TR gathered himself up. "Okay, I get it. A man's house is his castle, and Chuck wants a little peace and quiet. Okay, then. We'll give it to him."

Sara seemed reluctant. "So we'll arrange for you to get back home, maybe as soon as we pack your . . ."

TR jerked his arm into the air. She'd taken him out of context. "Hold on! I didn't say anything about going back home. I'm not ready for that yet. My house isn't even fixed! What I meant was I'll go run around doing your errands with you." Why was she doing this now? He didn't want to go. Not yet, not just as they were getting closer. He'd thought she felt the same way.

Sara sighed heavily. "Oh. Well, I just figured it was time. You have that guesthouse on your property."

"The guesthouse is too small!" He realized he was shouting and quickly lowered his voice. He didn't want old Chuck to come running. This situation was complicated enough without the sick husband inserting himself.

"Fine," Sara hissed. "Have it your way. But this can't go on forever, TR. Sooner or later you need to go home."

He mumbled something about needing to get dressed before they went out and shuffled to his room. This was disastrous. How was he going to make it so he could stay? If he left now, she might not let him back into her life so easily, and then where would they be? He was still intent on mending their fractured relationship. Being under the same roof allowed for an intimacy with his daughter that he couldn't obtain if he were elsewhere. Plus, there was the sticky situation with Marie and Bo. He wasn't ready to face them yet. One crisis at a time.

Tugging a long-sleeve denim button-down from a hanger, he hoped his daughter recognized the extra efforts he was making on her behalf. Dragging wet fingers through his pile of unruly hair, he told himself to play along. He couldn't afford to ruffle any more feathers. He still needed to stay; he needed time with Sara.

But as he tied his sneakers and made his way to Sara's waiting car, two more concerns nagged him. The first was, how long was he required to tiptoe around this Charlie fellow? And second, even more troubling, were Sara and her husband constantly arguing because of TR, or was his daughter the victim of an increasingly bad marriage? He didn't know the answer to either dilemma, and it bothered him.

The rational response to these household tensions would be for TR to move out of Sara's place altogether. To return to his oceanfront home and get his life back on track. His burn wounds had healed sufficiently too. Help was no longer vital.

But packing up and moving back home was far from simple. He didn't know where he stood with Marie, for one thing. He also didn't know if he wanted to go back to the same old situation with Bo—their discontent with one another had only escalated over the past year. Every day was some new irritation, TR suggesting how Bo could improve his art, Bo pushing back with attitude, and Marie shaking her head in the background. Frankly, the whole parenting thing confounded TR.

Just as everything between the three of them couldn't have gotten any worse, TR's life on the coast had literally gone up in flames. And though he hated to admit it, his pride was also at stake. It was foolish and pigheaded; he didn't need anyone to point that out. He hadn't forgotten that before the fire it was Marie who'd threatened to leave, accusing him of treating their son unfavorably and not living up to the supportive boyfriend and father she had in mind. TR hadn't taken the announcement well and, as a result, had gone off to sulk. Anger and alcohol had been his only companions. So, like an idiot, he'd exacerbated the disaster. Tenfold.

"Ready to go?" Sara asked, yanking TR from his brooding.

"Sure. Sure." Gingerly sliding into the passenger seat of her humming car, he kept his eyes ahead. Sara had enough troubles on her mind. No sense in burdening her with his.

The car shifted into drive. The two remained quiet as they slowly exited the tree-lined street of bunched-together houses. Stealing a sideways glance, TR noticed his daughter was lost in somber contemplation. His heart hurt a little.

It was strange to witness his Sara like this. He realized he didn't really know her anymore, but this wasn't necessarily the life he'd wanted for her either. Truth be told, he didn't see much of himself in his daughter any longer.

The vibrant, inventive little creature he'd once balanced on the edge of his knee and let pretend to steer the family car had vanished. He missed that open little hand that would grip his, accompanying him places, acting as his redheaded spark of inspiration. Had his leaving changed his daughter so much? Sent her on such a different and apparently unhappy course? Where was the zest for life? He supposed it had all gone out the window long ago, when Sara had been required to take care of Joanne. God knew that nutjob of a woman—may she rest in peace—had had the keen ability to suck the life from a person. Had he done this to Sara?

TR was suddenly sad for his daughter. And he was sad for himself. In his heart, TR understood, in more ways than one, he was the parent who had let his only daughter down.

Maybe that could be fixed. He wouldn't leave yet. He was going to stick around and try.

CHAPTER TWENTY-EIGHT
SARA

At five o'clock in the morning, Sara peeled herself from the couch. Both the penetrating chill of her home's front room and the giant kink in her neck caused her to wince. Sitting upright, she blinked back a burning behind her eyelids. Everything felt heavy. It was as if she were hungover, only she hadn't been drinking.

Spending the night on the sofa had been a bad idea.

With nothing more than a sweatshirt to cover her bare legs, falling asleep over the unyielding furniture arm hadn't been the smartest of moves. Riding out the night alongside an agitated and infirm husband, however, hadn't been ideal either. That's why she'd come out there in the first place. To get away.

The flu had turned Charlie intolerable.

Somewhere around midnight she'd thrown back the covers of her bed and tromped to the front of the house in search of uninterrupted sleep. Only now, in the predawn temperatures of a home with limited heat, did she regret doing so in a thin cotton nightgown. In the dim light, she caught a glimpse of crystalline frost that had gathered in the corners of the windows. Yanking her sweatshirt over her head, Sara shivered. November was moving in.

With coffee on the brain, she moved into the kitchen and turned on the machine. Returning to the front hall, she rooted around in a deep basket for shoes. Feeling the satisfying warmth of sheepskin, she retrieved a pair of lined slippers. Hastily, she slipped them onto her bare feet. She looked around. Maybe she should make a fire. It was normally a job she left for Charlie, as positioning the logs and little bits of old newspaper was usually her husband's area of expertise, not hers. The chill, however, was penetrating. Something about the way the home's heating system was set up (or not set up, for that matter) always pumped small amounts of warmth through the vents of the bedrooms but left the main room of the house with only a wisp of air. It was maddening, and Charlie promised he'd get it handled. But he never did. As a result, they relied on the natural wood fireplace in the winter months.

As Sara went about shoving chunks of chopped fuel onto the grate and searching around for matches, she thought about Bo. Were there means to heat the little guesthouse that he and his mother shared? Was there even a decent kitchen in there? She realized she had no idea.

Sara struck a match and watched a single, narrow flame transform from orange to red. With a slow crackle it caught and held, eating its way through the first fragment of splintered kindling. Leaning back on her haunches, Sara extended her palms and waited for the glowing heat to reach her.

Her thoughts drifted back to Bo. Was he lying in bed at that very moment, speculating about TR? Was he wondering about her?

The coffeemaker beeped, letting her know it was ready. She sprang to her feet, her slippers making a scuffing sound as she crossed the hard floor and entered the kitchen. She checked the back slider for Acer. The dog was not waiting at his usual spot. *Must be still curled up with Charlie,* she thought. A bitterness rose in her throat. Shifting back to her coffee, she recalled their earlier argument.

Charlie had returned home legitimately sick, and Sara should have known better than to engage when he was so cranky. But she'd gotten snared into bickering over the matter of her father all the same.

"I just wanted to walk into my own home and have the ability to unwind. Instead I've got your dad loafing around in his pajamas like it's the damn Shangri-La," Charlie had snipped from his propped-up position on their king-size bed.

Sara rushed over to make sure their door was shut before responding. "Keep your voice down," she'd hissed.

"Why should I? He deceived you, Sara. That's not okay. You should be angry too. Why aren't you?" Charlie's voice had escalated. The color in his cheeks was inflamed, his fever likely rising right alongside his anger. Sara tried to press a cold washcloth on him, but he resisted.

"Yes, I'm still angry. And I understand, Charlie. I told you I was working on it. It's not an ideal arrangement. I get that. But you don't get to come and go, with hardly any notice, and then expect the entire family to drop everything and walk around on eggshells upon your return. It's not fair."

His face turned a light shade of crimson. His teeth gritted together, making it clear he was having a hard time swallowing past the pain in his throat. Yet he continued his tirade anyway.

"Who said anything about walking on eggshells? I don't understand why you're defending him. You said you were getting your father out of here, back to where he came from. That obviously didn't happen. It was nice of you to house him for a stint, but it's been weeks, Sara. And that was before you discovered his secret family. I mean, do you realize how masochistic this all is? Don't you think we have enough problems of our own, without adopting your father's?"

Sara stared at him. How had they gotten to this point?

They'd gone to bed mad as a result. Eventually, the fighting died down and the lights were switched off. Nothing had been resolved. After tossing and turning and then being subjected to Charlie's congested snuffling, Sara committed to enduring the night elsewhere. She was too upset to fall asleep anyway. So she'd paced the living room carpet for a time before crashing on the couch. All in all, it had been a terrible night.

It was now Friday morning. The day she promised Bo she'd return. Blowing steam from her drink, Sara rested on the slate hearth and planned her day.

Sam would wake in a bit, expecting Sara to cook breakfast and drive him to school. Who knew when TR would surface? Some mornings it was before sunrise; others it was well past eleven. And Charlie would likely sleep as long as he could, considering his condition.

All she knew was that she had to get out of that house. Getting Sam sent off properly was her only concern. After that, everything and everyone else would have to fend for themselves. One of two things could happen in her absence: either TR and Charlie would stay on their separate ends of the house and not bother one another. Or the opposite would happen, resulting in a pissing match of sorts, and one party might possibly be inclined to leave. At the moment, Sara didn't care which scenario played out. She didn't want any part of it.

Snippets of her conversation with Charlie played on a loop in her head. Allowing herself to dwell on her husband's lack of understanding only caused her shoulders to creep up around her ears. Tiptoeing through the house, she noted a slender patch of yellow under the crack of Sam's door. Good. At least he was getting ready for school. After poking her head inside his room to tell him she'd left the bagels out, she sneaked back into her bedroom and ran a hot shower.

Once Sam was deposited at school, the drive to the coast was a quick one. Now that she was familiar with the curves of the road and identifiable mile markers, her time in the car sailed by. Just as she'd done before, Sara arrived and eased her car onto the gravel drive with an air of caution. Surprises weren't expected, but nevertheless she wanted to be careful. Once again, the place appeared deserted.

As her fingers wrapped around the car door handle, her phone vibrated from the depths of her purse.

"Where are you?" Charlie coughed into the receiver.

Sara's eyes darted to the dashboard clock. It read five minutes to eleven. No doubt both Charlie and TR were up by now, wandering around her small house and bumping into one another.

"I meant to tell you I'd be gone for the day."

"Okay. Are you at the store? Because I need some more cough drops."

She screwed up her mouth. It was by design that she hadn't revealed her plans to Charlie. She was still angry with him. And also, she sought space to untangle her feelings regarding Bo and Marie. Charlie knew none of this. Sara planned to tell him. Just not now. Not over the phone, and not when they'd parted on uncertain terms.

"No. I'm not at the store. But I can run that errand for you on my way home."

"So then where are you?"

She inhaled. "Sandpoint."

"Wait, what?"

"I needed to come here and check on a few things. I still haven't been able to reach the investigators, and I want to get a better look at the house's condition."

A rustle echoed through the line. Sara envisioned her feverish husband rooting around in the medicine cabinet. "I can hear TR showering in the guest room. Why didn't you take him with you? Isn't the whole point to drive him home? For good?"

"I know. I had to leave him there today. It's complicated. I—"

"Everything is complicated, Sara. We both agreed. Your dad needs to go home. Yet you keep making an excuse why that isn't possible. And you're leaving me in the dark." A hacking fit followed. Charlie was clearly exerting himself.

"You need to take it easy. That cough sounds nasty."

He cleared his throat. "I know."

"Listen, when I get back—" The rumbling of a motor drowned out her voice. The phone tipped as she craned her neck. In her periphery, Bo came into view riding atop a hulking metallic motorcycle. Roaring past her wearing a beat-up leather jacket, he threw a quick peace sign in her direction and steered the front tire toward the back of the guesthouse.

So that's why I never saw a car before, she thought. Bo had kept his means of transportation tucked out of sight.

"Sara?" Charlie was repeating her name over the line in exasperation.

"What? Oh, sorry. I have to go. But I'll call you later. I promise."

She heard him protest as she hit "End." He would have to wait a little while longer.

Jamming her arms through the sleeves of a rain jacket, Sara sprang from the car in search of Bo. A faint smell of exhaust hung in the air. The rocky ground beneath her boots was noticeably damp. But with a clear blue sky overhead, the usual coastal rainfall had thankfully dissipated. Quickening her pace, she went in the direction of the tire marks.

"Bo?" Sara called, rounding the corner.

"Yeah. I'm back here." His voice was slightly muffled.

Arriving around back, Sara discovered him parking the bike in an old shed. Behind him was a workbench of sorts, lined with a gleaming row of hand tools. Particles of sawdust covered the cement floor; a buzz saw lay nearby. Guessing this was where Bo worked, Sara took it all in, absorbing as much information about him as she could. She wondered what kinds of things he made back there.

Tugging a sliver helmet over his ears, Bo shook out his bushy hair. A sheen of sweat had plastered his sideburns against his temples. His boyish grin and edgy motorcycle jacket reminded Sara how young this kid actually was. Twenty-one years old, according to TR. He had his entire life before him. Sara quickly flashed back to when she was his age. What had she been doing? Figuring out her path in life, she supposed.

"Hey," she said, meeting his eye.

"Hey, yourself."

"Nice bike." She knew nothing of motorcycles, but it seemed to be the cool thing to say.

The grin widened. "Thanks."

"So, your mom still out on assignment?" Sara glanced around, her ear cocked for any other signs of life.

Bo hung the helmet on the handlebar of his bike and tapped a kickstand with his shoe. Smoothing down his matted hair, he stepped toward her. "Don't worry; you're safe."

The both laughed awkwardly.

"Oh, okay. Well, I came back like I said I would." She suddenly felt stupid, out of place.

"I see that."

"TR doesn't know I'm here. My husband does. That's who I was talking to on the phone when you pulled up. He's not very happy with me at the moment. Thinks I should have dragged my dad back here with me. We're kind of, you know, not seeing eye-to-eye on this whole thing." *Stop rambling!* Sara snapped her jaw shut. Why was she sharing all of this? He didn't ask about her married life, but here she was anyway, vomiting out her problems not five minutes after Bo's arrival. What must he be thinking? Sara caught his eyebrows knitting together, no doubt perplexed at her admission. She folded her arms across her chest and then let them drop again. His silent scrutiny was making her nervous.

"You seem a little on edge."

Her arms crossed again. "I guess I am."

He stared back at her, his brow still furrowed. "You know what you need?" Bo peered at her.

A strong drink? Things were going off the rails. The ability to relax in front of her newfound sibling was escaping her. "No. I'm not sure what I need, to be honest."

"You need a release. Something to take your mind off your problems."

"Um, okay?" What was he talking about?

"Come with me." He turned and strode away.

Sara remained in place. "Where are you going?"

Bo called over his shoulder. "To the studio. Come on. Don't worry so much."

Easy for you to say. Trotting to catch up, Sara met him at the base of the concrete steps. She watched Bo shove the swollen door. It opened, and his head disappeared briefly as he reached inside and flicked on the lights. With a grand gesture, he stepped aside and swept his arm, bowing. "After you."

Puzzled, Sara paused. "What are we doing?"

"I'm not doing anything. You, on the other hand, are pretty keyed up. In my professional opinion, you're in need of some creative therapy."

"Huh?"

"I've seen that same troubled look on TR's mug that you're wearing right now. Many times, actually. Whenever the old man is in a mood, he comes out here and gets his hands dirty. He calls it his creative therapy."

Sara reared back. "Who said I needed therapy?"

Bo held his hands out, feigning innocence. "No judgment here. All I see is a lady who has a lot on her mind. And sometimes the best way to sort things out is to put your hands to work."

"Is that what you do? With your woodworking? Clear your head?"

The corners of his mouth curled up. "Sure. If that's what you want to call it. I like to use my hands. I find it grounds me. Living in TR's wacky world, it keeps me sane."

She chewed her lower lip and considered this. "I'm not just some 'lady,' you know. I'm your sister."

"Right." His smile remained.

"What makes you think you know me so well?"

"Because I know TR. And from what I've seen so far, you're a lot like him. You've both got that stubborn attitude, and you like to push people to get what you want."

"Ha!" She scoffed. What did he know? TR was one of a kind, a wild card. Sara was nothing like him. She shook her head. "I'm not like him. Besides, what makes you think he'd be okay with me touching his things? Last time I checked, TR's studio was his castle. One usually has to be invited inside."

"*I'm* inviting you inside. Go on in. Grab a hunk of clay and just see what happens. Hang out and enjoy yourself. I've got some things to take care of. Come find me when you're done." With that, he tromped away, disappearing behind the guesthouse.

A twinge of envy vibrated through her. Bo may have been much younger, but he held a self-confidence Sara didn't quite possess. He didn't seek permission; he just did as he pleased. It must've be nice to walk through life that way, so certain of things.

At the moment, Sara was anything but certain.

Fidgeting, she hovered in the doorway. The logical thing to do would be to gently shut the door and take some final notes and leave. But she was TR's daughter, after all. And logic had a different idea.

CHAPTER TWENTY-NINE
SARA

The first thing Sara did was climb onto the high, circular stool. The rigidity of its surface soothed her. She let her fingers slip down and curve around the edges of the seat and held them there with a sense of expectation. *Hello again* came the whisper in her head. She knew this stool. It had been her seat before. In all the years, her father had apparently kept a few things from the old days. A sort of eerie familiarity passed through her as she sat there, remembering. It was like visiting ghosts of studios past. But she was very much in the present.

Standing before her was a rectangular wooden table. She knew what this was. The wedging table. Closing her eyes, Sara recalled her father, wooden mallet tucked into his belt loop, skillfully cutting and throwing down dense segments of clay. He'd then rock his hands into the earthy material, kneading it like a giant ball of sticky dough. TR would lose himself in the process. And Sara would get lost right along with him.

Reflexively, she reached out and trailed her index finger along the grain of the table's dusty surface. The smoothness pleased her.

Drawing her hands back into her lap, she surveyed the rest of the space. Old paint cans and tin cups were lined up on the workbench like little soldiers, containing various-size carving instruments. These were the same aluminum-handled shapers, needles, and carving knives that had dazzled her younger self. Each one with a power to impose change on whatever it came into contact with. Their pointy spearheads and angled shapers were still just as mesmerizing. For a flash, Sara felt that same little tickle she'd felt as a child, eager to snatch one up and press it into something malleable. Sara noted TR had collected an endless supply of tools over the years, but only a handful appeared well used. She smiled. It was so like him to just stick to a few favorites. Her father was never much one for change when it came to his work.

Rotating on the stool, she viewed the wall behind her. Along a far side, stacked onto the shelves of metal racks, were various works in progress, including sculpted busts, curled hands, and miniature human forms. Sara wondered how long TR had been working on each one, as some appeared abandoned.

The most recent image, not yet completed, was the face of a woman. The large, almond-cut eyes with finely molded lids emoting a somber expression were highlighted by gentle wisps of a prominent brow. Peering closer, Sara knew this to be the face of Marie. She tugged at her hair to keep from reaching out and handling the still-drying clay. She had the urge to rotate this face away from her own. She wasn't ready to deal with Marie yet.

It was odd to think of her father sculpting other women. Of course he had over the years. Why wouldn't he? But still, she knew Marie meant more to him than most. The idea floated in her gut, like something unsettled. Had Marie posed for this piece? It was difficult to fathom. The fiery woman didn't strike Sara as the patient type. But clearly TR had sought to capture his lover's beauty. From what she could tell, he'd done a nice job of it.

Tearing her gaze away, she looked down. On the concrete floor, beneath the racks, were piles of hulking gray blocks protectively wrapped in streams of waxy plastic. Sara locked in on these the longest. The flicker of temptation lit up. Blocks and blocks of unused clay were just sitting there, waiting to be made into something.

Spinning back around, she glanced at the room's filmy window. As far as she could tell, Bo was busy elsewhere. How strange, she thought, that he'd pushed her into the studio and expected her to know what to do. To help herself to TR's things and make herself at home. Other than being presumptuous, he had no idea whether Sara was the creative type or not. What did he know about what she needed? Yet his words lingered.

Therapy, humph.

She wiped moisture from her palms onto the front of her jeans and stared. It certainly was a nice studio.

Everything had its place, neatly organized, but not so much that it couldn't be put back if it were to be handled. Tapping her foot against the edge of the stool leg, she debated. No. She really shouldn't. What would be the point in moving things around, in *touching* them? This was TR's stuff. Not hers.

She was not the artist. Not really.

But something beckoned her anyway. Wheedling past her stubbornness and beyond her preconceived notion of why she'd come in the first place was a nagging desire. An appetite for something she couldn't quite identify. Perhaps if she just peeled back a small corner of the protective wrap, she might allow herself to feel the gratifying coolness of the clay. She'd just run a finger along the edge of the blocks for old time's sake. That would be enough. Surely.

Sliding from her perch, Sara made for the storage racks. *Just for a minute,* she told herself. *And nothing more.*

She followed the scent of damp earthiness. Her soles plodded along the cold ground, echoing throughout the vacant room. Rather than putting her off, the chilled temperature was invigorating, shaking off the funk from her long drive. Coming up on the first row of blocks, she leaned down and pinched the plastic sheets between her fingers. Lifting them, she revealed a sizable mass the color of pale ash.

Squatting down, she read the large print across the flap of an adjacent decapitated cardboard box. Her eyes widened. "Porcelain?" she said aloud. That was strange.

Her father had always sculpted with a type of oil-based clay, oftentimes followed by the construction of a wax casting, if he wanted the end product to be bronzed. But never something as refined as porcelain. That was for dishes and such.

This type of clay was something entirely new. And by the looks of it, this particular supply was fresh. She slowly pieced the clues together, her eyes traveling to the empty pottery wheel. *Of course.* TR had ordered a different type of clay with the intention of throwing pots. It made sense, but it was also bizarre for Sara to think of her father in this way. Creating vessels just wasn't his style. He was a disciplined artist, meticulously carving organic forms to represent life through his lens with fine-tipped tools, not cupping his hands to create a cylinder object on a wheel.

Had Bo not told her about the wheel and TR's interest in a catalog, Sara would have never guessed her father would have changed his ways. But then again, the old man's property was full of surprises. There was so much she still didn't know.

She reached out and splayed her fingers over the surface of the creamy clay. A tingle traveled up her arm. Sara closed her eyes, allowing the feeling to melt her rigid insides. A faint sigh escaped. She'd missed this.

Withdrawing her hand, she inched back and told herself this would be enough. Just the act of laying her hand on the material would sustain her. She certainly didn't need to disturb TR's collection just because Bo told her to.

What exactly did he imagine she'd do?

But then again, she thought, *there's so much of it.* She doubted TR would even notice if she nipped off a small piece for herself.

Gliding over to the workbench, she performed a quiet inventory. It took about two seconds to locate the wire clay cutters employed for slicing off material from the clay blocks. Snatching the set of wooden handles, she made quick work of crossing the room and sinking the thin wire into the flesh of velvety porcelain. She cut all the way through, a satisfying wedge tumbling onto the floor and falling at her feet. Retrieving it, Sara moved to the wedging table and planted it on the wood top with a giant smacking sound.

Stifling a laugh, she glanced around to make sure Bo didn't come running.

Seeing no one, she lifted the mound, turned it over, and slapped it down again with all her strength. Right away she felt better. Sara could almost sense the taut muscles in her neck giving way.

"Well, I'll be damned," she murmured. "Bo was right. This is therapeutic."

Not wanting the feeling to go away, she dove the heels of her hands into the clay and leaned down and forward, using the full weight of her body. Curling her fingers at the knuckles, she cupped her hands and rolled the clay over to perform the action a second time. Strands of hair cascaded down, escaping from behind her ears. Her lips sent a puff of hot air upward. Scooting in closer, she braced her hips against the wood frame for better leverage. Pushing down, she manipulated the material again until it felt pliable. A kind of ease took over, and she continued.

It had been a long time since she'd done something like this. The tops of her forearms burned slightly, the weakened muscles constricting and flexing as she went. Her hands gradually morphed into instruments, kneading and folding the clay over and over again. Pretty soon, a kind of hush filled her ears with only the sharp bursts of TR's instructions to "wedge out tiny pockets of air" sounding in her head. Giving over to the motion, she permitted months' worth of stress to gently slough away. A kind of rhythm picked up as she swayed and smacked until her once-geometric slice of clay had become a relaxed spiral. Standing back, she grinned. She'd forgotten how fun it could be.

"Someone's happy."

Sara jumped a foot. Her hand flew over her heart.

Bo stood in the doorway, arms folded and a cockeyed smile plastered across his face. A sliver of golden sunlight glinted behind him.

"Bo! You scared the life out of me." Her breath caught. She hadn't realized she'd been panting.

His heavy boots strode farther into the room. "Whatcha got there? Anything good?"

Sara leaned back and blocked his view of the table. A wave of guilt sent her hands into her back pockets. "Oh, just you know . . . checking stuff out."

"Uh-huh."

"How long have you been standing there?"

"Long enough. Guess you decided to take my advice after all."

Sara paused. She wasn't sure she should confess how gorgeously satisfying it felt to slam down a piece of clay and pound out her aggravation. But somehow she sensed Bo knew this already.

"Wanna have a go at the wheel?" He cocked his head.

Sara startled, her brow dipping. "What? Why would I do that?"

"Um, because it's just sitting there, being unused. And you seem to know what you're doing. Aren't you the least bit tempted?"

"I actually don't know what I'm doing."

But it was tempting. She'd been staring at the contraption for the better part of an hour. Every time she'd stop to roll the clay over, the wheel gleamed in her periphery. Her only experience with a wheel had been observing others use older versions, back when she was much younger. The kind of motorless kick wheels used by a friend of her father's back in the early 1980s that was propelled by the rapid use of one's foot and nothing more than a round plate of plywood. The one squatting in TR's current studio had an intimidating steel construction, a curious tray, and fancy toggles and switches. Just the act of turning it on might be enough for Sara to damage it.

"Well, you could've fooled me. You break that shit down exactly like your father." He eyed the spiraled clay in front of her. "You even made that 'ram's head' shape he refers to."

Sara perked. "You know about the ram's head?"

"Of course!" Bo exclaimed. Then he planted his feet wide apart, cradled an imaginary piece of clay in his two hands, and dropped his voice to mimic TR. "Boy, you've gotta cup it like this, see, then throw it down and make a tight spiral. Keep those—"

"Thumbs together!" Sara laughed at the uncanny imitation of their father, finishing his sentence.

"Exactly! It's the same speech every time, like I'm an imbecile who can't take direction."

"That's what he used to say to me all the time: 'Keep your thumbs together!' God, I can remember it like it was yesterday. So you guys hang out in here?" She swallowed back a small pebble of envy.

"Yeah, I've hung out in here with him before. I think the old man hopes some of his creative mojo will rub off on me. He's tried to teach me a couple of things, but woodworking is more my jam, if you know what I mean. The sculpting, not so much."

"Huh." This was all news to Sara. That TR had even taken the time to apprentice his new son meant TR trusted Bo enough to invite him into the secret lair. Not everyone got an invitation to TR's creative space. She felt a new kind of connection to Bo because of this.

"So did he teach you how to use the wheel?"

"Nah. But that's what YouTube is for, right? I looked up a video when TR asked me to unbox the thing and hook it up with electrical. It doesn't look so hard. You just get some water and throw on a glob of clay and spin. Presto."

Sara laughed. "Somehow I doubt it's as easy as 'presto.' But okay."

"Okay, you're going to try it?"

"Okay, I'll watch a video. Later. When I get some free time."

"Cool."

"Bo," Sara started.

"Yeah?"

"Why are you being so nice to me?" It was something she'd wondered since her first visit. His mother seemed to know some history, but she hadn't exactly been welcoming. And TR hadn't exactly encouraged the two of them to meet either. So far, all signs should be pointing Bo toward keeping his guard up, creating a distance between himself and the unwelcome stranger who was snooping around. But Bo had been quite the opposite. It was almost as if he was glad she was around.

He shrugged. "Why shouldn't I be? I mean, like you said, we are related. I know about the statue and how TR kind of left you and your mom after he hit the big time. You're the sculptor's daughter. I'm familiar with some of the story."

"I see."

"Besides," he said. "I can relate, if that makes any sense. My father situation is equally screwed up. My first dad didn't turn out to be who I thought he was. Besides not being my biological father, he didn't stick to the unconditional love part once he realized TR was my father." His voice dipped.

"I'm so sorry." Sara felt bad for this kid; having two dads who didn't live up to expectations must've been awful.

He shrugged. "It's okay. But TR and I don't exactly have the smoothest of relationships. So when you showed up, I thought you might be someone I could relate to. You just seem sort of, well, affected by this life. And that is something I can understand."

Who was this kid, with his gentle words and thoughtful insights? Normally it would crawl under her skin whenever someone said they'd read about her rocky history with TR. She'd never appreciated the very public invasion of her privacy. But when Bo said it, she'd felt consoled. Like he'd been trying to support her. As crazy as it was, Sara felt the thread of a connection wound between them. She suddenly was glad she'd come.

This must be what it feels like to have a brother.

CHAPTER THIRTY
SARA

Sara returned home later that evening under the dusky cover of an orange October sky. Parking the car, she let the lids of her eyes drop. The events of the day had sapped her. Fragments of her time spent with Bo played over in her head. The conversation, the workspace, and perhaps most surprisingly of all, the welcome sensation of gorgeous clay between her fingers. Sara left the property on a high of sorts. It was ironic, really. Rather than follow through with her plan to uncover mysteries of the charred home—and subsequent discord between its residents—Sara had been drawn by the lure of TR's art studio. Before she knew it, the hours had slipped away from her and it had been time to leave.

She was still contemplating how much of this to share with TR. So much had transpired over the past days, and her head was swimming because of it. Now home, she wasn't quite ready to face what was likely waiting to greet her.

No doubt Charlie was looming somewhere inside, prepared to pick a fight.

Guilt was taking hold. She'd left Sandpoint much later than she'd aimed for and, as a result, had been caught in the snarl of rush-hour traffic. Dinnertime had come and gone. Other than shooting a brief text to Charlie, reminding him a friend would drop Sam home after school, she'd neglected to touch base. This had surely not sat well with her husband. Not because Charlie wasn't used to looking after Sam—because he was—but rather that he'd been ditched by his wife and thoughtlessly saddled with hosting his difficult father-in-law.

Charlie's last words to Sara had been, "Your dad needs to go home." And she'd promptly ignored him. Being left alone to whip up a meal for TR had no doubt thrust Charlie into a foul mood. A mood that required significant energy Sara currently didn't have. And while she knew it was mostly her fault, she was growing to resent Charlie all the same.

Their marriage had become an ugly tally sheet of blame.

Peering up at the house, she caught a light in the window. Behind it, the electric-blue glow of a television screen pulsed. She wondered if Sam and TR might be into the video games again. It had become a sweet routine for the two of them, bonding over technology that her aging father didn't totally understand but embraced anyway. It dawned on her this was new for TR, spending time with a boy like this. He'd missed out on years with Bo, never really knowing him as a youth. Perhaps he was making up for lost time in a way. As far as Sara could tell, TR seemed to gravitate toward Sam more than anyone lately. This gave her a glimmer of happiness.

Squeezing the latch of the front door, she tried to tamp down the anxious feeling that bubbled up. She hoped Charlie was at least over the worst of his virus. Holding her breath, she prayed she wouldn't find him still in bed. TR was fine as a companion, but maybe not so much in the way of caregiver for her ten-year-old.

"Hello? I'm home." Just inside, everything was warm and smelled slightly of take-out pizza. Her mouth watered, salivating at the idea of food. It had been hours since she'd eaten. Following the aroma of gooey mozzarella cheese, she was drawn farther inside. Her boots were the first to go, clunking heavily on the hardwood floors. Her quilted jacket went next, fluttering onto the back of a chair.

She took stock of the house as she went, feeling as if she'd been gone for days. Most of the lights had been left to carelessly burn throughout the house. It was a small detail, but it irked her. Charlie always neglected to notice things like that in her absence. He'd probably left a pile of unwashed dishes in the sink for her as well. Sighing, she came to the back of the living room couch and flicked off an adjacent floor lamp.

"Hey, guys."

Two ruffled heads sat huddled together. Animated images jumped across a monitor in the background. Just as she'd predicted, her son and her father were up playing games.

"Hi, there, stranger," TR said, turning to greet her. His spotted hand shot up, revealing his grip on a bright cherry Popsicle. Sara tried not to glare as he dangled the drippy dessert precariously over her cushions.

She sagged. She was too tired to play disciplinarian.

"Hi, Mom!" Sam popped onto his knees and grinned. A bright stain of red ringed his small mouth. "Grandpa and I are playing *Minecraft*."

"I see that. I also see you introduced him to the box of Popsicles." She bent and pushed her nose to the crown of Sam's downy head. He remained still, allowing her to nuzzle him a bit longer before sliding back down again. Sam may have been getting too old for her to hold, but he still had his moments of little-boy sweetness. Sara relished them, no matter how minute. She knew they wouldn't last forever.

"I didn't realize what I'd been missing out on until Sammy boy here shared his dessert with me." TR made a slurping sound and grinned. This sent Sam into giggles, with TR playfully poking him in the ribs. Sara smiled. Clearly, they hadn't missed her presence.

"Long day?" TR asked, turning serious.

"You could say that." She flopped into a chair and rubbed at a sore spot on her foot. A hot bath was in order. But first she needed to find Charlie. "Where's your dad?"

Sam rotated back around and gripped the TV controller. "He's in your bedroom. Been in there all night."

"He has?"

"Except to come out and pay the pizza guy, he's been in there sleeping. I think." TR offered this bit of information along with a noncommittal shrug. Sara guessed he knew better than to get involved.

"Okay, thanks."

In an act of compassion, Sara got up and went to the kitchen to retrieve a mug of hot water and a bag of herbal tea. Clutching them both, she made for the master bedroom.

It was concerning to think that Charlie had been hiding out. Perhaps he wasn't recovering as fast as she'd expected. But then again, if he'd truly been asleep most of the day, he wouldn't have noticed her lengthy absence.

Charlie tended to withdraw whenever he got sick. She recalled a couple of years earlier when a rather nasty stomach bug had spread viciously among the airline staff. It had knocked Charlie sideways for a good week. Sara had slept on the couch, providing him with routine refills of sports drinks and cold washcloths. Perhaps now he was seeking comfort burrowed beneath the covers, just as he'd done before.

With her ear positioned gently against the door, she listened before easing it ajar. A stream of dim light leaked out from under the frame. No sound could be heard. Maybe Charlie had dozed off under the haze of cold medicine. If he was sleeping, she'd stealthily deposit the tea at his bedside and then tiptoe away. At least that way he'd notice she'd been in to check on him when he woke up.

Extending her arm, she swung the door farther open. To Sara's surprise, Charlie wasn't sleeping at all. He was hunched over the bed, jamming a pair of jeans inside a canvas duffel bag. Sara's cautious hope descended like a lead balloon. Her ever-mobile husband was packing.

"Charlie? I thought you'd be sleeping. What's going on?"

Sara noticed the whites of his knuckles as he shoved a pair of rolled-up socks into the bag next. "I'm going to a hotel, Sara."

"Why? For work?" It didn't make any sense that he'd be taking off for another shift so soon, but it was the only explanation that came to mind.

"No. Not for work. For peace. It's too crowded around here. And I need some space."

Space?

Her mouth hung in a stupefied gape. "To get over the flu?"

"No."

"Okay . . . ?" Though her feet were planted, she suddenly had the odd sensation she was floating. Her husband's blunt announcement had toppled out and loosened a tether, sending her adrift.

What was she missing? She tried to read his masked expression, to catch a glimpse so she might get a clue as to what he was possibly thinking. But Charlie appeared closed off. Her hands gripped the mug of hot tea for stability.

Her marriage was in real trouble.

How could he be leaving her? Like this? This departure of his felt acutely different. And it scared her.

Charlie continued packing.

"What then?" she demanded. The boiling temperature was beginning to burn. Annoyed, she banged the mug down on a nearby dresser. "I don't understand. Why on earth would you go to a hotel?"

Charlie paused. For a moment a look passed between them. A faint whisper of rising dread told Sara she might already know the reason.

"I just have to go. I need space to clear my head. This—" He righted and dropped his arms. "This hasn't been working lately. TR's crazy-ass world is completely consuming you right now. It's breaking you. I understand your need to try to help; it's in your very nature, and I love that about you; I really do. But you're blind if you can't see he's selfishly sucking you down with him, pulling you from your own family. And whether you admit it or not, you're letting him."

Sara steadied her knees. She could almost feel the blood escaping her body. Her lips failed to cooperate as she stammered out a weak protest. "Th . . . that's not fair. I'm doing the best I can. My dad is my family too. There are things that, well, it's just been a little complicated, that's all."

A troubled look splashed across Charlie's face. He let a partially folded undershirt slip from his hands. Sara struggled for what to say. This was happening too fast.

"We just need more time to work things out."

"I feel like we're deteriorating, Sara. We barely see one another. We don't talk. It isn't working. I'm not happy. And I have the feeling neither are you."

What?

Hot tears pricked the rims of her eyes. Charlie was punishing her for events that were out of her control. He was also blaming her for their separateness, when mostly his travel was the thing accomplishing that. If he'd just stay put for a minute, calm down, and give her a chance to explain, she could maybe turn this around. He was getting upset over something he knew nothing about. And now he was *leaving*.

She looked around the disheveled room, trying to figure out what to say. If nothing else, they had Sam to think about, for God's sake. And what about the two of them, for better or for worse? Didn't that mean anything? Despite the growing discontent, she didn't want to accept that they might be over. She'd spent her fair share of waking hours being angry with her husband, but that didn't mean she'd given up on them. She wasn't even being given a chance to save things.

"I'm here now," she urged. "We can talk tonight."

Charlie paused his packing. Behind his eyes was the darkly distinct shade of melancholy, like someone who'd already accepted defeat. "Are you ready to walk out there and insist your dad goes home? To finally pack his things and return to the coast?"

Sara hesitated. Charlie was pinning her into a corner. As much as she disliked the idea of an ultimatum, she wanted him to understand. Something in her needed to continue exploring a relationship with both Bo and TR. She couldn't articulate it quite yet, but one thing was for sure: Sara liked Bo. She could tell there was a level of goodness about him. And if he was the reason TR refused to return, if they'd had a conflict of some kind, Sara wanted to understand it. Because she was already considering Bo to be a brother. Charlie might not understand this, or maybe he would, but either way he didn't seem to want to stick around long enough for her to explain.

Sara understood deep in her soul that a shot at a whole family—really whole, not this fragmented unit she'd grown accustomed to having—was at stake. If she just could help bridge a gap, then maybe a real happiness would surface. Because what Charlie couldn't see was that Sara needed to fill the giant chasm that had been lurking in her heart for most of her adult life. That wide-open, lonely space that had taken up residence the day her father walked out. She desperately wanted the parent who had left to now apologize and stay in her life for good. And remarkably, she also wanted that man to be happy.

Gathering up her resolve, she looked hard into Charlie's face. "Not everything is so black and white, Charlie. There's other stuff my dad has to deal with before a move home can happen. If you just let me explain . . ."

"Uh-huh. That's what I thought." The response fell at her feet with flat indifference. He was being unfair. And it felt like betrayal.

With a final tug, he zipped up the duffel bag and hauled it over his shoulder. "Call me when you're ready to put your own family first."

As Charlie's words sank in, something snapped inside of her. A raw nerve had been struck one too many times. He knew how much she feared being walked out on, and he was doing it anyway. "That's really rich, Charlie! You've got to be kidding me! I'm the one not putting my family first? What about you? You can't even stand to be home for more than twenty-four hours before you're itching to get out of here again. You get to run off, hiding behind your job as an excuse while Sam and I are the ones left holding the bag!"

She noticed his jaw tighten as he hoisted the bag farther over his shoulder. "This is exactly why we need a break. I'm going before one of us says something we regret. Plus, I'm not going to fight with you with your dad eavesdropping in the next room. I'm leaving, Sara. I'll be at Sam's soccer game tomorrow afternoon. But for now, I'm going to a hotel."

And with that, Sara watched her once-steadfast partner turn and walk out without so much as a backward glance. There was nothing left to do but cry.

CHAPTER THIRTY-ONE

TR

Whatever was going down between those two wasn't good; TR could tell. It was like a proverbial boxing match, but without the punches. The walls practically vibrated with all their yelling. It caused poor Sam to cower and scoot closer under the security of his grandfather's arm. TR had a mind to jump up and put a stop to it. And then, not long after it started, things went silent.

Sure, his daughter and her husband had gotten into rather nasty snits before, but none that had sent ol' uptight Chuck—*Upchuck* for short—slamming out the front door in a veritable huff. TR had protectively crooked an elbow around the back of the couch, ready to shield Sam, who watched wide-eyed as his dad melted for a moment and muttered a kind of rushed goodbye to his equally upset son and then vanished. There had been bags and farewells before, but no sir, not like this one. The husband was taking off.

TR recognized that brand of indignation from a mile away. Hell, he'd *been* that indignation before. And he couldn't believe he was witnessing it right there in Sara and Sam's life. It was like a cruel record of the past. And it killed TR to see the crushing effect it had on the stunned little boy sitting by his side.

"Don't worry, Sammy boy," TR cooed reassuringly. He gripped the boy by the sleeve of his hooded sweatshirt and gently shook. "It's just adult stuff. Adults can be stupid sometimes. Did you know that?" He'd wanted the boy to laugh, to catch a bit of levity in an otherwise disheartened countenance of a suddenly somber ten-year-old kid. But all he got was a pitiful slant of a smile. TR huffed. It would have to do for now.

TR settled deeper into the couch, hoping his body language would be enough to tell the boy he'd sit there with him as long as was needed. *I'm not going anywhere, kid. Not tonight.* He rubbed his jawline. Who would have sat here with Sam if he hadn't been around? TR wondered.

Sara shuffled into the living room with red eyes. She attempted to comfort Sam, hugging his tiny shoulders from behind, trying to hide her face while covering up Charlie's departure with a lame excuse about work. But no one bought it. TR was grateful he was there. Someone needed to remain steady for the boy. His daughter, whose troubled appearance struck him, was currently not this person.

Sara mumbled something inaudible and drifted into the kitchen to heat a slice of pizza. TR craned his neck and watched as his stunned-looking daughter mutely worked her jaw over a mouthful of deep-dish crust. A large glass of milk was poured next, spilling over the sides as she dumbly gazed off in the distance. Without bothering to mop it up, she dragged the plastic milk carton across the wet counter and plunked it into the refrigerator. She gulped down the drink and went back to her pizza, her movements sluggish and leaden.

It wasn't like his otherwise pulled-together daughter to act in this manner. It was as if she were in shock or something very close to it. Clearly, this was the husband's doing. Whatever Chuck had said, or not said, before storming out had knocked the sense out of Sara. TR guessed this must have been their biggest row since he'd come to stay. Disturbed, he continued to examine Sara as she nursed her milk and stared, brooding out the window.

And then another thought came. TR found the backs of his legs bracing against the couch cushions with alarm. This must have been what it was like for young Sara when he'd walked out on Joanne all those years ago. She'd been the unknowing kid on the couch, just as Sam was now, silently watching as her parents brawled and then fiercely detached. Sara had been the one to endure the brunt of her reckless parents' behavior, just as Sam was doing now. Seeing the ugliness of it through the eyes of that beautiful boy, who regardless of it all still radiated a bright, unconditional love, practically made TR want to weep.

And here was poor Sara, going through it all over again. Another man in her life walking out, hitting that same raw nerve that surely was exposed once more. It killed him to know this. She deserved so much more.

He supposed the same could be said for Bo. That kid had been handed two fathers, yet he got along with none. TR was sorry for all the recent fights he'd had with Bo over his chosen career and inability to see his higher potential as an artist. The boy had real talent, yet he always pushed back with force against TR's suggestions. They never saw eye to eye. Marie always got involved, inserting herself into their arguing and chasing TR around the property as she hollered in stilted English about the need to support their son. That blasted woman could really sink her teeth into something when she wanted.

TR only wished Bo would pull his lazy head out of his ass and make something of his life, to recognize his unique gifts and do something profound with them. The objects Bo created with his bare hands were breathtaking. The kid could take a raw piece of wood and manipulate it, giving something as simple as a coffee table a surprising sense of fluidity. It was remarkable. But maddeningly, that stubborn adolescent refused to share his work with anyone else. True, he'd made TR a splendid worktable. And for just one day, the hope of intimacy between them had emerged. But it was snuffed out when Bo refused to do more. His son claimed he'd rather spend his days toiling as a handyman than trying to hock his furniture. TR had tried to make Bo see the error of his ways. He'd even gone as far as threatening to kick Bo out of the house, off the property for good, if he didn't try harder to harness his talent and maybe even earn a paycheck. But all that got them was a nasty feud.

Bo had dug in his heels. Words were exchanged, and emotions exploded. Then TR had hit the bottle a little too hard. Another mistake. He should have handled things better. It wasn't Bo's fault he'd had the rug pulled out from under him when he learned about his father. He'd been dealt a shitty hand.

But unlike Sam, Bo was practically a grown man. In that sense, he was far better equipped for the cruelties of life than a small boy. Bo had had time enough to figure out his place in the world. Well, sort of. TR rubbed his forehead. He couldn't think about that now. One crisis at a time.

Clasping the side of Sam's arm, he sighed heavily. What a mess they'd all made of this life.

"Hey." He leaned over. Sam smelled of pizza sauce and Popsicles. What a marvelous combination of things was this little boy. "What time do you usually hit the sack? You know, on a school night?"

Sam looked up. "It's not a school night. Tomorrow's Saturday."

"Ah. You're right. That's why they call you the smart one. Well, what time do you go to bed anyway?" He was hoping to scoot Sam off to brush his teeth in order to spare the boy seeing his mother like this. It was clear Sara was in a different stratosphere at the moment. If she were anything like her old man, it wouldn't be long before she gave up on the milk and craved something harder. Sometimes a little numbness helped.

"Eight-thirty."

TR frowned. "What was that?"

"Eight-thirty. You asked when I'm supposed to go to sleep. It's at eight-thirty at night."

TR squinted at the TV monitor, their video game set on pause. "That was twenty minutes ago, kid. Let's say you and I wander on back to your room and get the nighttime ritual knocked out together. Sound good?"

Sam scrunched up his angelic face, puzzled. "You mean get my pajamas on and read a book and all that?"

Grateful for the direction, TR pumped his head. "Yes! All of that. That sounds right. Let's do that."

"Okay."

TR heaved himself from the couch and followed Sam down the hallway. The boy stopped only once, casting his tearful mother an inquisitive glance, then kept going. Sara acknowledged the two of them with a weak but grateful smile.

"Oh," she exclaimed. Her watery eyes grazed over the pair of them. "You're tucking him in? Thanks, TR. Good night, Sam. Remember I love you. Your dad does too. Hopefully, you guys can FaceTime in the morning. Sleep tight, honey."

"Good night, Mom."

"Okay," TR replied, ushering Sam farther toward his bedroom. "We're headed off to brush our teeth now." TR gave a thumbs-up sign before shuffling away. He'd need to come find her when he was through with taking care of Sam. His daughter clearly needed a shoulder to cry on, based on her quivering chin. He had a feeling it would be a long night.

Sam scampered off, announcing to TR he needed to clear a path of dirty soccer clothes and debris before anyone entered his room. Sara normally kept that kid's bedroom as neat as a pin. But he supposed in all the confusion the normal household duties had been pushed to the side. Seems both parents had been gone a lot lately. TR was glad he'd been around as backup.

It struck him he'd never really been anyone's backup before. It felt good for a change. He figured it was the least he could do after staying with Sara's family all that time. He knew changing all those gooey bandages couldn't have been a walk in the park for his daughter. But she'd done it anyway. TR had never really expressed the sentiment at the time, but he was grateful she'd been around to take care of him as he healed.

"Sammy boy," TR said as he darted the corners of his grandson's rumpled sheets and neatened up the bed. "I'm sure glad I got to spend this time with you. You're my most favorite grandkid."

Sam scampered onto the twin mattress and grinned. "Aren't I your only grandkid?"

"Well, yeah. But that's not the point."

"It isn't?" He pushed his narrow, little feet under the covers and leaned onto the fluffy pillows.

"Nah. The point is even if I had a million grandchildren, you'd still be the best one. You've got your mother's good wisdom and, if I might add, your grandpa's artistic sensibility. Wrap that all up with your charm and good looks, and man, what a prize!" He winked as he pulled the bedding up and over Sam's chest, patting him on the head for good measure.

"If you say so, Grandpa."

"I say so."

"Grandpa?" The word enveloped him like a hug.

"Yeah, kid?"

Sam propped himself up on one elbow and looked up. "You're not going away, are you?"

TR frowned. "What makes you say that?"

"You said you were glad to spend time with me. Sounded like you're leaving or something."

TR swallowed hard. His heart swelled twice the size, gazing down on those big saucer eyes. "Nah. Just musing. That's all. You get some sleep now. There's a soccer game to be won tomorrow!"

"Good night."

"Good night, kid."

"Love you."

A piercing arrow shot straight through TR's heart. He paused, working his jaw around as he searched for the words. His lips seemed to be glued together, unable to form the right sentiment. Instead, he placed a palm over his heart and nodded somberly at his grandson. He hoped it would be enough. With a tender smile he flicked off the lights and shut the door.

He found Sara still at her place in the kitchen. The poor girl looked like she needed sleep. He noticed a line through her makeup where a salty tear had trailed but decided not to pry. She'd tell him when she was good and ready.

Hoping to lighten the mood, he went past her and hunted in the pantry before withdrawing a box of chocolate cookies he'd seen earlier. Handing her one, he smiled. "If you're going to sit there moping into your milk, might as well dip a cookie in there."

Her eyes flickered as she pinched the cookie and snapped off a bite. "Thanks."

It felt safe to continue, so he plucked out a second cookie and bit down. "That son of yours is a remarkable young man. Top notch! You should be proud."

"Thanks." Her voice cracked ever so slightly.

TR wiped crumbs from his lower lip. He studied his daughter. "I'm not sure what's going on between you and that husband of yours. And maybe it's none of my business, but you deserve to be happy. So does Sam. I'd hate to see your family break up in the unpleasant manner that mine did. I don't have to tell you what a disaster that was."

Sara cast him a blank expression.

Christ. He was botching it, he knew. He was never good at apologies. He wanted so badly to give Sara some nugget of sage advice, to reassure her it would be all right and she'd be able to get through the rough spots. She was a Harlow, and Harlows were strong. But standing here now, witnessing her tear-stained face, there was no eloquent way to console his crumbling daughter. She just needed to hang in there. But he knew that was nonsense. Her marriage was likely breaking up and maybe without her consent.

"What can I do for you, sweetheart?"

Sara finished her cookie and sagged. TR couldn't tell what she was thinking. Selfishly, he hoped she wasn't about to kick him out. But he'd go if that was what she really wanted.

"Anything?"

He nodded.

"You can tell me why you left and never cared enough to come back for me." There was a hitch in her voice, her green eyes pools of sadness.

TR's insides felt as if they'd been ripped clean in half. His daughter carried around so much pain. Fumbling for a stool, he collapsed. He regretted he'd never given her a decent answer, any truthful kind of excuse as to why he'd gone so long without her. It wrenched him to know this is what his little girl believed. "Is that what you thought this whole time? That I didn't care?"

"Yes." The quivering chin returned.

"Oh, sweetheart. Don't you know I never stopped loving you, even from a distance?" His hand reached over. He meant it sincerely. He was through playing defense, trying to hide the things of which he was most ashamed. It wasn't worth it.

"No," Sara murmured.

This answer turned his soul inside out. His poor girl. What had he done?

"Sara, I was young and impetuous and fed up with your mother. I walked away because I was too flawed to find a way to fix things. I was a fool. I'm still a fool! I'm truly sorry for the pain it caused you. But please, *please* believe me when I tell you it had nothing to do with you. Nothing to do with not *loving* you. I just didn't know how to handle it all. I was immature and prideful. Still am, I guess. But you were with me in my heart, always. I am so sorry. For everything. So, so sorry." The admission was like the crest of a large wave passing over the top of him, churning him over to forcefully wash him clean from all the miserable guilt he'd carried all those years. It hurt, and it took his breath away, but he didn't care. He only prayed Sara believed him.

His daughter appeared to be struck by something equally painful but faintly relieved at the same time. Her delicate lips trembled as her eyes and nose ran, but her grief was beautiful all the same. A stunning, beautiful sadness.

"Sara?" He wanted to know what she was thinking.

She remained pensive, quietly mulling over his words. TR prayed she wasn't considering shutting him out. He was underserving of her love; he knew this. But he so badly hoped for it anyway. When she finally spoke, he held his breath.

"Thank you," she whispered.

"For what?"

"Saying you're sorry. It's been hard." Another tremor passed between her lips.

TR swiped at his eyes. He didn't care how foolish he looked. "I know, sweetheart. I bet it was."

"You just vanished. So I never knew. There wasn't any closure, no explanation, just emptiness."

"Sara, I wrote letters and sent money. I don't know why Joanne chose to keep that from you. Your mother must have been very angry, I suppose. I'm sorry."

"Me too."

TR dropped his head.

"There's something else," Sara continued.

"Yes?"

"I like Bo. I've been to see him a couple of times now. Since he's your son and my brother, I want to know him more. And I can't understand why you don't. I can't understand why you don't want to go back and try to have a relationship with him. It's like you're abandoning your family all over again." She bit her lip and waited for a response.

TR understood the rawness to her words, the direct correlation his daughter had drawn between herself and Bo. His two children. It wasn't the same, but she didn't know that. Or maybe it was. Either way, he'd made a mess of things.

"I can see why you'd think that, but . . . Wait, that's where you've been? You were in Sandpoint?"

Her cheeks pinked. "Yes."

"Spending time with Bo?"

"Pretty much. Marie has been out of town."

Ah. He was beginning to understand now. Sara was testing out what it meant to have a sibling. "I see. And you like this brother of yours, you say? Think he's a good enough guy?"

"Yes."

"Well, then. Pull up a stool and tell me all about it. And I'll tell you as much as I know, too, which isn't a lot. I'm old and I'm scared and my memory isn't what it used to be. But that doesn't matter. Because Sara, my girl, there's nothing more important than being with you right now. And I mean that from the bottom of my heart."

Sara leaned in and blinked, as if awakening for the first time that day. She planted herself on the seat next to him and ran the heel of her hands along the bottoms of her reddened eyes. "Okay," she said. "I'm ready."

TR believed they both were.

CHAPTER THIRTY-TWO
SARA

After Sara had recapped her visits with Bo, her father nodded slowly and then said something that shocked her.

"I'm afraid to go home."

Sara was confused. "Afraid? Why? Because the house is unsafe? Or are you afraid of a confrontation from Marie?" Visions of TR's angry girlfriend with her wild hair and disapproving eyes came to mind. If her father did something to anger her, Sara had little doubt he'd be made to pay for it one way or another. Marie didn't strike Sara as the forgiving type.

"Nah. Marie I can handle. She and I have had our fights, that's for sure. And I'm fairly certain she's none too pleased with me at the moment. But it's more than that."

"What is it then?" She watched TR's mouth go twitchy.

"I'm afraid to go back and face what I've done. I'm ashamed, if you must know. The truth is I put my family's life at risk. It was pure stupidity. The fire started because of me, and I'm too much of a coward to own it. So I chose to run."

The breath drained out of her. This was big. Her father was admitting guilt, and he was terrified to face the consequences. She watched him nervously rub at his right side, itching his newly emerging scars. Sara supposed those wounds would be a constant reminder of how he had narrowly escaped death. And how he'd thrust Marie and Bo into equal danger.

But now a bigger question loomed. How did he start the fire? What did he mean, exactly? She recalled hearing TR on the first few nights he'd occupied the guest room. Her father had woken multiple times, yelping out from some sort of fierce nightmares. At the time she'd assumed this was due to the pain of his burns and nothing more. But now she understood. TR was frightened.

"I don't understand," she probed. "You were inside when the fire began, weren't you?" She imagined him trapped by thick smoke and growing blaze. She wondered how long he'd remained inside before fleeing, when the flames attached themselves to his right side and sent smoke into his lungs. Had he tried to stop and put them out or just run away instead? Had he looked for Marie or Bo? It must have been harrowing.

"I wasn't awake when it started," TR said.

"So you were in your bed? Alone?" This part piqued her interest, considering how much she didn't know about Marie. She wouldn't put it past that woman to act out in some kind of vengeful rage, an impulsive move in a lover's quarrel. Just look at the way she'd come after Sara during that first visit.

TR shifted his eyes to the floor.

"TR?"

"I was upstairs in my study."

"A study?" It dawned on Sara she'd never asked what was actually on the second level of the house. When Bo had taken her inside, she'd been too preoccupied with all the damage on the first floor.

"Yeah, I work in a studio on the side of the house. But my study is actually where I keep my art books and papers and that sort of thing. Lately I've been doing a little oil painting up there when the mood strikes me. The natural light can't be beat. It's quiet, and I have a terrific view of the Pacific Ocean."

"Sounds nice."

"It is," he said, gazing off in the distance. Sara supposed he missed his private space: an area to act on whatever whim struck him on any given day. She even envied it a little. "There's also a decent-size sofa. And sometimes when Marie and I have a particularly nasty row, well, I've taken to sleeping up there."

"Okay, so you and Marie got into it, so you decided to sleep in your study for the night? Was she being, um, violent?"

TR chuckled and rubbed at his jaw. "Ha! That depends upon your definition of the term. She's a hot-blooded woman. Got a mind of her own. It's invigorating to be around her passion. But every once in a while, she lets her emotions get the best of her. And then, not so much. But no, she's never tried to hurt me, if that's what you're asking."

Sara tried to picture their relationship. Stormy and tempestuous is what came to mind. But the way TR's eyes glinted when describing his girlfriend made her think he still loved Marie. She just wondered whether the feelings were mutual. "So what did you two fight about that night?"

"Humph! Same thing we always fight about: Bo. Marie's got a soft spot when it comes to that kid. She insists she's doing him a favor by coddling him, but she's not. The kid's got talent. He just doesn't use it, that's all."

Sara tried to imagine how Bo had reacted to TR's gruff sentiments. There had been frustration edging Bo's responses when they'd talked about their father. But she also sensed her brother hadn't given up on their relationship altogether. Otherwise, surely he would have left.

"So, anyway," TR continued. Sara could tell he was anxious to get back to the story. "Bo and I had been butting heads. He's just as damn stubborn as his mother. I got hot under the collar and rescinded the offer to let him stay there. It was rash and unfeeling, I know. But I was frustrated. As a result, Marie and I got into it pretty bad. I went to bed upstairs with a bottle of Jack Daniel's and eventually passed out. The next thing I knew, an inferno had practically surrounded me. I bolted and barely got out with my life."

"And Marie and Bo? How did they escape?"

"Well, they were out in the guesthouse, away from the flames. Marie didn't want to see me that night any more than I wanted to see her. I knew she'd wandered over to sleep in Bo's extra bed. Thank God they were at a safe distance."

"And then the firefighters found you facedown on the cove below hours later?"

"I'm afraid so. I looked around to make sure no one else had come back into the main house, but then like a selfish jerk I just fled for safety. After that, I passed out from the pain, I guess. Plus, I'd had copious amounts of whiskey. The rest is just a blur. So you can see now why I'm afraid to go home and face the music. I really messed up. Big time." There was heartfelt regret in TR's voice. Sara understood the tremendous level of culpability he must be carrying.

She rested her chin in her hand and leaned against the counter. The lines around the truths she once held were now fuzzy.

TR had also grown quiet, perhaps thinking the same thing as Sara. Where did they all go from here?

The dark night sky had moved in, dimming the room and her father's features. Acer snuffled softly, lying stretched along the tile floor, his furry belly rising up and down with unburdened sleep. Obscured by the lack of light, the tick of a wall clock sounded across the room. Sara's mind drifted briefly. Where was Charlie? Was he already fast asleep somewhere, glad for the solitude? Or was he tossing and turning with uncertainty over leaving his family?

She squeezed her eyes hard, producing little stars behind her lids. If only she could wish a different outcome.

Surely her husband wasn't really *leaving*, was he? Sara refused to dwell on the possibility. She'd left him a couple of messages earlier, but so far there'd been no response. She knew if she considered all the possibilities of why he wasn't calling back, it might propel her into further darkness. So, for the present, she'd focus on what she could control. And solving TR's problem seemed to be the best choice.

"What about the investigators? Surely they've come up with some theories on the matter," she said, breaking the silence. "They visited you here one day. What did they say?"

TR grunted. "Not much." He'd made it perfectly clear from the start that he held little regard for authority. Maybe that was why the police hadn't been keen to share information with Sara. Maybe because they considered TR a suspect, they believed speaking to his daughter might hinder the case.

"They must have said something. Did they say what even started the fire?" Surely they had to have given some small detail during their visit. It couldn't have been all questions and no answers. She couldn't imagine TR would let them get away with that.

"They mentioned a few things."

"Like what?" She was beginning to get exasperated again.

"Well, I smoke, for one thing. Not often, but I like a hand-rolled cigarette from time to time. And when I'm drinking, I often like it more than usual."

"Okay . . ."

"And then there're the supplies I keep upstairs. You know, for painting."

Sara rolled her hands over one another, gesturing for him to keep going. It was like playing the most maddening game of charades.

"So they questioned me about that stuff. The paint thinner, the oily rags, all the materials that were flammable or could, I don't know, combust."

"Ah." She was beginning to piece it together. TR's study was primed for disaster. "So are they saying the fire was your fault?"

"I don't know!" Shadows flew across the walls as his arms shot up. "I'm not a fool! I know how to handle my own paint. I've been at this work for two-thirds of my life. You think I don't know how to store my own supplies?"

"I know, TR I know. But let me get all of this straight. You and Bo fought. Then you and Marie fought. Followed by the fact you went up to your studio, finished off a bottle of whiskey, followed by a cigarette or two, and fell asleep amid a pile of highly flammable materials. Is that right?" *Good grief.* Of course something terrible happened. How could it not? TR's entire household of tense fighting and unchecked inebriation was just one powder keg away from explosion. The way he explained it, it had only been a matter of time until disaster struck.

"Yeah, I guess that about sums it up."

"Shit."

"I know."

Inexplicably reenergized, Sara slid off her stool and went for the light switch. Digging in the back of the refrigerator, she produced two cans of soda. Popping the tops, she placed one in front of TR and inhaled a fizzy sip from the other.

"Pop?" Puzzled, her father arched an eyebrow.

Sara nodded and pushed the can farther in front of him. "Yes, I'm giving you a soda. I think we can conclude that hard alcohol is not your friend right now. I don't think it's mine lately either. Bad things tend to happen when we imbibe too much. Wouldn't you say?" She shot him a look that told him not to test her. "So why haven't the investigators been back or at least tried to call you?"

"Oh, they have."

This was news to Sara. "What?"

"They've called your home phone a couple of times. I answer it sometimes when you're not home. The lead cop said they're ruling it an accident. Closing the case. My insurance company is supposed to take it from here."

"TR! What the hell?" Here she'd been pulling her hair out day after day over some big mystery when TR had casually known the truth all along. He couldn't do his daughter the courtesy of informing her?

He colored. "I've liked being here with you and Sam. I wasn't ready to move on quite yet. I missed out on so many years with you, Sara. It's been like making up for lost time."

Her anger dissipated, and warmth spread into Sara's chest. She'd waited so long to hear her father say this. "We've liked having you here too." It was all she could get out for the time being. Any more sentiment beyond that would cause the choked-up feeling she'd been fighting all evening to resurface.

"Thank you." TR seemed sensitive to this and continued with his explanation. "The long and the short of it is that the cops think I got drunk and drifted off to sleep with a lit cigarette." He paused to roll his eyes at the audacity. But Sara could tell he accepted the blame.

"And the fire started just like that?"

"Yeah, I guess. I'm slipping in my old age. A danger to myself in my own house. I got careless. I hate to admit it. It's shameful. How could I have been so idiotic? I've agonized over facing Bo and Marie."

Sara empathized. She knew how stubborn he was, and admitting he was wrong must have been excruciating. "And now? How do you feel now? Do you feel ready to face your family? To return and make amends?"

"I do feel better now that I've talked it over with you. If you hadn't gone out there and met Bo on your own—and pushed me to own up to my own mistakes—who knows where I'd be?"

Sara nodded, appreciating his gratitude. "And what about Marie?"

"I reckon she and I have some talking to do."

Just like Charlie and me, Sara thought. She tapped her lips, choosing her words carefully. "So I'm considering going back out there again. To the coast. Thought I'd take Sam. He could see where you work and get a close-up look at the house. He's asked a lot of questions; a visit might answer some of them. Plus, it might be nice for him to meet his uncle Bo. What do you think? Maybe the three of us could go together?" Her breath caught. It was awfully presumptuous; she knew that. But it also felt like it was time to bridge TR's two worlds together.

"Oh yeah?" TR asked, perking slightly. "Going back to spend time with your brother?"

"Yes. I'd like that. And I was wondering how you'd feel about me spending time in your studio. I kind of like it in there." She squeezed her fingers together in her lap. It was important to have his blessing.

A spiderweb of leathery lines spread at the corners of TR's eyes. The brightness of a smile flashed. "That sounds nice, kid. I'd like that."

CHAPTER THIRTY-THREE

SARA

They'd driven up the next morning, the three of them together in a contemplative mood. Outside a light drizzle fell, the scenery pale and overcast. Mossy green pines bordered the road, winding them through the forest and eventually delivering them to the sea.

After hashing out the particulars with TR—who'd been hesitant but willing to go as long as Sara was to remain on standby if things went south—she'd notified Sam. Her son had been given the choice of whether he wanted to miss his soccer game for a chance to see his grandpa's place. It was up to him. There was no pressure either way. Sara was sure the details of TR's increasingly messy life would be a lot for Sam to understand. But surprisingly, he agreed enthusiastically.

Making the phone call after breakfast, she'd dialed Charlie's number on the pretense of a change of plans. But when he answered, she'd launched into questions about whether he was coming home.

"I'm not ready to talk yet, Sara," he'd responded, his tone both flat and impatient.

"But we need to talk. This isn't the way things are supposed to go."

"And how is it they're supposed to go?" he asked. "You, me, Sam, and your disruptive father are all supposed to hold hands and sing 'Kumbaya'?"

"No, I—" She swallowed before pressing on. "I love you, and I want to work on things between us, but my roots are important, too, and I need you to understand, to meet me halfway, to be there for me and Sam."

"I understand what you're saying. And I don't want to fight right now. But I need some time. That's all."

"Fine. Well, I'm taking Sam to the coast for the day. Maybe we can talk when I get back?"

She thought she heard Charlie start to ask a question, but he only responded with a "maybe" and then claimed he needed to go. Sara was left holding the phone, wondering whether she should have said more.

Before leaving her neighborhood, Sara had also tapped out a text to Bo, informing him they were on their way. She and Bo had swapped phone numbers during her last visit. Sara thought it was only fair she gave him warning that she'd be returning so soon, with TR in tow. She supposed Marie was back, and Sara didn't want either one of them to be taken by surprise this time around.

When her car pulled onto the gravel drive, she placed a hand on TR's arm and told him to keep steady. She knew he was apprehensive about confronting his girlfriend and his son, both of whom he'd parted from on bad terms. But TR squared his jaw and stepped out of the car with his head held high. Whatever weakness lingered just beneath the surface, her father wasn't willing to reveal it.

She coached him as they walked toward the guesthouse. "Try to be open, TR. You don't have to like everything you hear today, but you need to at least listen. And remember, apologies go far. Look at us." She nudged him, knowing by his look that he understood the sentiment. His apology to her had brought them there.

TR nodded and reluctantly moved out from her, toward his waiting family.

Sam, who was following behind, scurried to catch up now that TR had marched off. "This place is pretty big," he said, swiveling around to take in the setting. His eyes traveled across the trampled landscaping, the burned house, and the path that led to the two outer buildings. She wondered what he was thinking.

She'd briefed him earlier that morning, the best she could. Without going into too much detail, she'd shared that TR had more family than just them. He had a girlfriend and a grown son who lived at the coast. Sara confessed she'd only just met them and TR needed to smooth over an argument with these people. But they were TR's family, so it was important they drive him back home to try.

Sam had taken this new information in without expressing judgment, the way only young children can. *If only adults could be so willing,* Sara had thought.

"Yes," she replied to her observant son now. "Your grandpa's place is big. The main house isn't safe to walk around inside, though. Too much fire damage. But we can go everywhere else. Want to see more?"

Sam pumped his head, picking up his stride. Together they wound around the side to the art studio. Pushing the door aside, she inhaled the familiar smell and waited for Sam's reaction. He didn't say anything, but Sara noticed his lips part, perhaps a little awestruck by the sight of TR's workspace. Gently, she ushered Sam inside and got busy flipping on lights and turning the knob on a tiny space heater. Sam planted himself in the center of the room and stared.

"Pretty cool, huh?" she asked, coming over to the wedging table to set down her purse and laptop computer. Dried fragments of clay the size of breadcrumbs were scattered across the surface. She must not have cleaned up very well during her last visit.

"I'll get you some clay," she offered. Sam perked. "While I'm doing that, why don't you help yourself to some of those special sculpting tools hanging over there? I bet you can figure out what to do with them."

"Okay!" Eagerly, Sam scooted across the studio and began perusing the collection of instruments. Sara pretended not to notice as he thoughtfully examined the assortment, running his index finger over various shapes and sizes before plucking one from its hook. Sara concealed a smile as she spotted a double-sided wire tool clutched in his hand. It was one she recognized, used for turning and fluting clay. By the looks of its well-worn wooden handle, it was also one of TR's favorites.

Sam returned and cast curious glances as Sara went about setting up a makeshift work area for him. He settled in quickly, fingering a newly cut slab of clay and testing out different tools on its malleable surface. Sara stood back and watched for a few moments as he went to work, shaping what appeared to be a tiny creature with fur.

Who needed video games, Sara wondered, when a kid had an entire art studio to explore?

Turning her attention back to the wedging table, she began her own setup. This time she'd come prepared with a hard drive full of downloaded instructional videos and a journal containing notes from home. She'd stayed up half the night doing research after TR had given her permission to try the wheel. He'd kind of gushed encouragement at her, actually. When he was done sharing what he knew about the accident, Sara admitted she'd nosed around in his studio and helped herself to his things. To her happy surprise, TR said he was glad to hear it. Sara supposed her father had hoped for this all along for his children. And while Bo wasn't too keen on being a clay artist, Sara couldn't wait to dive back in.

~

Sixty frustrating minutes later, the dazzling fantasy she'd concocted in her head wasn't exactly turning into a golden reality.

Sara braced her knees around the sides of the pottery wheel and huffed. Long drips of pasty water ran down her forearms and puddled into the wells of her elbows. Gray splatters decorated the canvas apron secured at her waist. The only thing keeping her energy up was sheer determination and the cold trickle of salty air that entered through the crack in the front door.

She'd made four or five attempts now to get it right, but no dice. Her lower back ached, and the unused muscles along her bare arms throbbed. Still, she pressed on. The wet, lopsided lump of clay sitting before her resembled nothing more than maddening failed tries. The video she'd uploaded earlier had made it look so simple. Just jam your thumb into the middle and spin. Yet Sara still couldn't figure out how to center the monstrous thing. Throwing on the pottery wheel was proving much more difficult than she'd thought.

But it felt astonishingly good, despite her lack of skill.

Sitting cross-legged on a nearby bench, Sam observed and giggled. He pushed the now-dirty sleeves of his fleece sweatshirt off his wrists and clucked. "Wow, Mom. That's pretty bad."

Sara playfully stuck out her tongue. "Some help you are."

"Maybe you should watch that video another time."

"You think?" She'd only watched it half a dozen times already. She'd made a habit of hitting the pause button every few seconds to jot down more notes.

"Or maybe don't use such a big piece of clay." He held up his own piece, no bigger than a pack of gum. Perhaps her son had a point. Sara had sliced off more than she could handle.

If that wasn't a metaphor for the past month, she didn't know what else was. It had been a wild ride up until that point. Reconnecting with TR and stepping once more into his world was a journey she'd never believed she'd have. Who would have thought that one day she'd be sitting in her estranged father's art studio alongside her son, trying something new? Certainly not her.

But here she was anyway. Open and willing.

Sara took Sam's suggestion and scooped off a chunk of excess clay. With a swift motion, she lobbed the slick glob into a nearby bucket of scraps. Sam flicked her a glance of approval and went back to his own work. They didn't say much, but she knew he was enjoying himself. Whatever unease existed over Charlie's leaving, the time spent in the studio was proving a decent distraction. She was grateful.

It was nice to witness her son contentedly testing out his own creative limits. Sam bent over, pointing his bump of a nose down in concentration. His fingers manipulated bits of clay, twisting here and there to form funny little alien creatures. The bodies were compact, with spindly arms that hung too low at the sides. He'd used a needlelike tool to dig out features on each one—a set of eye sockets for one and a line for a mouth for another. Even from far away Sara could tell he'd given each one a little personality.

"Looks like you may take after your grandpa, after all." She cocked her chin at Sam's clay figure. "Very impressive."

"Thanks." Sam beamed.

Turning back to her own work, she squinted. Where did she make a wrong turn? Contemplating, she arched her stiff back and dug her dirty knuckles into a sore spot. Her body wasn't used to bending this way. Looking beyond Sam, her eyes traveled out the low window. Somewhere out there, TR was talking to his other family. Sara prayed, for everyone's sake, that it was going well.

Slouching back over her dreadful attempt at a vessel, she agonized. This was not shaping up to be anything remotely like the coffee cup she'd hoped to craft for Birdie. She thought it might be such a nice way to tell her friend thank-you for all the support she'd given. She imagined a sizable mug, complete with an ergonomic handle and sturdy base, which would hopefully be fired in TR's kiln and glazed just enough to be pretty. TR promised he'd help with the end product if she could get started on her own.

Sara inaudibly cursed the group of enthusiastic potters from the videos she'd studied. There was no way she was anywhere near coffee mug status. That much was glaringly clear. The most she could hope for that afternoon was a crooked little pinch pot. And even that was going to be a stretch.

But even amid her growing disillusionment, Sara was not deterred. Because though she had no idea of what she was doing, it was satisfying nonetheless.

The very act of plunging her wet hands into a bucket of murky water and then dropping them back around a gooey mass of adaptable clay was enlivening. The touch, the feel, and even the backbreaking exertion of it all were why she'd come.

Working there, in her father's studio, Sara was able to do something she hadn't before. She was able to harness all her built-up angst over Charlie, the stress over her father, and her longing desire to protect Sam, and channel it into something tangible and good.

As she cupped the cylinder, contouring the soft clay with the heels of her hands, something inside of Sara stabilized. With keen focus, she braced her forearms over her thighs, and her right foot tapped gently, prodding the machine's pedal. Nothing but the soft whir of the wheel and the faint splatter of wet clay sounded as she bent over and pushed deeper into the process. The only thing that mattered in that moment was the form in front of her. Her burdens sloughed away with each turn of the wheel. And in the quiet stillness of her creative bubble, Sara found peace.

When she was satisfied with her effort, she tapped the pedal once, halting the electric spin of the wheel. The circular tray slowed gradually, her creation coming to rest off-center. Looking across the room, Sara caught Sam's eyes darting away as he held in a laugh. What a sight he was there, perched just below the window. Dappled light bounced off his shiny head of hair. An army of sculpted figurines sat gathered on the bench around him, comical and crude but beautifully creative all the same. Sam had taken to the work.

Sara followed his amused gaze back to her own concoction. While it had been quite involved to mold, the wobbly shape before her told her she had a long way to go.

"Oh boy." She sighed. Sam's funny look snared her, and they both chuckled. It really was a sight.

"What is it?" Sam said, cackling. His little voice echoed off the concrete floors and spread throughout the room.

The clay body in front of her had sprouted up and out to one side, resembling a wonky, tubular version of the Leaning Tower of Pisa. The sides were constructed of an uneven thickness, and while the lip was uniform, it was inappropriately weightier than the base. The whole thing was tragic.

"I don't really know," she mused. "Maybe it could be a funky pencil holder?"

"Wow, Mom. That's a pretty crazy pencil holder!" He clutched his sides and lost himself in laughter. Sara leaned back and nearly knocked over the bucket of water. Splashes flew up and hit her in the face. This of course sent them both into another fit of roaring hilarity. Sam rocked back and forth, nearly bumping his assembly of clay people. The leg of the bench tipped as Sam almost toppled off.

Gathering her breath, Sara dabbed at her tears. She didn't know if she was crying with joy or relief or both. But what she realized in that moment was she wouldn't give up this memory with her son for anything.

CHAPTER THIRTY-FOUR
TR

Knocking softly before stepping over the threshold of the guesthouse, TR steadied himself. The nerves that Sara had helped to quell now returned. He'd come to face the music and to seek forgiveness, but he was scared. How would Marie and Bo react? Would he even be welcome? There was only one way to find out.

"Hello?" He gently pushed the weathered door aside and peered into the semi-lit room. Woodsy rosemary mingled with tangy tomato sauce to fill the tiny space as Marie's inviting cooking aromas lured him farther inside. Once all the way in, he saw the two of them and froze.

Standing side-by-side were his girlfriend and his son, arms folded and looking back expectantly, as if they'd been waiting. The shame came immediately; TR acknowledged one, then the other in silent greeting. Marie was clearly simmering at a low boil; he recognized the smoldering agitation in her eyes. It had been so long since they'd talked, he feared what she might have to say. Bo appeared hesitant more than anything else, but he nodded still, granting TR access into their sanctuary.

"Hello." Marie was the first to respond, her voice edged with bitter regard; however, she released her locked arms and gestured to him. "Come in."

Despite the lack of an affectionate welcome home, TR melted at the sight of her. Had he really stayed away for so long? "Ah, you're a sight for sore eyes."

"Thank you." Her lips curled up cautiously, and his heart skipped. He noticed she had on her good dress underneath her cooking apron. The one with the green collar that highlighted her delicate neck. Her dark hair was down and wild, and a bit of black mascara had been smudged at her temple, perhaps from chopping an onion or even a recent crying jag. But she looked beautiful. And she'd made an effort. TR took this as a good sign.

Bo fidgeted beside his mother, the hem of his sawdust-flecked jeans skimming just above the floor. TR caught the slightest movement of Marie's hand against her son's side, as if to tell him to behave. *This is going to be tough,* TR thought.

"Hi, Bo. You're looking well," TR said, making sure to deepen his smile. He wished for a clean slate, a chance to start over, and prayed his countenance might convey that to his son.

"Hey, TR," Bo replied. It wasn't as warm as his mother's greeting, but he'd take it. TR wondered if his son had been pressured into being there against his will. Was he even open to hearing his old man out? TR didn't blame him if he wasn't. He'd been a lousy father over the past four years, more so if you counted Sara. Hell, who was he kidding? His whole life.

"Smells great in here." He inhaled and patted his stomach in approval. His eyes drifted over to the single-burner stove that was simmering in the kitchenette. Thick drips of marinara sauce trickled out and over the sides of a pot. A cutting board with sprigs of freshly cut basil lay nearby. TR felt his knees go weak. He was a sucker for Marie's cuisine.

Marie noticed him ogling and lifted her chin as if to indicate she wasn't going to forgive and forget all his many transgressions over a mere compliment. With a guarded gesture, she indicated they all sit down. Bo and Marie lowered, simultaneously, onto the edge of a twin bed. TR glanced around and chose to sit across from them, on one of the room's two stick chairs. With an abrupt motion, he scooted closer to them, positioning his boots on either side of Marie's crossed legs. He watched to see if she'd lean away from the sudden closeness. She didn't—a good sign.

"Before either of you say anything—because I'm sure you have plenty to say—I'd like to go first. That is, if you don't mind." He waited and cleared his throat, summoning the courage his daughter had given him.

"All right," Marie said. "Go on."

TR looked to Bo to make sure there'd be no objections. His son's focus remained steady. After a beat, he continued. "I've come to ask for your forgiveness. The fire was my fault, and I put you both in harm's way. Please believe me when I tell you it wasn't intentional. But I caused it. And I am so very sorry."

Marie sucked in her breath, and Bo blinked hard. TR realized he'd never really said sorry to them before. Ever. They must have been in shock.

"I've made mistakes. A lot of them, in fact. And I'm not proud of the kind of person I've become. I've turned rigid and reckless, and it's caused a great splintering in our family. I suppose that getting to be an old man has frightened me in some regard. If I can't accomplish the things I want, pass down my legacy, and be of some kind of inspiration, then what am I anymore? To myself or anyone else, for that matter. That fear has caused me to become ugly and angry at the world. I can't imagine the toll that's taken on both of you, the ones who have remained here despite it all. Despite my foolish stubbornness and careless ways. It's a miracle, actually, that you're both hearing me out now, as you are." He tried to swallow past the choked-up feeling that kept rising.

Marie didn't move. Her mouth was pursed in indignation, but her eyes were softening. TR believed her anger was subsiding slightly.

Fighting back tears, he rotated to face Bo. "Son, you are important to me. I am ashamed of how I've treated you, how I've tried to push you in a direction you weren't interested in going. I've had time to reflect. Time to realize how much I missed out on your growing up, and that saddens me. I'm terribly afraid now that my actions have driven you away, and I'll miss out on even more of your life because of it. Please know that I love you no matter what. You are an amazing young man. You will be whether I'm in your life or not. I hope you can accept my apology." TR had never been sincerer. He was proud of this kid and wanted so much for him.

"Thanks, TR," Bo said quietly.

Without thinking, TR reached over to where his hunched-over son was sitting and brushed a swoop of hair away from his brow. "Bo? Can you ever forgive me?" TR asked, peering down.

Bo raised his elbows from his knees and sat up. His eyes were wet. And while he appeared too emotional to speak, he pumped his head in agreement.

"That's a yes?" TR asked.

Bo dragged a sleeve under his dampened nose and sniffed. "Yes."

TR inched forward to grip Bo's leg and squeezed. He'd try for a hug later, but right now he needed his son to know he was grateful.

"And Marie," he began.

"You almost burned us to the ground!" she snapped, apparently having held her tongue long enough.

"Yes."

"And you took off for weeks with not so much as a word! Who does that?"

"Well, I—"

"I'm not finished!" she said. "You put our son's life at risk. My life at risk. What would you have done if something had happened to one of us? Forget us forever? Move back with your daughter and pretend we didn't exist? You know we had to be the ones who broke the news to her? Sara said she didn't even know we were out here! TR! How could you?"

TR fell to his knees on the cottage floor. "Marie!" Shame overwhelmed him. "I was an idiot. I don't know what I was thinking. You are my family, *mio amore*, the mother of my child. Please forgive me. If you leave me, I'll understand, but if you stay, please know that I want to make things different. Life is too short to ignore the beautiful gift of family. You and Bo and Sara and her son are my family. I love you."

Marie didn't say anything. She let TR stay slumped that way, sniffling into the folds of her skirt for what felt like an eternity. All the shame he'd felt for so long over Joanne and Sara, Marie and Bo, all came cascading out into a big release. Saying he was sorry was the best thing he could have ever done. TR knew he didn't deserve love, but he had to try. If reconnecting with Sara had taught him anything, it was that family was the most important thing. And second chances were possible if you tried.

Suddenly Marie was crouching down beside him, slipping a gentle arm around his shaking shoulders. *"Il mio amore,"* she murmured. "My love. You are right. You are a fool. But you're my fool. I love you too."

They sat that way for a long time—TR and Marie huddled on the ground, Bo hovering just above them—until the tears slowly receded. After a time, Marie encouraged them to get up. She scooped bowlfuls of pasta for each of them, and they sat on the twin beds, eating and talking of the fire and the damage and the repair work that needed to be made.

When the meal was done, TR paused and looked around. The windows were fogged from the room's warmth, dirty spoons lay idly alongside empty dishes, and contented faces leaned back onto pillowed beds. This was TR's home, his family, and he had never been more grateful for their existence. From time to time, he'd cock his head and tried to detect what his daughter and grandson might be doing in the next building over. He hoped it was something fun.

"Well," he said, breaking the dreamy post-meal trance at last. "What do you both say we go out and find Sara and Sam? I'd sure love you to say hello and meet my grandson. I have a feeling he and his mother will be spending more time here, if that's okay with everyone."

"Sounds good." Bo smiled.

"I see you've bonded with your daughter at long last," Marie said.

"I have. She's a great kid. And she's helped me see the error of my ways, among other things."

"I like her then." Marie laughed. And together, the three of them went in search of the others.

CHAPTER THIRTY-FIVE

SARA

Later that night, Sara tipped back on a patio chair and gazed up at the stars. The dense gray clouds had parted, taking the rains with them. What was now revealed was a deep, navy sky, dotted with fine specks of faraway light. Tugging at the edges of a wool blanket, Sara smiled. It had been a good day.

Witnessing her father, a sixty-nine-year-old man with a lifetime of regret and fractured family ties, interact with Bo and Marie earlier that afternoon made Sara appreciate something she hadn't before: despite the fights and the hurt feelings and bitter blame, family members could still find a way to come back together in a way that was surprising and extraordinary.

TR had spent a long time inside the tight quarters of his guesthouse that day, confronting Marie and Bo. Sara didn't know all that was said, but she had an idea. TR wanted to come clean, to confess he was the one who started the fire. His anger and his irresponsible intoxication had sent them all into ruin. He was sorry. Sara knew this to be true.

Throughout their afternoon at the coast, Sara and Sam could hear outbursts travel across the property. It was usually snippets of a high-pitched lecture from Marie. They couldn't make out the exact words, but the sentiment was clear: TR was getting a tongue-lashing. Marie was no doubt upset about her boyfriend putting all their lives in danger and then taking off without warning. As odd as their makeup was, they were a family. And maybe for the first time, Sara was happy her father was there for them.

After she and Sam had entertained themselves in TR's studio for hours, sufficiently tuckered out from fits of endless laughter and messy attempts at the wheel, they'd gone to find the others. Coming to the front of the guesthouse, Sara found them all outside.

She wondered about the exchange between Bo and TR. She hoped they could somehow find common ground. The long, engrossing hug the two men held one another in at the end of the day told her they'd chosen forgiveness. Sara let go of a long breath. She was happy for the two of them.

Standing on the sidelines, dumbfounded by the exchange of emotion, Sam looked on silently. Sara put her arm around him as they watched Marie pat both men on the shoulders and murmur something in their ears. TR's lined face grew serenely smooth, his drawn-down mouth releasing. Sara saw that he'd found a sense of calm somewhere in their conversation. She recognized this relief as a sign of forgiveness of himself.

Afterward, TR called them over, introducing his grandson with a clap on the back. Everyone gathered in a kind of jovial crowd, and handshakes were exchanged. TR stood over them all, beaming.

Sara smiled back and made her way around the circle, connecting with each set of eyes. Even Marie made an effort and reached across the group to squeeze Sara's hand. The proud woman didn't say much, but Sara took it as a peace offering anyway. Marie then hiked up the hem of her skirt and bent down. A slew of Italian came out in a singsongy voice as she pinched Sam's cheek. Sam raised a curious eyebrow, and they all laughed. If there was any ice left among them, it had now been broken.

That's when it hit Sara. The ties of family were a profound phenomenon.

"What did you say back there?" Sara had asked TR after they'd driven away. Her father sat beside her on the passenger seat, wearing a buoyant smile.

"I told them I was sorry, for one thing. And I told them I wouldn't be there if it hadn't been for you."

"Me?" Sara turned to face him. "Why me?" All she'd done was drive him there. TR's willingness to face Bo and Marie was all his doing.

"Don't you know by now that this old man of yours would still be shuffling around in some hospital facility if it weren't for you? You saved my life, kid."

Sara swallowed and turned back to the road. "That's not true. You saved your own life by running down to that cove. I wasn't even there the night of the fire."

A warm hand came to rest on her shoulder. Sara fought the urge to close her eyes.

"Ah, sweetheart," her father replied. "I was dying when you found me. That damn fire had nothing to do with it. You and this beautiful boy of yours came back and saved me from myself. I was rotting from the inside out in that hospital bed. And that was something that started long ago. You arrived like an angel in the darkness. You brought me back into the light. I was so low about all the ruin I'd caused—to you, Bo, and Marie. But you helped me see that wasn't the end, that forgiveness was still possible. And now I have a second chance. You'd better believe I'm going to take it."

Tears pricked her eyes. She'd waited so long to find a way toward forgiveness. She felt it then, there inside the front seat of her car. The last brick in the wall that had been built up between them came tumbling down. An overwhelming wave of relief washed over her.

"Thanks, Dad. I do forgive you. I really do." Sara's mouth ran dry as a sob gathered at the back of her throat.

Her father emitted a tiny gasp.

Sara realized why: she'd called him TR for so long, but somehow that no longer felt right. She didn't dare utter another word. Anything more would send her to the side of the road in a soggy mess. She felt his hand clasp down and then let go. The rest would remain unspoken for now, but understood all the same.

Glancing once in the rearview mirror, she caught Sam hovering in attentive observation. Sara was grateful her son had finally gotten to know his grandpa. It was something she'd never fathomed, but it happened anyway. Getting him in touch with his father would be the next thing. Sam deserved that too.

When they arrived home, TR announced he was headed off to bed. But before he said good night, he told Sara he hoped she and Charlie could find a way to work things out. "I know I'm not the shining example of commitment. And getting advice on your love life isn't something a daughter necessarily wants to hear from her old man. But honey, I know one thing. Life is fleeting. You've got to snatch up as much of the goodness as you can while there's still time. Charlie may have his faults; heck, we all do. But if you believe that he's worth fighting for, then I wouldn't hesitate. That little boy of yours needs two happy parents. If that happiness can happen with you two still together, that's a good thing."

"Thanks, Dad." She dipped her chin. TR planted a peck on her forehead before wandering away. She hugged her middle and tried to hold on to all the things he'd said.

If TR's family could find a way back to one another after so much drama, then maybe she and Charlie had a fighting chance. Of course, Charlie had to want this too. Sara was only one side of the equation. She couldn't keep them together all on her own. But they'd been happy once before; why couldn't it happen again? She knew she had to try.

Now, with her dad and Sam asleep, she huddled in her backyard and drew up her knees. Her right hand slipped down to her side. The hard surface under her fingertips confirmed her cell phone was still tucked safely inside her pocket. Before stepping outside, she'd checked it and rechecked it to make sure it was fully charged. The call she was expecting was too important to miss. Especially tonight.

Sara took in the cold night air as she waited. It must have been somewhere north of ten o'clock, and the temperature was dropping quickly. Faint light from the crescent moon overhead was the only thing illuminating her blackened yard. The bushy silhouette of a maple tree could be seen, as well as the long, jagged line of a wooden fence. Acer had also wandered outside. And while Sara couldn't make out his wiry body in the dark, she heard him rustling through the grass, sniffing out any creatures that might still be awake.

Turning, she looked in the direction of Birdie's house. A single table lamp glowed in a living room window. Her friend was likely still at the restaurant. Eileen was in the habit of leaving a light on until her partner crept home in the wee hours of the work night. Sara made a mental note to call Birdie in the morning. Maybe they could have coffee together. It had been too long.

Slipping into a dreamy state, she reclined and allowed her thoughts to drift over the sequence of the day. There were so many things she wanted to share with Charlie. Although she was still upset and hurt by his recent actions, Sara yearned to hear his voice. He was the person she used to talk to at the end of the day. She realized she wanted that back.

Charlie would call soon. Sara had texted him earlier, asking if they could speak. Within only a matter of minutes, he'd messaged back. He'd be glad to talk.

Sara pictured her husband at his generic hotel, cashing in his travel points for a bed that wasn't his. He was likely unable to get comfortable in the foreign surroundings of a room that was just miles from their house. Sara guessed her husband had probably eaten dinner alone, channel surfed for a while on the room's television, and then decided that a workout might take his mind off his mounting restlessness. Charlie was used to the fast pace of travel, but Sara knew he was not accustomed to moving forward without a plan.

Charlie had acted rashly and taken off unfairly, without giving Sara a chance to explain. But she'd had time to reflect. The distance, the stress, the unannounced plans had all contributed to their troubles. If she was honest with herself, Sara must admit she also had a part to play in the untethering of their marriage. She'd been strict and unbending about raising their son, and not easy at times when it came to Charlie's work schedule. Adding TR and her obsession with him into the mix had only exacerbated things. She owned that. Neither of them was perfect. There were things that needed to be said.

A vibrating buzz ran up along her side now. Sara eagerly pressed the button on her phone. She didn't bothering reading the screen. "Charlie?"

"Hey." His voice was cautious but tender. A beat of hope struck her heart.

"Hi. I'm glad you called."

"Yeah, me too." He was trying to remain neutral, but Sara could tell by his softened tone he'd shed a bit of anger since their last argument.

"Charlie . . ." She hesitated. Where should she begin?

"How was the coast?"

"Good. Really good. My dad is moving back there."

"Oh yeah?" Sara imagined him brightening on the other end. She knew this was what he wanted, but it was more than that. The news meant she'd taken what he'd said to heart. Moving TR out of the guest room meant things had taken a shift.

"Yeah. He's going to camp out in his guesthouse with his girlfriend while the big house gets remodeled. It's tight, but it will do."

Charlie was silent for a minute. "You okay with that?"

It felt like an olive branch. "Yes. I think I really am."

"And your brother? You okay about him too?" Sara was grateful for Charlie's concern. He knew the discovery of TR's family had been a blow, and he was worried about its effect on her.

"I am. Bo is nice. You'll meet him sometime—if you want, that is. I think you'd like him. He was living with TR and Marie, but after today he's decided to get a place in town. He's moving out so his parents can have the guesthouse. He's also pretty good with his hands and offered to do a lot of the repair work on TR's house. It will be a good project for him and my dad to do together. I actually think they're looking forward to it."

"Wow. That's quite a lot of progress. I'm guessing your dad has you to thank for getting everyone together. I'm happy for you." He paused and then added, "If you're happy."

"I am. It's good. Really good." She rubbed at her eyes, the day catching up with her. "It's a long story, and I want to tell you all of it. But we need to figure out what's going on between us first. Don't you think?"

"I do."

"Charlie, I'm—"

"I know," he said, cutting her off. "I'm sorry I said the things I did. You've had a lot going on, and I realize it all kind of came crashing down at once. I just . . . I just haven't been very happy."

Sara bit down. The statement stung. He'd said this twice in a matter of days. "I want you to be happy."

A sigh passed through the receiver. "I want the same for you, Sara. But we don't communicate anymore. I know I'm always gone. And that's on me; I agreed to pick up my schedule. But when I am home, you're off somewhere else. You're booked with volunteer meetings or running around with Sam, and that's fine. Except when we are both home, we don't talk. I come home from trips, and I feel you're resentful over my absence, but it's my job, Sara. And I'm trying to do the best I can. In the middle of all of this, your dad moves in—again something we never discussed before it was literally happening—and I feel like it was one more distraction pulling you away from me. Or maybe vice versa. I don't know. My point is for the past several months, it hasn't felt like we were ever on the same page."

He was right. The weight of her own judgment hung heavy. They'd been slowly pulling apart for months. And if Sara was honest, she *was* resentful over his job. She knew who he was when she married him: a pilot who was required to be away much of the time. But talking about it and living it were two different things. The stress of having her husband away so frequently exasperated her. He'd work hard shifts and return depleted, not able to fully engage with her and Sam whenever he was home. At first she felt bad that Charlie was always so tired; she could understand why all he wanted to do was throw on a pair of sweats and watch the ball game for hours on end. But after a while of this, her empathy faded, and irritation settled in. She assumed most of the household duties and began leaving Charlie out of the loop entirely. What was the point? Life had to go on, whether he was around or not. Looking back, Sara could see where he'd be put off by her lack of communication. She was just as much to blame as was Charlie.

They both could do better.

"I know." She pulled the receiver in tight and closed her eyes. "I'm sorry it hasn't been good. To be honest, you're right. I am resentful of how much you work. When you mentioned you might be working more, I should have said that I didn't want you to. But I wanted you to want the same thing. With all the extra shifts you've taken on, and that you don't seem to mind, I've been scared that maybe you found happiness elsewhere." She was afraid to finish that sentence.

"Elsewhere? You mean like with someone else? Is that what you've been thinking? That I hooked up with another woman?" He sounded wounded.

"Well, the thought did cross my mind. What would you think if I was voluntarily choosing to spend more time away from my family?

And it's not just me. It's Sam. Maybe you needed space from me, but that goes hand in hand with not being around for Sam, and that made me angry too. I assumed the only logical reason was there was someone else you preferred to be with." The concern caught in her throat.

"Sara." He paused. "Honestly, I haven't. That's not who I am. Yes, things got sideways, but I didn't go that far from you. I won't lie; flying is lonely, and with you pulling away, it's been lonelier. Sometimes I'll grab a drink with a flight attendant after work. But that's the extent of it. I swear. I would never cheat. This is me you're talking to." He sighed. "And about Sam, you're right. I let my own hurt feelings get in the way of me being the best dad I can be, and for that, I'm ashamed. I want to do better for him. I want to be there for him."

"What about me?" she asked, her breath in her throat. "Do you want to be there for me?"

"I do, Sara. But honestly, I don't know if you'll show up when I am there. This marriage of ours has to be a two-way street, and no matter how much I want something or how much we both want it, that doesn't mean it's going to work out. I don't know what our future holds. We have to more than want it; we have to work for it."

"I'm sorry. For everything. I'm here now. Maybe we need to find someone to talk to. Like a counselor. I mean, I'm willing if you are?" The question dangled, and she worried he might say no.

"Yes. Okay."

Sara hugged her knees again. "Okay."

"Now what?"

"Maybe you can come over tomorrow to see Sam, and then we can go out to lunch, just the two of us, and talk. TR's here for a couple of more days. He can stay with Sam for the afternoon so we can have some time alone. We could even go to Birdie's restaurant. I think it would mean a lot to her if we showed up. She'll be busy working, so it will still just be us for the most part, but it would be a nice gesture. And she makes that good tuna poke bowl."

"You know how much I love her tuna poke bowl." His chuckle was warm, even over the phone. They set a time to meet the following day. Sara said good night and then paused, unsure. In that short moment, she realized that if there was one thing TR taught her, it was that you didn't wait to make things right. Even if Charlie didn't love her anymore, even if the problems in their marriage were too big to come back from, she didn't want any regrets or uncertainty that she hadn't been fully honest with the people she cared about. That she hadn't done everything she could to show them how she felt.

"I love you," she said softly, almost a whisper.

"Me too." His tone was hesitant, but he'd said it, and Sara was grateful.

She pressed the phone to her chest to hold on to that feeling just a moment longer. It was a small step, but she was grateful nonetheless. She knew all the hurt feelings and uncertainties wouldn't be patched up overnight. But Charlie had agreed to try, and that was the most important part. They were going to try.

Calling Acer, she retreated into the warmth of her house. Going room by room, she flicked off the lights. Pausing outside TR's door and then Sam's, she listened. All was peaceful. Moving down the hallway, she wished the same peace for Charlie and Bo—and even Marie. Just as TR said, she had to snatch up the goodness while she could. And that was exactly what she intended on doing.

～

Three weeks later, Sara walked confidently through a set of double doors and took a seat on the last remaining chair in the room. Glancing around, she silently congratulated herself for being there. It had taken a bit of courage to announce her plans to her family. To her happy delight, Sam, Charlie, TR, and even Bo all responded with boundless encouragement. And now here she was. Ready to step into the next phase of her life.

Slipping a nearby canvas apron around her waist, she waited. The buzz of excitement traveled up from her shoes and extended into the tips of each one of her fingers. She was so happy she could burst. Faces surrounded her and smiled in nervous greeting. A familiar earthy aroma tickled her senses. Her palms splayed across a smooth wooden surface, the gray, dusty film pleasantly reassuring.

It was like being home again.

A bohemian-dressed woman with gentle eyes and a long skirt entered and addressed the class. Sara liked her instantly. "Welcome, everyone," the woman said. "This is Pottery 101, and I'm your instructor. We're going to have a lot of fun in here, so find a wheel, and let's get started."

A short little man next to Sara leaned over and whispered, "I'm so excited!"

Sara felt as if her whole insides were smiling right back at him.

"Yes," she said. "So am I."

ACKNOWLEDGMENTS

The first thing I do when reading a new book is go straight to the acknowledgments page. I know how much effort goes into publishing a book, beyond the writer's work. It takes a whole tribe. I should know. Without my tribe, in particular, I wouldn't be here.

Thank you first and foremost to Abby Saul. You are the best agent I could ask for. Thank you for plucking me from the slush pile and being my champion, editor, truthsayer, and all-around talker-off-ledges. Thank you to Danielle Marshall, who took that coffee meeting in Seattle and said yes. I'm forever grateful. Thank you to the entire Lake Union team, especially my editor, Alicia Clancy. Tiffany Martin, your talent and (sometimes) relentlessness pushed me to make the pages the best they could be.

A shout-out goes to the Ladies of the Lake and all my friends at the Women Fiction Writers Association. So many of you paid it forward, helping give sage advice (Kerry Lonsdale!), and I hope I can do the same for other writers along the way. Thanks also to my hive of "Bees." You know who you are, and I love you. To Molly Carroll, my literary sister, a big hug.

Finally, thanks to my husband, Greg, and three kids, Natalie, Lauren, and Ben. You put up with all my shushing and writerly determination with love and support. My heart is full.

ABOUT THE AUTHOR

Nicole Meier's previous novel is *The House of Bradbury*. She is a native Southern Californian who pulled up roots and moved to the Pacific Northwest, where she lives with her husband, three children, and one very nosy Aussiedoodle. Visit her at www.nicolemeierauthor.com.